There's No Place Like Gnome
Love in Larkspur Series Book 1

Katie Stearns

Chapter One
Lacey

I roll my tense shoulders back and growl out a sigh that materializes on the inside of my windshield. I angrily turn up the defroster and scowl out at the highway stretching into darkness beyond the illumination of my headlights. Snow dashes and streaks through my high beams and has been for the last hour. I wouldn't usually be driving on a rural highway at night during what is beginning to feel like a snowstorm. I have more sense than that. But my usually innate common sense has been suspended tonight because all I can think about is the multitude of things I would like to say to a certain someone who I've worked with for years. A certain someone, who earlier tonight, became my former boss.

Things like, *I hope every time you bite into a chocolate chip cookie, it's actually oatmeal raisin.*

Or, *I hope every time you get your nails done, they smudge before you even get home.*

And, *I hope both sides of your pillow are always warm.*

Yeah. That would've shown her. That would've been better than what really happened, which was me instantly tearing up and apologizing while she attempted to let me go nicely.

Yvette was never easy to impress. She was a boss who pushed you and expected your best every time. That, in and of itself, is admirable, I think. Especially because, thanks to Yvette's stringent expectations, I *did* become a better design stylist and a better marketing assistant. I worked my tail off to prove I could be more than just a fashion design student who knew how to use a sewing machine. I was proud of how far I had come within Yvette's company, Style by Y, her baby, her own proof that she was a successful businesswoman. Style by Y became the thing my whole life revolved around. I devoted hours of my free time to go above and beyond what my job required, and I quickly moved away from sewing things and having my hands on the fabrics as they were sewn, to designing pieces as well as following, and setting, the trends of the season.

Was it stressful and I barely slept more than five hours a night for years? Yes. Was it worth it? Well, if you had asked me yesterday, I would've said yes. Tonight, after being fired for pushing what ended up being *not the trend* of the fall season, I definitely say no. Honestly, it wasn't all my idea. It was *her* decision to choose my designs. I shouldn't be fired for her decisions...right?

If there's anything I've learned working for a corporation like Style by Y, it's that trends are super tricky to foresee. There's so much pressure to be the next big thing in fashion, and obviously every decision can be a flop or a huge success. Unfortunately, this latest one was a flop. My flop.

I guess people just weren't ready to embrace their inner cottage-core because those demure, pastel dresses and patterns were not the thing to bring in the money this season. No love for *Little House on the Prairie* vibes apparently.

And Yvette said, if you can believe it, "Oh, honey. This will be good for you. Now you can spend a nice long holiday with your family! Think of it as a vacation. After the new year, I'd be happy to put in a good word for you somewhere."

Put in a good word for me? That's laughable. Why would she put in a good word for me when my designs were what lost her thousands of dollars in revenue? I have a feeling she wouldn't be very diplomatic with a potential employer.

Also, she doesn't know a single thing about my family or personal life. She doesn't know that things between me and my dad aren't that great since he married Mariah, or that I haven't seen him for Christmas in two years and neither of us have minded.

I glance over my shoulder into the back seat where my suitcase sits. To be honest, I forgot all about Christmas this year. I didn't even realize it was this weekend until Yvette mentioned her dumb bright-side idea.

Ever the optimist, right?

Except, *Yvette*, how am I supposed to enjoy the holidays when I'm unemployed?

After I got the axe, I packed some things and immediately called my best friend. Lindsey lives in Sioux Falls, unfortunately, so that's what has me driving all the way across Minnesota to see the most supportive person in my life. She has wallowed with me through two break ups, with both wine and a pint of ice cream, as well as been there for me when I was dragging myself through the funeral preparations for my mom five years ago because my dad was too busy being a surgeon to be a decent father or widower. She's the best a girl can get, and that's why I'm headed to spend Christmas with her and her fiancé. I haven't seen her in more than a year because I've been working so much, and I can't wait to see her. She'll help me get a plan together for what the hell I'm going to do next.

Ugh.

How could Yvette do this? I worked so hard...and now it's all for nothing. What am I going to do? Relocate to Sioux Falls? Try to find another design firm in Minneapolis who will hire me?

I hate not having a plan. And I hate driving at night. And snowstorms. And radio stations that go in and out. And—*what the hell was that*?!

I try to swerve. I slam on my breaks. I scream like a banshee in heat. But I still hit it.

Thump.

My car slides to a stop on the snowy highway, and I finally get myself to stop screaming. My heart is pounding, and I am positive that if the thing I hit isn't dead, I will be.

I say *thing* because it wasn't a deer, or bear, or stray dog, or any sort of animal I've ever seen before. I swear, I just hit a baby Yeti with my poor Kia Sorento.

It was *white. Snow white.* With *horns.* And *red eyes.*

Do Yetis have red eyes?

Doesn't matter. I saw *red eyes.*

I peer over the steering wheel, my little ticker still going crazy, but I can't see anything, Yeti or otherwise, on the road in front of me.

Okay. Okay, Lacey. What's the plan?

I take a few shuddering deep breaths and try to get myself together. I glance out each window and around the interior of the car.

This is fine. I'm not hurt. My car is probably not totaled. I still have my phone and my suitcase. And I still have my favorite snack in the whole world—Little Debbie Oatmeal Creme Pies.

Wait—

"No, Debbie!" I exclaim, and lurch to the right to snatch my slightly mangled treats from the floor of the passenger side. I clutch a few to my chest and look out the windshield again.

Still nothing.

What the hell did I hit?

Listen, I'm not afraid of much. I can kill a spider. I held a snake once at the zoo in middle school. I don't believe in ghosts or aliens or the boogeyman.

But whatever is out there has red freaking eyes.

I don't know anybody who wouldn't be afraid of that.

Okay, but, a plan, Lacey.

Right. A plan. What do I do now?

There's a little bit of steam emanating from under the hood that makes me nervous to drive any further, so I turn off the car and remove my keys. Then, I reach for my phone, where I had attached it to a phone holder on the dash so I could use the navigation. According to the route I'm on, I'm only about five miles from the nearest town. Thank goodness for that. I open my phone app to dial 911 because I am definitely not walking five miles at night in this weather, but then a flood of headlights approaches my car and slows to a stop alongside me in the opposite lane.

I quickly roll down the window and a flurry of snow hits me in the face.

"Be careful! I think it's a Yeti!" I shout out the window, still clutching my Debbie snacks in one hand.

"Are you okay, ma'am?" comes a deep, male voice over the wind whipping between our vehicles. It's then that I see the emblem on the side of the car. *Larkspur Police Department.*

Oh, what luck!

The car door opens, and a policeman in full uniform steps out, his stern face directed at the front of my Kia.

"Hi! Yes, I'm okay, but I don't know what the hell I hit—I swear it wasn't a normal—"

"Åh nej," he exclaims, staring. "You hit Albie."

I shiver from the cold pouring in through the window. "What in the world is an Albie?"

The policeman swings his gaze toward me with widened eyes. He waves me out, and I roll up the window before opening the car door and stepping out onto the snow-covered highway, smooshed Debbies still in my hand.

He points with a gloved hand towards the front of my car, where a deer-sized furry white body is laying in front of my front driver's side tire.

I gasp and quickly dart behind the policeman. "What's an Albie? Is it some kind of monster? Tell me. I can take it," I assure him, even as I cower behind him.

"He's an albino deer," he says, with a bit of shock in his tone. "He's sort of a living legend around here—has been for nearly a decade." He whistles low and steps a bit closer. I scurry to follow, still using him as a shield. "Mamma always says if you kill one, it's bad luck."

"But it isn't going to eat us, right?"

"What?" He looks over his big shoulder at me, and I finally see brown eyes and a pinched expression. His serious face is smooth and cool, with dark slashes for eyebrows that indicate he's not necessarily a friendly human being. "He's dead. You killed him." He gestures for me to look closer, and I begrudgingly do so.

When I catch sight of the antlers, I realize he's right. It's just a deer. A very white deer. Phew. Wait—what about the eyes?

"Are you sure it isn't a Yeti? I saw red eyes and—"

Mr. Policeman scoffs and turns around to face me. "Yeti? You sure you're alright? Did you hit your head?" He looks me over for injuries, his eyes pausing on my fist full of Debbies as he does.

"No, no, I'm fine. Wait, what did you say about bad luck?"

He sighs. "Mamma believes a lot of crazy things, don't worry." Then, he picks up the radio attached to the shoulder of his uniform while keeping his eyes on me. "Townspeople aren't going to be happy though when they find out Albie's dead."

"But—but it was an accident," I explain helplessly.

He shrugs two broad shoulders. "Steve, can you call in Lars to come tow a car into town?" he asks into the radio as the cold and snow swirl around us.

I glance at the police car again. Guess I'll be spending the night in Larkspur and not in Sioux Falls with Lindsey. Bad luck *indeed.*

"Do you need an ambulance?" comes a staticky male voice from the radio. Mr. Policeman looks me over like he's double checking.

"No, the driver is in good condition, just a little shaken up."

"Alrighty. Hold tight."

Ah, bobbins.

I should've waited till the morning for my little road trip. Now my car needs to be fixed, and I hit a Yeti-deer hybrid, whose death has bestowed even *more* bad luck upon me. 'Cause getting fired wasn't bad enough.

"Lars will be here in a few. You can warm up in my car if you want. Grab your belongings, ma'am."

"Lacey," I introduce, and do as he says, quickly collecting my suitcase, purse, and the rest of my snacks from the front seat. He opens the back door of the cruiser for me to slide in, and I pause with a chuckle.

"I've never been in one of these."

He gives me a slightly unamused look, snow moving on the wind between us. "Good. Get in."

I do, and once he's closed the door on me and my things, I watch him take a walk around the perimeter of my car. When he's inspected it enough, he stalks back and gets in the driver's seat.

"Can you hand me your license, ma'am?"

"Lacey," I remind him, and fumble through my purse and then wallet for it. I slide it through the grate that separates the back seat from the front. "You'll be pleased to know that I've never gotten a ticket," I boast as he enters my license number into his fancy police laptop that's mounted next to the driver's seat.

He says nothing, so my mind goes back to what I was thinking about before he rolled up. What was that? Right. Making a plan.

I'm in the middle of nowhere basically, with a banged up car, at night. Hopefully Larkspur has a hotel with vacancies. You know what? A hotel doesn't sound half bad at the moment. I could handle a nice hot bath, room service, and cable television.

"Do you have family around here, Miss Murdock?" he asks, interrupting my relaxing thoughts.

"No, I was on my way to Sioux Falls to see my best friend," I explain.

"That's two hours from here."

"Yeah, I was planning to drive straight through from Minneapolis when Albus—"

"Albie," he corrects.

"Right, when poor Albie jumped in front of my car and doomed me with bad luck."

He grunts in reply, or maybe it was a groan. It was probably both, actually, if his gruff personality so far is any indicator.

"Is there a hotel in town?" I ask this nameless policeman.

"No."

"No?"

He shifts enough to look over his shoulder at me. "No," he repeats firmly. "You won't find a Holiday Inn or Starbucks or Target in Larkspur or anywhere around here."

I blink. No hotel? A little bit of panic rises up from my stomach to the back of my throat. If there aren't any hotels, then what else is there? "Uh, does the jail have any open beds?" I joke weakly.

He sighs, taps my license against the grate to indicate that I can have it back, and then turns forward again. His dark eyes glare at me through the rearview mirror for a split second, and then he presses his phone to his ear.

"Get a room ready," he says into the phone without a greeting. "Yes, for a customer, who else? Me?"

Wait—a customer? Does he know somewhere I can stay for the night? I rub my thumb over the smooth plastic surface of my license as I continue to listen in.

"She's just passing through, but she hit—" He breaks off abruptly, his eyes finding mine again in the mirror, "a deer, and Lars is towing her car in."

Hmm. I think he just kept a secret for me so that whoever he's talking to won't get upset about Albie. This tough guy might be nice. Interesting.

"We'll be by in a few." He hangs up without saying goodbye and then sighs heavily, like that conversation cost him a year of his life.

"Where are we going in a few, Mr. Policeman?"

He eyes me through the rearview mirror again. "The only bed and breakfast within forty minutes of here."

"Oh." Nothing wrong with a good B&B. I stuff my license back into my wallet. "Thank you, Mr...?"

A few seconds of silence later, he answers, "Christiansen."

"Thank you, Mr. Christiansen."

He shakes his head. "That's weird. Lee is my first name."

"Nice to meet you, Lee," I say brightly.

He says nothing to indicate it's nice at all, but that doesn't bother me. It took me almost a month to get a simple thank you out of Yvette. I'm used to working for people's affection, including my dad's.

The interior of the police car lights up with the arrival of the tow truck then, and Lee gets out. He shakes hands with the tow truck guy—Lars, did he say on the phone?—and then comes over to open my door.

A chill comes over me as soon as he does, and I shiver involuntarily. The snow hasn't let up at all since my little accident, and the wind seems to have only picked up.

"Oh, lady," the tow truck man says, "you're in for a world of trouble once Larkspur hears about Albie."

I grimace at him apologetically.

Lee smacks his arm. "Nobody needs to know, alright? Just take her car in."

"You know better than anyone that I can't keep a secret."

Lee sighs, and I continue to shiver with the door open as these two men talk. I'd peg them both around thirty, if I had to guess. Lee is all muscle and bulk with that bossy personality while Lars holds himself much more casually, with longish brown hair peeking out from under the bright orange winter hat he's wearing. It's a funny dynamic watching these two very different young men who seem to know each other so well.

"And *you* know better than anybody how riled up Mamma is going to be if she finds out."

I fight back a smile. This rough and tough policeman is afraid of his mother. That's just perfect.

"Come on, Lars. It won't be a lie if we say she hit a deer."

Lars studies me, but it's with far less sourness than Lee. He sighs in resignation.

"*Fine.* But you tell Mamma C to make me a *semmeltarta* for my birthday this year."

Lee growls. "*Fine.*"

And then, they shake hands. I guess that's how it's done out here in Larkspur. Hand shakes, promises of birthday cake, albino deer, no hotels...

Oh, Debbie, I think to myself, *we're not in Minneapolis anymore.*

Chapter Two

Will

Phew, what a day.

I'm very much looking forward to getting into bed and zonking out until morning because today is only one day full of many, many Christmas preparations for not only Mamma, but also the whole town.

The week of Christmas is always the busiest for me. On top of my normal duties at the inn, which is a lot of work for just one person even when it's vacant, I also help my family and community members get ready for all the festivities that take place around town. And really, my defining quality as a human being is that I don't say no to helping, especially to people I care about.

My parents raised all of us kids to be the ones who help, but between me, my older brother, and my younger sister, it's usually me who does the most. Lee is a police officer, so that kind of excuses him from too many extra things my parents might need. Svea is the baby of the family and is much more prone to pranks than chipping in. By default, that leaves me, who can never say no. Most of the time, I really don't mind. Doing things for people is how I show that I care. But the holiday season always wears me out because there's just so much to do.

Mamma needs help baking spritz cookies and delivering them to the elderly who live in Silver Estates. Pappa needs an elf for the Santa story time appearance he does at the library every year. The City Council always needs help putting up Christmas lights and wreaths around town, as well as setting up for the Holly Ball and Christmas Day dinner at the community center. Sometimes, I even get roped into helping shovel the sidewalks on Main Street. Whatever needs to be done, I'm usually the first there and the last to leave.

And today, I was bouncing all over town in my truck, hauling a load of pine boughs to the community center, picking up groceries from the store for my parents, helping my sister put in new light fixtures at her boutique, and then shoveling the sidewalk in front of the inn, which was probably useless because it's supposed to snow through the night.

I let out a huge yawn as I go through the main level of the inn, switching off lights as I go. Every bit of this place is familiar to me. I could navigate it with my eyes closed. Everything is spotless, as it always is and always was before I took over from my folks.

Larkspur Inn was my parents' venture for twenty years. There isn't a single wall or floor or piece of furniture in this house that wasn't touched by them. Those oak beams up there on the vaulted ceiling were nailed up by Pappa. These hardwood floors were stripped and stained by him as well with my help. Every dish and plate in the open concept kitchen once belonged to someone in our family.

Everything in this house was put here to make people feel like a welcome guest in someone's home. Nothing is cookie-cutter or hum-drum. Mamma's Swedish heritage has permeated every room with *Dala* horses made by Pappa, little decorative clogs, and most notably, a gnome in every room. And yes, I had to talk her down to that number after they retired. She finds them charming, and it reminds her of her mother, but to anyone else who isn't from Larkspur, it's just a silly gnome. Not a magical creature who protects farmsteads and homes from disasters and bad luck. But whenever she stops over, I always find an extra one hidden somewhere that she snuck in.

When they were ready to retire two years ago, they gave it to me to run. Was it my dream to take it over and be the town innkeeper at the age of twenty-seven? No. But they didn't ask, and even if they had, I wouldn't have been able to tell them what it was I wanted to do instead. The inn is the family business, and it's an honor to keep it going, but I'm not psyched to dust and clean and do laundry day in and day out.

Truly the only thing I like about running this charming little bed and breakfast is the breakfast part. I think I get that from Mamma, who taught me much of what I know about cooking. I won't be winning a Michelin star any time soon, but I do like how my usually long list of things to do just goes away when I cook.

I pile two logs into the wood stove in the living room with a weary sigh and close the door partway. Tomorrow will be filled with more tasks and errands, but tonight, I will be climbing those creaky stairs and getting my butt to bed. The only nice thing about being busy all the time is that I usually sleep like a rock.

I switch off the living room light and admire how the Christmas lights strung on the porch eave outside shine in through the glass front door as I pass it for the stairs.

And unfortunately for me, that's when my phone rings. It isn't unheard of for Mamma to call me at ten o'clock at night, and at this moment, I consider not answering. But because I love my family and can never say no, I reach into my pocket and pull out my ringing cell phone.

"What the?" I mutter to myself in surprise when I see Lee's name on the screen. I can't even remember the last time he called me on the phone. "Hello?" I answer curiously.

"Get a room ready," he says without pretense, always in that same gruff tone.

"A room? For who?" Who in the world would need a room at this time? "You mean for a customer?"

"Yes, for a customer, who else? Me?" my older brother growls. "She's just passing through, but she hit—" he stops for a breath and then continues, "a deer, and Lars is towing her car in."

I let out a little sigh. So much for hitting the sack and calling it a night. "Sounds good. I'll get right on it."

"We'll be by in a few." And then he hangs up without a goodbye, in true Lee fashion.

Svea told me once that he doesn't say goodbye because he secretly is a softy at heart who can't bear to say goodbye to anyone he loves, which is just our family because he's too surly for anyone else, but I think he's just that grumpy and sour. It's only mildly endearing that he's such a Grinch, but it's fun to mess with him so he gets all riled up. Once a little brother, always a little brother, even though we're adults.

I pocket my phone and quickly turn all the lights back on, unlock the front door, and flip the porch lights on as well. Then, I slog upstairs to get a room ready for my unexpected guest.

There are four rooms available, but only two of them have ensuite bathrooms, so I take an immediate right at the top of the stairs. This is my favorite room, actually, because it overlooks the front porch. The room is furnished with a four-poster queen bed dressed with a deep blue quilt made by Mamma. I turn on the overhead light as well as the lamp on the nightstand, and then I straighten each corner of the quilt. The bathroom is fully stocked on towels, but I double check to make sure there's plenty of soap. Thanks to my usual tenacity for keeping things in line at the inn whether there are guests booked or not, everything seems to be in order.

I head back downstairs and look over the living room. It's the week of Christmas, so there's a small Christmas tree settled in the corner adjacent to the wood stove, decorated with little gnomes and stars woven from grass. When my parents ran this inn, the place was always decked out with Christmas things, but being that I didn't have any guests in the books for this week, I didn't do too much. Now, I'm glad I at least did a little something.

I don't imagine my guest is going to be hanging out down here tonight, but I still want her first impression of Larkspur Inn to be a positive one. Lee said she hit a deer and had to have her car towed, so I'd like to think that stepping into a homey living room and a cozy bed will be very welcome after the night she's had.

I glance toward the kitchen, and my heart leaps.

Someone to cook for tomorrow.

That thought is all it takes for the gears in my mind to start turning. Should I go sweet or savory? I could do Swedish pancakes, or I could do the classic bacon and eggs. I could do a frittata or egg bake or muffins.

Anticipation rushes through me, and, despite my exhaustion, I already can't wait for the morning.

The flash of headlights announces Lee's arrival, and I glance down at the black, long-sleeved t-shirt I'm wearing with my jeans and stocking feet. I usually try to look more presentable, but it's late, and this reservation is definitely last minute.

The snow is coming down in sheets now, already filling in the sidewalk I shoveled only an hour ago. I'm definitely going to be helping the town dig out tomorrow. Just one more thing on my list.

I watch the dark shape of my big brother get out of his police car on the street and then open the back door. I smack my forehead with one hand and chuckle.

"Really?" I say to myself. He put her in the back?

I open the front door and stand on the threshold of the snowy porch as he leads a woman around the hood and then up the sidewalk. "Lee, did you really make her sit in the back?" I call out to him as they trek closer, the wind and snow chilling me. "Did you give her a ride, or did you arrest her?"

"You're not funny," he calls back, lugging a suitcase up the porch steps. At least he had enough manners for that. "And don't you dare tell Mamma," he grumbles.

I laugh and reach for the luggage. Behind him is a woman dressed in a puffy black coat and black boots that were made for style rather than function. Brown hair flows out beneath a lavender colored beanie, but it's the beautiful brown eyes peering up at me with genuine sweetness that catch me off guard.

"I've been hearing a lot about Mamma," she says teasingly with a glance at my brother. Lee, as usual, doesn't respond to teasing.

"You gonna let us in or just stand there?" Lee demands crossly.

"Of course. Come in, get out of the weather," I say, and bring the suitcase in. My brother and guest follow, and she gives me a polite smile that I return easily as she comes inside and stomps her cute boots on the rug. I set her luggage down to close the door, and when I turn back, Lee is already disappearing up the stairs with the suitcase.

"First door on the right," I inform him, even though he says nothing in reply. I bring my focus back to my guest. "Sorry for my brother. There's a reason he isn't the one running this place," I say with a chuckle.

"No worries," she assures me, chuckling too.

"I'm Will Christiansen. Welcome to Larkspur Inn." I extend my hand, and she shakes it with cold fingers.

"Nice to meet you," she says warmly. "I'm Lacey. I was panicked when Lee said there wasn't a hotel anywhere near here. So glad you had a vacancy."

"Yeah, me too. Hell of a night to be out. Glad you're alright."

Lee tromps down the creaky stairs then, and Lacey smiles up at him.

"Thanks for coming to my rescue, Mr. Christiansen." There's a lilt of amusement in her tone that has me immediately liking this woman.

My brother side-eyes her as he walks by but says nothing as he opens the door.

"Watch out for Yetis!" she calls out as the door closes behind him, and then she gives a little satisfied sigh. "He's delightful," Lacey says to me, and I laugh softly.

"You have no idea." I gesture with one arm toward the stairs, about to start the introductory Larkspur Inn spiel, but then what she said to him registers. "Did—did you say *Yetis*?"

She sighs and places two fists on her hips. "Lee said it was an albino deer, but I *swear* it was a baby Yeti," she explains, and then her face instantly fills with dread. "Shoot. It was supposed to be a secret! I didn't mean to hit him, okay? I didn't. He just jumped in front of my car."

"Oh no," I whisper in concern as her story makes sense. "You didn't." Not Albie. Mamma says it's good luck if you see him on Hunting Opener.

She grimaces at me. "I know. I'm the worst, and apparently, it's bad luck to kill one and I've already been fired from my job, so I really don't need any more bad luck." Her coffee-colored eyes go wide. "I didn't mean to say that—about being fired. I mean, yes, I was fired, but you didn't need to know that, and you honestly didn't need to know about Albie either. Lee said something about keeping it a secret because Mamma would be upset."

That has me laughing. "Lee would rather die than get in trouble with Mamma. But don't worry, I won't say anything, okay? It stays between you and me."

"Thank you," she says in relief.

"Come on, let's get you settled," I say with a smile, and gesture up the stairs.

"Please tell me there's a bathtub," she pleads as I follow her up.

"Yes, you have an ensuite bathroom with a bathtub and a shower curtain as well."

She turns toward the open door to the right once she gets to the top of the stairs and gasps when she goes inside. "Wow, this is beautiful!"

I stay in the doorway and watch her as she takes in the bed, dresser, and nightstand, all of which are technically family heirlooms. Pride wells up in me when she runs her hand over the quilt. She gasps again when she notices the lace curtains hung on the window and immediately touches the delicate fabric with gentle, reverent hands.

"These are...wow," she whispers.

"My gran made them," I say, smiling softly at the way she inspects each tiny knot. But once the words are out of my mouth, her brown head whips toward me.

"What?" she asks in exasperation. "She *made* them? By hand?"

My eyes go to the curtain, and I nod. Her mouth pops open.

"Oh my gosh. Oh my—I'm—I can't even speak." Her hands cover her cheeks for a moment as she processes what I said. I try not to laugh. "She *made*—do you know how hard it is to make lace by hand? You need a special loom thing with—" Her hands drop into a prayer pose in front of her. "Oh, please tell me she lives somewhere in town."

I give her a sad smile. "Unfortunately, she died four years ago."

She returns my smile with one of her own, full of regret and grief. "I'm so sorry. It would've been such a treat to watch her create something like this." She turns back to the window to touch the curtain again, and I can't help but think that Mamma would love to know how much this stranger appreciates her mother's handiwork.

"No one has ever said anything about the curtains," I say, more to myself than to her.

"The average person probably wouldn't, but I'm in the fashion and textiles industry, or...I *was*, so I have an eye for this kind of stuff."

Hmm. Guess that explains the fancy boots.

"Isn't it sad that most people don't recognize beauty in things like this?" She sighs. "This probably took her weeks and weeks to make." She takes another moment to enjoy my gran's talent, and I find that it really means a lot.

Sometimes, guests can be overly critical of the accommodations, like they're expecting to walk into a 120 year old house and find everything you would at a Hilton. The whole idea of the Larkspur Inn is that it's supposed to feel like home. It's supposed to be a place where you can relax and feel welcome in a way that big chain hotels can't seem to do.

"Mamma made the quilt," I say, and smile when Lacey gives another little gasp and immediately inspects it lovingly. She hasn't sewn in a long time due to arthritis. "Sewing is kind of in the family. My little sister makes clothes, actually. She's opening her boutique after New Years."

She looks up at me with interest. "Her own boutique? That's amazing."

"Yeah, she's been working pretty hard to get all of her inventory done before opening. I think she's almost there."

I swear I see stars in Lacey's eyes. "Does she need help? It's been a minute since I've manned a sewing machine, but—I mean, well, if I'm still here. Lars said he would let me know tomorrow about my car and how long it'll take to get it fixed."

I nod. "Well, if you end up sticking around for a bit, I'm sure Svea would love some help."

She does a cute little clap with her hands. "Awesome. I'd love to even just see what she makes. Maybe I can consult her or something."

Her enthusiasm for helping out my sister warms me up inside. How many strangers offer to help like that? Lacey's the only one I've met, and I've met quite a few strangers in my time running the inn. A woman who teases my grumpy big brother *and* offers to help my little sister...Lacey seems alright.

And she's your guest, you idiot.

I clear my throat. "Well, make yourself at home, okay? I usually serve breakfast around eight, but if you'd like coffee or tea before that, just help yourself." I sort of skipped the spiel, I guess, but it's late, and I'm tired.

She sets her purse down on the bed and smiles at me. "Thank you so much."

"If you need anything, just dial one on the landline," I instruct, pointing to where the phone is sitting on top of the dresser next to a gnome statue with a yellow hat. "Good night."

"Good night, Will."

I give her one last smile and then close her door behind me. It's then I realize I never gave her a key, so I snatch it off the hook to the right of the doorframe and knock.

"I don't need a bedtime story," she calls from inside, and I chuckle. The door opens, and Lacey stands there in a purple blouse, her coat placed on the bed behind her.

"I forgot—here's your room key," I say, and hand it to her.

"Oh, right. Thanks."

"We'll take care of the rest of the check-in details in the morning. I just need you to sign something and get a credit card on file."

"Ah, and here I thought Lee was going to pay for it."

I laugh at that, and she grins at me. "See you in the morning." I give her a friendly nod and turn around to go back downstairs to turn off the lights.

"I hope you don't dream of Yetis with red eyes!" she says cheerfully, and then as the door closes, I hear her mutter, "cause I probably will."

Chapter Three

Lacey

The morning wakes me gently with the sun rising through those gorgeous lace curtains, and I realize that I actually feel rested for the first time in years. Because I actually got a full night's sleep. Because I don't have a job.

Despite the delicious comfort of this double bed and the amazing bath I took before I went to sleep last night, my temporary relaxation is spoiled when I think about the state of my poor life.

I've always had dreams of becoming a famous, or at least successful, fashion designer. I was a kid who loved clothes and colors and textures, and when I watched a competition show on television about designing and sewing clothes, I instantly felt like my life had a direction. Sewing became my true north, and I learned every tip and trick I could from anybody. College was a blur of threads and fabrics and sewing needles, and then I landed my first real job with Yvette.

But now, I'm back to square one. Back to feeling like I've just graduated and unsure where to go with my passion and talent.

My hand drifts over the beautiful quilt around me, and I sigh. What I said to Will last night is true—people don't appreciate the art of things like this. I wonder what kind of things his sister makes? Even if I get my car back this afternoon, which, let's be honest, I probably won't, I should still try and connect with her.

I sit up with a yawn and stretch my arms over my head. I glance around the room, taking in the wooden dresser which definitely isn't one of those IKEA things you put together from a kit. On top of it sits the house phone and a little gnome with a pointy yellow hat. Everything in this room feels personal and...*homey.*

Style by Y's office spaces were so sterile and bleak that I often found my best work was done at home where I felt more comfortable and relaxed, even if my little studio apartment is a bit messy with all my stuff.

But here at the Larkspur Inn, I feel transported to somewhere safe and comfy. It's honestly the perfect place for me to have ended up after the whole Albie fiasco last night.

When I called Lindsey before bed to let her know what happened and that I'd taken a slight detour, she howled with laughter when I told her the story. She also told me to get Lee's number, which made me snort. The strong and silent thing isn't really my type, but it was fun teasing him.

I've always been more attracted to men with a sense of humor and a nice smile, not someone who grumbles and grunts their way through a conversation. Not that it matters because dating has sort of been put on the back burner while I was working for Yvette. I dated a guy for a few months last year, but he broke it off because I was too busy and basically saw him four or five times a month. Can't really blame the guy.

With a sigh, I heave myself reluctantly out of that cozy bed and step into the bathroom to brush my teeth. The bathroom is beautifully restored, with what I'm sure are original tiny white hexagonal tiles on the floor, and then a vintage oval mirror hung on the light blue painted wall over the vanity.

A girl could get used to this.

But I won't. Because the plan was to spend the holidays with Lindsey in Sioux Falls, and this girl needs her best friend. It was great to talk to her on the phone last night, but she has the best shoulder to cry on.

After I do my business and sling my hair up into a bun, I rifle through my suitcase for a shirt and jeans. I packed pretty haphazardly, so really nothing goes together that well. I settle on a white Henley and a Kelly green scarf to go with my jeans. As I'm pulling one boot on, I smell something sweet wafting up through the old hardwood floorboards, and my stomach instantly groans.

"Alright, alright," I mutter, patting my hungry stomach, and then grab my phone off the nightstand.

I don't bother to lock the door to my room before heading downstairs. As soon as I hit the bottom step, the smell of cinnamon and sugar has me drooling. I wipe at the corner of my mouth with no shame and turn to the right, taking in the adorable living room that I swear I could live in for the rest of my life.

The wood stove is roaring away, blasting out heat into the house and adding so much charm to the whole space that I actually smile at it. There's a Christmas tree with some wrapped presents beneath it in the corner blocking most of a built-in bookshelf filled with books, and in front of the wood stove are two royal blue couches, one facing the stove and the other perpendicular to its twin. I would love to dive into one of those couches and forget about the upheaval of my current life.

But first, breakfast.

My gaze follows the room to the right where a dining table sits, and on the other side is a kitchen island surrounded by beautiful oak cabinets. There stands Will, his back to me as he works on something at the stove. I smile upon seeing him in the kitchen because my dad couldn't cook to save his life. After Mom died, I basically kept him fed until he met Mariah. So, I definitely admire a man who can cook.

My stomach groans again as I make my way over to the kitchen. Will glances over his shoulder at me with a welcoming smile that his brother doesn't seem to have, and I smile back.

"Morning," he says in the same friendly tone of voice he used when we spoke last night. He's wearing a pair of jeans and a blue Larkspur Inn t-shirt that pops against the cabinets around him.

"Morning. Smells amazing." I take a seat on a bar stool at the island.

"Hope you're hungry. Would you like coffee?" he asks, holding polite eye contact with me until I answer him.

"I'd love some. I can get it so you don't have to step away from the stove."

"Thanks. Help yourself." He smiles and nods toward the fridge to my left, where the coffeemaker sits on the counter next to it.

"What's on the menu?" I inquire cheerfully as I get up and find a little rack of adorable white coffee cups next to the coffeemaker. I take one off the top and quickly fill it.

"Have you ever had Swedish pancakes?" he asks from behind me.

"I haven't. What makes them different from regular pancakes?" I turn to face him with my steaming coffee and bring the mug close to my face so I can blow on it.

He waves me over to see what he's doing, and I oblige. "Swedish pancakes are more like crepes but a little thicker," Will explains as he flips a thin layer of batter on the pan.

"Ooh, I love crepes."

He grins at me. "Perfect, you'll love these then," he says happily, and moves the pancake from the pan to the pile of them he has on a plate next to the stove. "Mamma always eats these *pannkaka* with powdered sugar and jam on top, but I like them with whipped cream and cinnamon syrup." He gestures to a small saucepan on the back burner with an amber liquid warming inside that smells heavenly. "My feelings won't be hurt if you try Mamma's version," he adds with a wink that turns me into a teenage girl on the inside.

I've been trying not to notice, okay? But Will is cute. He has the same high cheekbones as his brother, but his green eyes are just...*pretty* and framed by long reddish eyelashes. And his smile is all friendliness. There's a handful or two of faint freckles across his open and unguarded face. And from his trim waist and his filled-out shirt sleeves, it's pretty obvious that the dude doesn't sit on his butt all day eating potato chips. There's no doubt in my mind that if this guy doesn't have a girlfriend, he probably isn't hurting for applicants.

"Alright, grab a seat there, and I'll put everything on the island. Or would you like to sit at the table?" he asks, snapping me out of my very obvious perusal of the burnt gold streaks tucked throughout his brown head of hair.

"The island is fine," I answer. "Can I help? Here, I'll bring this," I say, and set down my coffee to reach for the plate of pan-crepes.

Will's green eyes cut to me in what appears to be mild surprise. "Yeah, thanks," he says gently.

I beam at him and take the warm plate, not even hiding the big sniff I take in as I turn and place it on the island. They smell like butter and love...like something my mom would have made on a Saturday morning.

Thinking of her dampens my excitement as I go around the island to sit back down on my stool. I can almost hear her laughing in my ear about how I just ogled this poor man in front of me. I can see her brown hair flying back with her laughter as she eats these Swedish pancakes beside me. Ugh, I miss her so much.

"So, no pressure here, I swear," Will says as he puts down the saucepan on a trivet and then follows with a little bowl of whipped cream.

I force a smile on my face to take me out of my sad thoughts. "If Mamma is as fearsome as Lee made her out to be, I better try her way." I wink at him. "But I'm definitely hungry enough to have a second one your way, too."

"So diplomatic," he teases as he brings two white plates and sets one in front of me.

I chuckle, not sure but kind of hoping that he's flirting with me. Not that it matters. I'm out of here as soon as my car is fixed...but it's nice to feel like I'm not totally intolerable to the opposite sex.

"So, show me how it's done," I say, gesturing to the spread of deliciousness on the island. Next to the little saucepan is a jar of raspberry rhubarb jam and a small metal sifter with powdered sugar in it—one of those old-fashioned ones with the crank on the side.

Will rubs his hands together and does exactly that. He puts one pancake on his plate and folds it in half and then in half again, and adds a dollop of whipped cream on top. Then he raises his eyebrows at me like "are you ready for this?" and slowly pours cinnamon syrup over the whole thing from at least two feet above the plate, because, apparently, he's being fancy. And I eat up the whole show because, as I said, he's really cute.

"You made that look irresistible, so don't tell Mamma—" I wink at him, and he laughs, "but I'm trying your way first."

I follow his instructions to the letter, even pouring the syrup from high up, and when I take that first bite of syrupy, cinnamony, whipped creamy Swedish pancake, I'm sold. It's freaking delicious.

I point at my food with my fork. "Okay. I don't want to offend your mother, but I don't know how her version can be better than this."

The look of pleasure and satisfaction on his face almost makes me blush. It's clear that he takes pride in the food he's just made for me, and knowing that I validated that for him is just...awesome.

"Don't worry," he says with a chuckle as I cut myself another bite. "We all like our *pannkaka* different. I like them this way, Pappa likes them with bananas and chocolate chips, Svea likes them with Nutella and peanut butter."

I pause my cutting, trying not to smile as I ask, "And Lee?"

Will rolls his pretty green eyes and smirks. "One single pat of butter on top."

We both crack up at that, and the sound of our mingled laughter filling up the kitchen makes me feel like we have been friends forever. Like we've always teased his brother and eaten breakfast together in the morning. I don't know him at all, but he's one of those people you feel instant camaraderie with. I can see why he runs this place. His welcoming, friendly personality puts people at ease.

I dig back into my pancake and get two mouth-watering, cinnamony bites down before I look up and catch Will's eyes.

"So," he says, trying not to smile, "did you dream about Yetis last night?"

I laugh and move a bite of pancake around in the extra syrup on the plate. "I actually don't remember. As soon as my head hit the pillow, I blacked out."

He smiles and reaches for another pancake, having finished his already. "I'm glad you slept well. The beds are one thing I've never had a complaint about."

"But you have had complaints?"

He shrugs, and I watch him give me a little smile as he pours the syrup from high up again. "Some people come here and expect that the internet is going to be 5G or that there will be more than basic cable. Once someone called down to complain that the toilet flushed too loudly." He shakes his head and shrugs again. "There's no pleasing everybody, but I try to make sure everything is clean and in working order."

"People are dumb sometimes," I comment. "My former boss was tough to please, and that's actually what got me fired. Turned out my designs weren't on trend, and it reflected badly on her, even though she was the one who approved them." I sigh and stare down at the last lonely bite on my plate.

"That's awful," he comments.

"Yeah. So now I don't know what I'm going to do, and—" My phone's ringtone cuts me off, and I grab it off the countertop next to me. It's a number I don't recognize, but I gave Lars my information last night so he could call me. Maybe it's him. "Excuse me," I say with a glance at Will, and then pick up. "Hello?"

"Hey, this is Lars calling from Janssen Auto. Is this Lacey?"

"Lars, hi!" I greet, and immediately feel nerves snaking around my tummy full of Swedish pancake. "What's the prognosis? Is Kia going to make it?"

I hear a sigh come over the line and brace myself for the worst. "Well, your radiator is punctured, and you're gonna need a new one."

"Okay."

My coffee cup appears in front of me courtesy of Will, who noticed that I left it over by the stove. I give him a smile of thanks, and he nods back.

"Trouble is, we don't have one here at the shop to replace it, so we have to order one. And with the snow last night, the highways might be a little clogged up today. And then with it being so close to Christmas... Well, what I'm saying is, you're not getting your car fixed this week. We're probably looking at getting the new radiator in next Monday."

My eyes widen. A whole week? Oh, bobbins.

Oh, bobbins and thimbles and thread.

This is so not what I planned. I was going to spend Christmas crying all over my best friend and eating anything and everything. I was going to wallow. Now I'm stuck here without a car and won't be with anyone I love for Christmas.

"That's...not great. But I guess there isn't much you can do about it," I reply in a glum tone.

"Sorry, Lacey. I wish I had better news."

"It's okay. It must be Albie's revenge."

Will chokes out a laugh around the pancake in his mouth, and it makes me smile at him.

"Must be," Lars agrees. "I'll keep you updated though if anything changes. I'm sure I'll see you around town."

"Thanks, Lars."

"Take care."

"Bye." I hang up and turn a disappointed face towards Will, who returns it with a sympathetic expression.

"Worse than you thought?"

I nod. "I hope you have vacancies for the rest of the week 'cause it doesn't look like I'm going anywhere soon."

His eyebrows rise. "The rest of the week? Damn, Lacey. Albie did quite the number on your car."

I nod and reach for my coffee. "Mamma was right about the bad luck thing."

"Well, you're the only guest on the books here, so you're welcome to stay as long as you need to. Speaking of which—" He grabs a paper from the other end of the island. "Sign this sometime today, okay? So we can get everything squared away."

I take the paper from him and set it next to my coffee. "Of course."

"And you know, you couldn't be stuck in a better town for Christmas," he says cheerfully. "Larkspur has stuff going on all week, and everyone is really involved."

I swallow down my coffee and set the mug back on the counter. I have to call Lindsey and tell her I'm not coming for Christmas. That thought makes me incredibly sad. I was really looking forward to seeing her and spending the holiday with her.

"And, hey," Will adds, this time sounding genuinely hopeful, "now you can help out my sister."

I sit up a little taller, perking up at that thrilling thought. "That's right. I can."

"I'll text her right now," he says, reaching into his pocket for his phone.

I thoughtfully watch him as he types out a text. I guess things just aren't going to be what I hoped they would be for Christmas, and for my job, but I guess if I have to be stranded, at least I'm in such a lovely inn with a cute innkeeper. Maybe I'll get to meet Mamma and make friends with his sister. Maybe this will be okay. Maybe sometimes, plans are meant to be canceled, or changed.

Despite everything that's happened in the last twenty-four hours, things could definitely be worse. Let's just hope Albie's bad luck has run its course.

Chapter Four

Will

I wasn't expecting to have a guest all week, but I'm not upset about it, even if it means more things to do on my list. From the two conversations I've had with her, she seems pretty easy going. I do feel bad though that she can't be with her friend for Christmas or her family. Whether she intends to stay around the inn most of the time or partake in the Christmas events happening around town, I'm going to do whatever I can to make her feel welcome. It's technically my job, but I also just can't help but want to make this situation better for her. Chalk it up to my Christmas spirit.

After breakfast, she helped me put a couple of things away in the fridge, even though I told her she didn't have to, and then disappeared back upstairs while I went out to shovel. The porch, steps, and sidewalk were completely covered in a heavy blanket of snow, but at least the wind had died down.

When I came inside an hour later, Lacey greeted me happily from one of the couches, where she was curled up with a book she selected from the bookshelf. Despite her current predicament, I've noticed that she still seems pretty cheerful. The only time I haven't seen a smile on her face was when Lars called.

And it's one hell of a smile. The kind that lights up the room and makes your heart skip a beat. Whoever has her heart is a lucky man.

I let out a sigh as I pull on a pair of jeans after my shower. There isn't room in my life for a relationship, and I don't see that changing in the foreseeable future. It doesn't matter whether I'd like to settle down with someone or not, because not only are the pickings pretty slim in a small town, but it wouldn't be fair to date someone when I couldn't spend much time with them. Mamma always told us growing up to not devote yourself to someone if you don't intend to love them with everything you have. In other words, go all in or stay all the way out. Don't mess around with the hearts of others.

I guess I can date when I'm dead.

I pull on a t-shirt and my old Larkspur High sweatshirt, and reach for my phone where I left it on the bed. The little green light is blinking at me, so I plug in my pin number and find a text message waiting for me from my sister.

Svea: WHAT??? YES. I *would freaking love the help. I don't care who this woman is. If she can sew, send her my way pronto, okay? If you don't, I may not sleep this week.*

I chuckle at her dramatics, but she probably is pretty sleep-deprived. Svea's been basically attached to her sewing machine the last week. If she can get some help with finishing her inventory, she might just look like a normal human being and not a zombie. I'm proud of her, though. She's starting her own business and doing the work to make it happen. Not many twenty-five-year-olds are willing to chase their dreams like that.

I grab a pair of socks out of the top drawer of my dresser and then plod down the hall to the stairs. The door to Lacey's room is part way open, and I rap my knuckles on the doorframe.

"Come in," she calls from inside.

I push the door open all the way and step forward into the doorway. Lacey is standing at the foot of the bed with her suitcase open, a gray cardigan in her hands. She gives me that pretty smile, and my knees twinge with weakness.

"Hey. Just wanted to tell you I heard back from my sister. She says she'd love the help, if you're still interested."

Her brown eyes light up. "Really? Awesome. I'd love to." She quickly folds the cardigan in her hands and places it on the bed next to her suitcase. "Let me just—oh—" She stops, frowning towards her feet. "I don't have a car."

"I can give you a ride. I have to head into town anyway," I offer, and her excitement returns as her eyes meet mine again.

"That would be so great. Thank you."

I smile at her. "You're the one helping out Svea."

She beams back at me with a smile that I feel all the way to my toes. I'm already figuring out that Lacey is a sweetheart, but she's a guest. An out-of-towner.

Go all in or stay all the way out.

In this situation, I have to stay all the way out.

I take an awkward step back. "Let me know when you're ready to go, okay? I'll be downstairs."

"Great, thanks Will."

I give her a friendly smile and a nod of acknowledgment, then head downstairs. I take a seat on the couch to put on my socks, and then my phone starts ringing. One glance at the screen and I see it's Mamma.

"Morning, Mamma," I say, and get up to close the door to the wood stove a little.

"*God morgon*," she answers in Swedish. "Are you shoveled out already?"

"Yeah, are you guys?" I straighten up and wander through the dining room and into the kitchen, memories of breakfast with Lacey coming back to my mind as I do.

"Pappa is working on it, but he could use a hand. Can you stop over?"

I bite my tongue. I wasn't planning on getting over there until this afternoon to pick up the spritz cookies she's making today for the Silver Estates folks. Guess my list of things to do is getting a little mix-up because I can't say no to my mom. Even though I'd much rather point out that Pappa has the shoveling under control, because I know he's in good enough shape to be doing that. But that's not the point according to Mamma.

I hear the stairs creaking as Lacey comes down, and I make my way toward her.

"Sure, Mamma. I'll be over soon."

Lacey visibly perks up when she realizes who I'm talking to, and that just makes me even fonder of her.

"*Tack*," she replies warmly, which is "thank you" in Swedish.

"See you in a bit." I hang up and sink my phone into my pocket as Lacey clasps her hands in front of her in excitement.

"Was that the infamous Mamma on the phone?"

I chuckle and reach down for my still-wet boots near the door. "It was. She asked me to go over and help shovel them out, so I'll drop you off at Svea's first."

"What? I don't get to meet her?" Lacey asks in a half-teasing, half-serious tone.

I focus on tying my laces so I don't give away how much I enjoy her interest in my crazy mother. "The second you get in that house to say hello, she isn't going to let you leave. She'll want to *fika*, and then you'll never get over to Svea's." I stand all the way up and find a puzzled look on her face.

"Feek-what?"

"It's a Swedish thing. It's basically coffee and cake and conversation, but it's more of a big deal to Swedes than how simple that sounds. It's sort of hard to explain."

Her brown eyes glance around me, to the Christmas decorations and artwork on the walls, and then back to me. "You're Swedish. Is that why there are gnomes everywhere? Are gnomes a Swedish thing?"

I chuckle. "Yes, and Mamma takes them pretty seriously."

She smiles at me. "I would love to meet her, but I already said I'd help Svea. So...maybe I can meet Mamma another time? I *will* be here all week."

This girl seems great, and I know Mamma will love her. I can already see them at the kitchen table chatting away like old friends. I'm sure she'll tell Lacey every embarrassing story from my youth, because that's what moms do. Even though that idea has me mentally cringing, I can't say no to that hopeful face.

"Of course," I reply, because, apparently, I can't even say no to a stranger.

My truck bumps along the roughly plowed road toward Main Street where my sister's boutique is located. Lacey sits quietly in the passenger seat with that big puffy black coat swallowing her up, pointing her face at every passing house and building. Everything is covered in thick, glistening snow, making Larkspur seem quieter and more peaceful.

While it's definitely a beautiful sight, all I can think about is how much time it will take to shovel the sidewalks. As I turn onto Main, I notice that a few of the lighted snowflakes hung up on the light poles have been knocked down by the wind, and I frown.

"This is the most charming little town I've ever seen," Lacey says in hushed excitement. "It's so far from what I'm used to in Minneapolis."

"I bet."

There's no skyscraper in sight here, just brick buildings and antique-looking streetlights. Larkspur takes a lot of pride in keeping the original brick in good condition. The only structure that's been renovated to look newer is the grocery store down at the end of Main Street. Everything else has a warm, historic sort of feel to it.

"Are all these businesses family-owned? I don't recognize any company names," she says as I slow to a halt at the four-way stop.

"Yeah, pretty much. A lot of businesses just stay in the family, like the inn."

Janssen Auto is back down the other way, just off the highway. The Llewellyns own the grocery store. The Karlsons have run the butcher shop and the bakery for generations. There's so much heritage here, and sometimes I forget that it isn't like this everywhere else. I like that Lacey has opened my eyes to it again.

She looks over at me with a pleasantly interested expression. "The inn is a family business?"

I nod, keeping my eyes on the road. "My parents ran it for twenty years, and when they retired, they turned it over to me," I explain, and gently brake as I turn to park in front of Svea's. "Here we are," I add, gesturing to the set of glass doors in front of us. There's a closed sign hung on one door, and on the other is a white sign that says, "Svea's Boutique."

Lacey squeaks excitedly and opens the truck door before I've even turned off the engine, which makes me smile. It's nice to meet someone who's so eager to help, just out of the goodness of their heart and not to get anything out of it. Most of the townsfolk are that kind of people, but it feels different with Lacey because she's a stranger with nothing personal to gain from helping.

I slam the door closed and see that she has paused at the sidewalk because it's covered in eight inches of snow. I have the crazy thought of trudging over there and carrying her into the shop, but I mentally shake that thought away and gesture for her to step in my footsteps. She does, not seeming terribly worried about her city boots, and follows me inside.

Svea has worked hard to get things up and running, but the shop still looks a little out of sorts. The lights I helped install bring things together, but the racks of clothes aren't yet placed where she wants. The walls are painted a neutral light gray, but the fixtures and clothes racks are black. On the hardwood floor in the corner next to me and Lacey is a small pile of light pink rugs that my sister intends to put beneath each clothing rack and in front of the counter, which sits against the back wall. A small hallway just to the left of that leads back to the office, restrooms, and door to the parking lot. Just outside of that door is the staircase that leads to the upper level, where Svea lives. I can faintly hear the sound of her whirring sewing machine from here.

"Svea-Bee-a?" I call out, and catch Lacey grin at the nickname.

"Did you bring reinforcements?" she shouts back, and I chuckle. Where Lee is the quiet one, Svea is the loud one.

"Follow me," I say to Lacey, and lead her around the racks of merchandise to the hallway. I peek into the office where my sister is sitting at a table with her sewing machine, her dirty blonde hair a mess of frizz pulled into a careless ponytail on the top of her head. The dark circles under her green eyes make me worry even more about how hard she's been working, and I'm even more glad that Lacey is here to help.

"Hey," I say as Lacey joins me in the doorway. "This is Lacey, she—"

"Oh, thank God!" Svea exclaims, and immediately abandons her sewing machine to come and literally hug this stranger.

Lacey's brown eyes widen a bit, but she looks pleased and not weirded out at all. In fact, she hugs my sister back like it's the most natural thing in the world.

"I don't care what level of skill you have," Svea says when she steps back, "I'll find something you can help with. Thank you, thank you, thank you, thank you."

Lacey beams at her with that amazing smile that makes Svea's chaotic office feel much less stressful. "I was in the fashion industry. I think I can help a lot."

Svea's eyes go round. "The *fashion industry*? You're a literal Godsend!" Then, she drops to her knees and clasps her hands together in prayer. "Thank you, thank you, thank you, thank you," she mutters to God with her eyes squeezed closed.

Lacey laughs sweetly at my sister and then reaches down to help her up. "We can pray when we're done."

Svea laughs too and slings an arm around Lacey the Godsend. "I like her already," she says to me, and I give her a small smile before looking back at Lacey.

"Do you mind if we exchange numbers? Then you can call me when you're done and I can come get you."

"Good idea," Lacey says, and steps forward as she pulls her phone out of her purse. She sighs as we switch phones to enter in our information. "I feel like a teenager again without a car."

"Don't worry, Lace," Svea says affectionately, apparently already calling her a nickname. "My brother doesn't mind playing Miss Daisy. Do you, bro?"

I smirk at her, but on the inside, I feel just another weight come down on my shoulders to be responsible for something or someone else. The only one in my family not to ask something of me is Lee, and that's because he's stubborn and would rather cut off his arm than ask me or anyone else for a favor.

"Here you go," Lacey says brightly as she hands me my phone, and I hand hers back.

"Have fun," I say as I take a step back, and then I give my sister a serious look. "Go easy on her, okay? Don't be bossy."

Svea scoffs and pulls Lacey over to her sewing machine. "It's in the name," she says, pointing at a sign on the wall that says "Boss Babe." I chuckle and lift a hand in farewell.

"See you later."

"Bye! Say hi to Mamma!" Lacey calls out as I turn back down the hall.

Something tells me that Lacey is going to be considered part of the family by this time tomorrow, especially if she meets my mom. She won over my sister in two seconds flat. Even Lee tolerated her teasing last night. I won't be surprised if she winds up spending Christmas with us. Honestly, she should. I can't imagine going over to celebrate with my family and leaving her at the inn by herself. I suppose I should just get my head around that idea right now, because I know it's the right thing to do. The kind thing to do. And I think Lacey deserves some kindness if her willingness to help out a stranger means anything.

I get on my way to my parents' house, noting some branches down on the corner when I turn onto 5th Avenue. I can stop and put those in the back of my truck when I leave later. When I approach my childhood home, I see Pappa out at the end of the driveway with a shovel, little puffs of white exiting his mouth with each exhale.

I honk at him and park on the opposite side of the street. He waves his shovel at me with an appreciative smile, and I waste no time in getting to work with the shovel I always keep in the back of my truck.

"Quite the storm," Pa says, huffing slightly as we work side by side.

"Yeah, it was a good one." I sling a shovelful of snow to the right, and he slings one to the left.

"Lee said he had to give a ride to an out-of-towner last night. Terrible night to be out driving."

That surprises me. Usually, Lee doesn't keep my parents up on all the ongoings of the police department.

"Yeah, she's staying at the inn while her car gets fixed."

Pa nods like he's been told this information already. "Everything good over there at the inn? Make sure that wood stove pipe isn't getting blocked up."

"I check every couple of days, Pa, don't worry."

He nods again, and we continue.

Out of all of us, Lee is the most like our father. While Pappa isn't as gruff and grouchy, he is on the quiet side, and like Lee, is protective. He also adores Mamma, and swears it was love at first sight. I'm sure whenever Lacey meets my mom, she'll tell that story.

Really the only one of us kids who even likes that story is Svea, but if you ask her when she's going to find a significant other, she'll answer the same way I do. Too busy.

And, well, Lee is probably going to die an old curmudgeon. He will for sure if he doesn't get up the guts to go after the girl we all know he's in love with. Emma Mackenzie is the local librarian, and the shyest person I've ever met. I know for a fact that Lee only reads as a hobby because he can check them out at the library, and in doing so, catch a glimpse of his dream girl. Tomorrow, she's hosting Christmas story time at the library with my dad as Santa and me as the elf, because, again, I can't say no.

It's a little sad to me when I think about us kids. All of us are too busy or too stubborn to find the kind of happiness my parents have. Mamma has been asking us for grandchildren since each of our 21st birthdays, but there are no spouses or babies in sight for the Christiansen kids.

At this rate, I won't settle down until I retire. My stomach squirms. Is that what I want? To hope that the right person will be available when

I'm in my sixties? That thought downright depresses me. But what am I supposed to do when I love my family too much to tell them I need a break? That maybe I need a *change*?

"Something on your mind, Son?" Pa asks as we continue to clear the end of the driveway.

"No, why?"

He shrugs his broad shoulders, the same shoulders he passed on to me and Lee. "You seem lost in thought."

I shrug too. "Just thinking about everything there is to do before Christmas."

"Yeah, busy season, isn't it?" he agrees, and pauses his shoveling to lean an elbow on the end of his shovel handle. "If you need a hand with something, just holler."

"Sure," I say, avoiding his eyes as I dump the last shovelful of snow on the mound I've been making. He knows I won't. I know I won't. But it's a nice gesture.

"Come on, let's go in. Mamma's already got the coffee on for *fika*," he says, patting my shoulder as he turns towards the house.

I almost turn him down. Main Street needs some help, but he's my dad, and maybe I can get out of hanging around all day if I help Mamma finish her baking, too. So I plod behind Pa, wondering when I'll ever be in control of my own life.

Chapter Five

Lacey

Svea is officially my hero.

She's been telling me all about how she got started with her business and how she, like me, has had a love for fashion and sewing since childhood. She's been selling pieces since high school and even made her own prom dress. She's definitely a girl after my own heart, and that instant camaraderie I felt with Will, I also feel with his sister.

She showed me the pieces she has left to finish, and I love every single one of them. She has a simple style, but the details are elevated. And everything is made from quality materials. I think she isn't going to have any trouble being a success with her boutique.

When I first sat down at the sewing machine, I was filled with a giant rush of emotion. Like I was visiting an old friend I hadn't seen in years. The purring of the sewing machine eases every worry I have about the current state of my life. And the feel of the flannel beneath my fingertips as I guide it under the needle takes me back to the first time my mom showed me how to use her sewing machine.

I don't know how exactly I got away from this aspect of fashion. I think I was so eager to prove my worth that I threw myself into design and marketing, which by default put me in front of my sewing machine less and less. Instead of putting a whole piece together stitch by stitch, I was suddenly looking at swatches of fabric and approving them to be passed off to the sewing team.

What would have happened if I hadn't taken the job with Yvette? What if I had had the courage to do something like Svea's doing? Ugh, I admire her so much. I'm pretty sure she's my spirit animal.

I lift my foot off the pedal and turn the wheel at the end of the sewing machine to raise the needle out of the fabric so I can remove it and cut the thread. I hold up the dark blue flannel I was hemming and smile at it. I forgot how satisfying it is to finish something like this.

"Perfect! It's done! I can't believe how fast you are!" Svea exclaims looking up from where she's hand sewing buttons on a pair of jeans across the room from me. She has green eyes like Will, but her hair is a little lighter, like a darker dirty blonde. I see the resemblance between her and her siblings, but Svea is definitely spunkier than Will. She's been so much fun.

I've been here for two hours, and together, we've managed to get done half of what she has left. I'm so proud of myself. And it feels good to work with my hands like this. I forgot how much I love it.

I smile at my new friend, because ten minutes into sewing, she decreed me her friend, and stand up to hang the shirt on a hanger. I then place it on the rack next to the others I've completed, and that pride fills me up again.

"Svea, I know I'm the one helping you out, but I feel like I should be thanking you," I say with a little smile. She looks up at me with one eyebrow higher than the other. "I'd forgotten why I even got into fashion. It was because of *this*," I explain, pointing at her sewing machine trailing white thread and the rack of clothes we've done. "*This* is what it's supposed to be. Creating."

She smiles at me and puts her jeans aside. "For sure. I've been working so hard, I was starting to wonder if this is all worth it. Like, am I crazy for doing this? You know?"

I chuckle and nod. "I totally get it."

She looks behind me at the rack. "I can't believe how much we've gotten done. You're literally an angel." She gives a little excited gasp. "Oh my gosh, I might actually get a full night of sleep tonight!"

I laugh sympathetically at that. She's been working her fingers raw, and I love that I've met someone who understands my passion. Dad certainly never has. Since I had no interest in medical school, all he cared about was whether I was staying off the streets and making some kind of money. I have the vague idea to call him and tell him where I've ended up for Christmas, but that information changes nothing for him. I'm sure he'd say, "Oh, glad you're alright," and then change the subject or get off the phone because Mariah needed something.

A ringtone chirps from somewhere on Svea's desk, and she quickly rifles through the small pile of clothes and fabric filling it to get her cell phone.

"*Hej*, Mamma," she greets, sounding far less stressed than when I first walked in. "Oh my gosh, Ma, you're not going to believe this. I'm halfway done! Yeah! Lacey is—" She stops abruptly, like she was interrupted, and listens for a second. I trail my fingers affectionately along the rack full of finished clothes. "Honestly, I *could* use a break. I'll bring my friend Lacey." She smiles at me when I perk up. "She's really the only reason I even have time for *fika*." She grins. "You'll love her, Mamma; I know you will. We'll be right over." I grin back at her. "Bye, Ma." She hangs up and lets out an exhausted breath. "*Fika* calls," she announces, and reaches for our coats.

Fika, that's right. Will mentioned that this morning.

I try not to squeal with excitement. "I get to meet your mamma?" I already told her about Lee giving me a ride to the inn and how both of her brothers had mentioned her with a healthy amount of both respect and fear. Svea thought that was hilarious, and it made me feel like I had made a friend for life.

Svea hands me my coat, and I quickly slip it on. "She's a treat, trust me."

"Oh, I can't wait," I say with a giggle, and follow her out to the front door. She pulls her keys out of her coat pocket and uses one to lock the door, and then she turns to go back towards the office.

"She's a little crazy with traditions and stuff, but I wouldn't trade her for anyone, or Pappa," she tells me as I follow her back through the shop to the back door at the end of the little hallway.

"You guys are all pretty close then?"

She opens the door for me and smiles as she locks it. "Super close. I love my family."

Outside is blinding compared to the hallway, thanks to all the snow that fell overnight. I have a feeling that if I hadn't hit Albie, I might have gotten into a car accident because the roads would have deteriorated even more. I might have had to spend the night in my car or walk for help. It sucks for him, but it probably worked out the best for me.

Sorry, Albie.

I still feel bad that I hit him, but Svea hasn't said anything about it, so at least I know Will can keep a secret.

Svea and I pile into her little two-door car, and then we're off to Mamma's. She turns onto Main Street and drives back in the direction Will came from earlier.

"What about you? What's your family like?" Svea asks as her little car sputters on through downtown.

"It's just me and my dad. And his wife Mariah, who I honestly don't know that well," I explain, trying not to compare her close family to my not-so-close one.

"Bummer you won't get to see them for Christmas," she laments, glancing at me with a pinched brow.

I shrug. I actually *shrug* at the fact I won't see Dad. If that doesn't say it all, I don't know what does. I don't usually think about the distance between me and him, but it really is sad. Mom would be heartbroken if she were here.

"You're not close with them?"

"No, not really."

She shakes her head. "Sometimes I forget not everyone is like our family. Sorry, Lace."

"Oh, it's okay. Don't worry about it." I wave her off and she falls silent as we come to the end of Main Street.

Larkspur is such a cute little town. I googled it last night after I talked to Lindsey, and the population is barely one thousand people. There's a school, a couple of churches, one grocery store, two gas stations, and as Will verified earlier, mostly locally-owned businesses. It's absolutely nothing like where I grew up, and maybe that's why I'm so captured by it. Everything here is historical in some way, even the people.

Svea turns off Main Street, humming to the Christmas song playing on the radio, and then a couple of blocks down, she turns into a shoveled driveway. Will's truck is parked on the street, I notice, and I feel a little zip of happiness that I don't want to examine.

She turns off the car, and we both get out. "Now, I'll give you a little warning. Mamma can be a lot," Svea says to me as we shuffle to the front door, but even though her tone is serious, her eyes are amused.

"I'm so ready, girl."

She chuckles, and I follow her into the house.

My first impression is *wow*. I feel like I just walked into the Larkspur Inn, but smaller. There are similar color schemes going on—blue, yellow, and white—and even similar Christmas decorations on the Christmas tree settled in front of the window to the left. Gnome decorations hover in the branches, and there are several other gnomes throughout the room. There are two couches and a recliner facing the television mounted to the wall in the opposite corner, and a beautiful woven rug covering the hardwood floor. There are also two different signs that say, "*Välkommen.*"

The only thing that makes this room different from the living room at the inn is the absence of a wood stove. But, oh, it feels homey. And the tantalizing scent of vanilla and sugar accosts my senses as I remove my coat.

"Mamma, Mamma," Svea calls out in a sing-song voice, toward the entry to what must be the kitchen or dining room.

"*Hej, Dotter,*" comes a cheerful woman's voice from out of sight. I reach down to undo the zipper of my boots and step out of them as Svea removes her boots, too.

"Are those spritz cookies?" Svea shouts back. She nods her head toward the opposite entryway with a smile, and I follow her.

"Of course they are."

My anticipation mounts as we move from the living room into the next room, which is the dining room. A blond-headed man in his sixties is sitting at the table with a cup of coffee and a newspaper, a pair of readers perched on his nose. His upright posture and big shoulders remind me immediately of Lee, and I smile, because this is apparently their father, who I've heard much less about than the woman to the left, who's standing on the other side of the kitchen island.

"Looking good, Pappa," Svea says with a smile. Her father lowers his glasses slightly like he's going to give her laser beam eyes, but instead, his brown eyes are warm and amused.

Mamma is short—shorter than Svea or me—with graying brown hair hanging past her shoulders and the same green eyes as her daughter and middle son. She has a stocky build that she carries effortlessly as she moves around Will, who's standing at the counter with a tray in his hands. When he looks up at me and my eyes meet his, I smile easily.

"Mamma, look who I brought," Svea says as she goes into the kitchen and hugs her mother, even though she's wearing a floury apron. She hugs her daughter with one hand, the other clutching some kind of metal device, and then she spots me standing in the dining room.

"Lacey this is our mom, Elsie, and our dad, Fredrik," Will introduces. "This is Lacey. She's the one staying at the inn this week."

"The one who's literally saving my life by helping me with my sewing," Svea adds, winking at me.

I beam at them all and then point a smile at Fredrik, too.

"The one who hit Albie," he says calmly, like he's talking about the weather. He even turns a page in his newspaper, ever so casual.

All eyes in the room swing to him, and then I feel everyone look at me. Blood rushes to my cheeks at the shocked expressions on Elsie's and Svea's faces.

"Ah..." I start to say, but Will speaks at the same time.

"I swear I didn't tell him."

They turn to Will in unison.

"What?" Svea exclaims.

"You *knew*?"

Will and I grimace at each other.

"It...was an accident?" I explain awkwardly, wringing my hands. "I really did try to swerve..."

Elsie sets down the metal thing and then places both hands on the counter. She lets out a low sigh. "Oh, dear. Killing an albino deer is terribly bad luck."

"So I've heard," I whisper. A weird sort of shame comes over me. Maybe I attracted Albie with my own bad luck. "Maybe I should go...I don't want my bad luck to rub off on you."

"You're the opposite of bad luck," Svea assures me. "You helped me more today than I thought was possible."

My heart warms at her positive point of view, and I give her an appreciative smile that she returns. When I look back at Elsie, she's giving me a thoughtful look that makes me nervous. After a tense moment, her expression changes. She gives me such a sweet, motherly smile that I feel like a little girl again.

"*Välkommen*," she says in that same friendly way Will speaks, like she didn't just find out I'm the reason Albie is dead.

I blink.

She comes around the counter toward me, and I'm so caught off guard by her sudden change in demeanor that I can only stare at her. She's a beautiful woman, with her graying hair and laugh lines. She takes my hands in her floury ones and smiles at me in a way that reminds me of her two present children.

"You are very welcome in this house, dear," Elsie says gently. "Your misfortunes are a reason to stay, not a reason to leave." She squeezes my hands, and I finally relax. "Will and I were just cleaning up. Then we *fika*."

I smile at her, and she lets go of one hand to gesture toward the dining room table where her husband still sits.

"Are you sure I can't help?" I ask instead of sitting down.

I can feel Will's eyes on me, and when I look over at him, the tray still in his hands, he gives me a cute smile that has my stomach fluttering.

"Oh, aren't you sweet?" Elsie grins and pats my hand. "Will can finish up. Svea, will you bring the cookies? Freddie, the coffee?"

Everyone immediately does as Elsie says, leaving poor Will to wipe down the counters and fill the dishwasher as the dining room table fills up with plates of not only cookies, but also what appears to be cinnamon rolls, some kind of cake, and a full pot of coffee.

Svea puts a coffee cup down in front of me and then slides into the chair beside me with a cup of her own. She yawns and reaches for the coffee. I smile as she fills up my cup, and then Elsie thrusts a little white plate into my hand with a butter cookie shaped like a wreath on it.

"Have you ever had spritz cookies?" Svea asks as she accepts one from her mother as well and shoves the whole cookie into her mouth at once.

I examine the cookie and think that maybe I've had store-bought ones a long time ago, but I'm sure these are way better.

"They're Will's favorite," Fredrik says as he helps himself to a slice of cake.

Svea snorts and sips her coffee. "Remember when you caught him extruding the cookie dough straight into his mouth, Mamma?"

I chuckle and look across the room to Will, who has paused and tilted his head back at the ceiling like he can't believe his sister just blurted that out.

"Grounded him for a week," Elsie says with a smirk as she reaches for a cinnamon bun. I take a bite of the spritz cookie, and it melts in my mouth. Yummm.

"Who do you think he learned it from?" her husband says with a loving smile that makes me ache. My dad used to smile at my mom that way.

Elsie's face turns a little red, but she says nothing, choosing to sip her coffee instead with a flirtatious glance at the man she married.

"Are you done embarrassing me?" Will asks as he wipes his hands on a towel.

"Never," Svea answers around another mouthful of cookie.

He sighs and comes to join us at the table with a cup of his own. He sits beside Elsie and across from Svea. His presence at the table completes this little group, and it dawns on me suddenly how I'm sitting here with his family, like a welcomed friend even, despite what happened to Albie.

I smile at him when he glances at me between bites of his favorite cookie, and he smiles back. As the conversation begins again, I lean toward his dad, keeping my voice low.

"So, who told you about Albie?"

He chuckles and shows me the brown eyes he shares with Lee. "Lars's dad is a good friend of mine." He winks, and I shake my head slightly with a soft smile. Of course, word gets around quickly in a small town, right? "Lars couldn't keep a secret to save his life."

Next to me, Svea sits up a little straighter. "He's right. Don't tell Lars *anything* you don't want him to repeat." She slumps in her chair and swirls her mug around as she looks into it. "Especially when he's your big brother's best friend."

"Pretty sure you're just as bad, Svee."

She scoffs, pointing lowered eyebrows at Will. "And you aren't?"

He looks at me and then back to his sister. "Hey, I knew about Albie and didn't say a single word."

I smile at the pride in his voice, and then I chuckle when his mother gives him a light smack to the back of his head. "You get bad luck, too!"

"What? Why?" Will rubs at his head, playing it up.

"You were a co-conspirator," Svea agrees, lifting her cup in his direction like she's giving a toast.

"Oh, no," he disagrees, pointing a finger down on the table. "If *anyone* is a co-conspirator, it's Lee. *He* was the first to know."

"Åh nej," Mamma mutters and covers her face with one hand.

"Pretty sure he told you not to tell her," I whisper across the table to Will, who shrugs, looking pleased with his mother's dramatic reaction.

"Älskling," Fredrik says soothingly, reaching for his wife's wrist.

"It means *darling*," Svea whispers to me, and I turn my head to see a content and warm look on her face.

"That's adorable," I whisper back, and she nods at me, smiling. When I look back at her parents, Fredrik has his head in close to his wife's, and they're speaking softly to each other.

Ugh, that's just too cute.

I've never had something like that, but deep down, I've always wished I did. Someone to come home to at the end of the night. Someone to share myself with. Someone to take care of who will gladly take care of me, too. But work has been the priority, so until I make a relationship a priority, I'll never have what these amazing people have.

Everything is so different here, and even though I've just met these people, I feel how much I wish I was a part of what they're a part of. Community. Family. Love. My life has been completely devoid of all these things that are literally what life is all about. How have I gotten it so wrong? How did I not realize how much my job had blinded me?

For the first time, I wonder if losing my job was a blessing in disguise. Maybe it's for the best because even just one taste of the life I wish I had is enough to make me consider never taking another corporate-type job ever again.

The good thing is, I'm twenty-six. I have time to change the things I need to change. It isn't too late for me to love my life. I just need to start filling it with things that make me genuinely happy. I need to fill my life with things that are good for me as a whole, not just good for my resume.

Maybe my time in Larkspur will help me put things into perspective, so that I can make plans for the future that will make me happy. Maybe I can learn a thing or two from the Christiansens.

And as I stay and have *fika* for another two hours, I feel it in my bones. These people have it right. I want what they have.

I definitely have some thinking to do.

Chapter Six

Will

"Well, we should probably head out," I say hours later, trying not to stress about the things I didn't get done this afternoon. I never got back to Main Street to fix those snowflake lights, but maybe the city is working on it.

"I told Karen you'd be by with those cookies," Mamma reminds me needlessly, pointing at the counter where I've already packed them up in a few Tupperware containers.

"Don't worry. I'll stop on the way back to the inn." I shove my chair back and get to my feet. Mamma hands me her cup to take into the kitchen, and I do so without a word.

"You can't take her yet," Svea says, and when I look up from the sink, she has her arm around a pleased-looking Lacey.

"She'll be here all week," I tell my sister.

"And I'd love to help out some more tomorrow," Lacey offers generously, and my stomach flips. Her helpfulness is going to be my undoing; I just know it.

"That would be amazing. I'll get your number from Will." They hug and stand up, and my parents do as well, causing a cacophony of scrapes on the hardwood floor.

"Don't be a stranger, dear," Mamma says kindly as she rounds the table and gathers Lacey up in a big hug. I grab the containers, and as I move closer, I barely make out Mamma saying something else to her. "Your bad luck will be short-lived, Lacey. I'm sure of it." She pulls back and gives her a big smile, receiving one from Lacey as well.

"Thank you for having me over. Your family is amazing."

Mamma pats her shoulder. "Too bad Lee wasn't here. Maybe next time."

"Don't worry about Albie, okay?" Pappa chimes in, coming over and pulling Mamma into his side. "I'll make sure no one in town gives you a hard time." He winks and then looks over at me. "Look after her, Will."

"Yes, Pa."

Svea, who snuck around our little circle to bring things to the kitchen, sidles up to me and puts a travel mug in my hand. "For the ride," she says with a grin, and then turns to hug Lacey again. "See you tomorrow, you angel of thread!"

Lacey giggles and steps back.

"You all love her more than me," I mutter, but Svea hears me.

"Of course we do. She's amazing." She points at me with a glint in her green eyes. "We just tolerate you."

I roll my eyes and elbow her as I leave the room. "Later, family."

"*Adjö,*" Mamma says.

"*Hej då,*" Pappa says.

"Bye, buttface," Svea shouts cheerfully as I move into the living room. Lacey chuckles behind me.

"Bye, Svee," I call back.

"You guys are so fun," Lacey comments, still chuckling, as she pulls her coat on. I set the containers and travel mug down on the end table next to the Christmas tree so I can do the same. "Makes me wish I had siblings."

"Oh! Lacey!" comes Mamma's voice again, and she rushes into the living room with a serious expression. "Come here, and touch this *tomte.*"

I barely stifle my groan. Mamma and her gnomes.

"Touch *what?*" she questions, glancing at me to translate, but Mamma takes her arm and pulls her across the room to her favorite gnome. It's the one she swears watches over our home and everyone inside it as long as we respect him or something. She gets her superstitions from *Mormor,* her mother, and takes them very seriously.

Mamma takes the gnome off the shelf and puts him in Lacey's uncertain hands. The red paint of his stone hat is worn in places, but Mamma says she loves him that way. He has a big round nose that peeks out from beneath the red hat, and his body is plump around the middle and painted blue.

"This *tomte* has been in our family since I was a little girl. He protects our family and our home. Once you stepped into this house, his protection covered you as well."

I get my boots on, feeling awkward for Lacey, but there's no stopping Mamma. I would be embarrassed, but I love my mom. Her heritage and culture are something she holds dear, and I'm not so terrible of a person to deny her that. Even Lee has touched that *tomte* a time or two simply because she told him to.

"Your bad luck will end soon," Mamma assures her with a confident smile. "I'll have Freddie make you a *Dala* horse, just in case."

"Oh, okay," she answers politely, giving away that she has no idea what a *Dala* horse is. "Thank you." Lacey places the *tomte* back into my mom's hands. "Thank you again for having me."

"Take care, dear. We'll see you soon, I'm sure." She pats Lacey's cheek affectionately and then lets her go to get her boots on. "Give those cookies to Julia at the front desk, okay?" she says to me. "And tell her *God Jul.*"

"I will, Mamma. See you tomorrow at the library."

She blows a kiss at me and then turns to put her *tomte* back on the shelf. I pick up the containers and travel mug and then follow Lacey out. The afternoon sun is just beginning to lower to the west, yet another reminder that I have things to do when I get back to the inn.

"Sorry about that," I say as I fall into step beside her down the driveway. "My family is a little..."

"Swedish?" she teases with a glance at me.

I chuckle as we cross the street to my truck. "Thanks for just going with it."

"Oh, don't thank me. I love them. I haven't felt so at home since my mom died," she says warmly.

I pause at the driver's side door and watch her walk around to the other side, my heart sinking a bit. I get in, and Lacey takes the containers of cookies from me. "I'm sorry about your mom," I apologize gently, and set the travel mug in the cup holder so I can dig out my keys from my jeans pocket.

"It's alright." She settles the containers on her lap and fastens her seatbelt. "I miss her, but Mamma hugs just the way she used to. Best Christmas present I could ever get, really." She has a soft smile on her pretty face that's both sad and grateful.

I frown slightly as I fire up the truck. I don't know what I would do if I lost one of my parents. It's inevitable, obviously, but I'm still hoping that day is a long way off. Mamma and Pa are both still in good health, even though they've slowed down a bit in recent years. But I was glad to see them retire because they've always worked hard. Mamma worked in the kitchen at Silver Estates for decades as well as helping Pa run the inn, and he definitely kept busy around town and with us kids. It's good to see them resting more and enjoying their days more, even if it means extra work for me.

"Your family is something really special, Will," she adds, giving me that sweet smile I've already become so fond of.

I nod, returning her smile, and grab the travel mug Svea made up to take a sip before getting on the road. But as soon as the coffee enters my mouth, my tastebuds are completely overwhelmed with salt. Choking and trying not to gag, I quickly fling open the truck door and spit out the disgusting mouthful.

"Oh my gosh—are you—" Lacey starts to say in concern, but I get out of the truck before she can finish.

The front door is ajar, and my sister stands there, laughing so hard she's bent over.

"*Vad fan*, Svea!" I shout, which means "what the devil," still spitting as her laughter carries across the snowy yard. I should've known, honestly. She's always pranking one of the family, but it's usually me or Pappa. Mamma and Lee don't forgive as easily.

"I'm so glad I got to see that!" Svea cackles.

"Just wait, you brat! I'll get you back," I threaten, but she just laughs more and closes the door.

I get back in the truck and slam the door shut.

"What did she do to your coffee?" Lacey inquires, sounding equally amused and worried.

I put the truck in drive, avoiding her eyes as I pull out into the street. "She salted it. Tasted like she made coffee with seawater." I wish I had something to rinse my mouth out. "She's always pranking me; I should've known."

She chuckles. "Wow. That's brutal."

I raise one eyebrow at her as I turn the corner. "Still wishing you had siblings?"

Lacey grins at me. "Don't worry. I'll help you get her back."

"You will?" I ask in surprise, and pull onto Main Street. I cast my eyes around to see if the snowflake lights have been fixed, and I see someone on a ladder down the block. "I thought you and Svea hit it off?"

"Oh, we definitely did. But I like a little fun. We'll think of something," she assures me confidently.

Hmm. It's kind of nice to be in cahoots. Every time Svea pranks me, I can never get Lee to help me retaliate. He's too busy being the mature firstborn.

"Thanks."

She smiles at me, and I try not to let it affect me. But seeing her fit in so well with my kooky family was so endearing. She laughed with Svea and Pa, listened intently to Mamma, and smiled at me in between. She's a beautiful woman inside and out, and she makes friends like Lee has never been able to.

What a shame she's from Minneapolis. But even if she wasn't—even if she was part of this community—it wouldn't matter. I'd still be just as busy and just as difficult to date. My mind goes back to what I was thinking about while I was shoveling with Pappa. Everything I do is because someone else needs something, and I don't know how to turn people down. And while it bogs me down, I still don't take a vacation or even a day off to do something just for me.

And Lacey just reminds me of everything I wish I could have instead of the long to-do lists and endless errands or favors I do for my family and the community. I wish I could learn how to say no when I need a break, and then not feel guilty about it. I wish I could devote myself to one thing, and not *everything*.

After Lacey and I drop off the cookies at Silver Estates, I take us back to the inn. As I get to work on cooking something for dinner, I realize I'll need to get to the grocery store at some point tomorrow since I'll have a guest to make breakfast for each morning this week. It's been about a month since I've had any guests stay longer than two nights. Usually in January, a couple groups of snowmobilers come through, but for the most part, the inn is pretty dead between the church's fall and spring retreats. Which just means the usual chores (dusting and wiping down surfaces), and cooking for no one but me.

I glance at the clock, realizing it's too late for Lacey to order any take out for dinner, so I pull out my phone and send her a text.

Will: *Just so you know, all the restaurants who deliver are closed.*

I set my phone on the counter and begin measuring out the seasonings that go into Swedish meatballs. I cap the allspice, and then my phone buzzes.

Lacey: *Oh.*

For half a second, I consider offering to drive her somewhere for dinner, but why would I do that when I'm about to make more than enough food for dinner?

Will: *I'm making dinner, if you want in. It'll be about a half an hour.*

Lacey: *Are you sure? You can put it on my tab. *winky emoji**

I chuckle.

Will: *It's on the house.*

I put my phone in my pocket and go back to the spices.

Only thirty seconds later, the staircase creaks beneath Lacey's descent into the main level, and I look up at her as she comes closer.

"The least I can do is help you make dinner," she says with a smile that I instantly return. She's removed her green scarf and let down her hair and looks relaxed and friendly.

"Sure." I put away the nutmeg and allspice in the cabinet behind me, stir the onions cooking in a pan on the stove, and turn back to see she's standing across from me at the island where I've got all my ingredients out.

"Do you usually serve dinner here, too?" she asks curiously, her brown eyes taking in the boiling pot at the stove behind me.

"Just breakfast, but I guess I can be persuaded to serve dinner as well." I wink at her and then hate myself a little. I shouldn't be flirting with her, but it's so easy to do when she reciprocates so comfortably.

She watches me as I put the ground meats in the glass bowl with the spices. "What are you making?"

I smirk at her. "Swedish meatballs, of course."

Lacey grins that pretty smile and laughs sweetly. "Of course."

"It's Mamma's recipe."

She rubs her hands together. "I don't usually cook that much, but if you show me what to do, I'm sure I'll catch on."

I grab a measuring cup from the middle drawer of the island and then hand it to her with the container of breadcrumbs. "One of those in the bowl," I instruct, nodding towards the glass bowl.

She grins and immediately rips the lid off the breadcrumbs. Her enthusiasm makes me smile as I turn to stir the onions one last time, and then I move them aside to cool. I use the same wooden spoon to give the boiling potatoes a stir as well, and as I do these things, I feel every bit of stress evaporate. The kitchen is my happy place, where I forget all the things that need to be done and all the responsibilities I've shouldered. I can breathe when I cook, and everything feels okay.

My parents' ages and endless demands, the community needs in getting ready for all the Christmas festivities, the small bit of festering loneliness, the wishing for something else....it all just quiets down into a whisper I can ignore.

I turn back to Lacey as she caps the breadcrumbs container.

"Can you crack eggs?" I ask, sliding the egg carton toward her.

"I can, indeed," she answers proudly, and I snicker.

"Two, please."

"Yes, sir." She carefully cracks two eggs in the bowl as I add the meat, and then she gets up to dispose of the shells and wash her hands. "Do you like to cook?" she asks me as she dries her hands on the towel and hangs it back on the oven handle.

"I love it," I reply, and bring the pan of onions to the island so I can add them to the bowl. "It's my favorite part of the job."

"Really?"

"Absolutely. Life is nothing without food—good food. It brings everybody together. And not just at the same table, but also across the world." I place the onion pan back on the stove. "I mean, until today, had you ever had any authentic Swedish cuisine?"

"I've had frozen Swedish meatballs once, but those were definitely not authentic," she replies with bright eyes.

"Exactly. And through these family recipes, you're eating the same thing that our relatives are in Sweden." I grin, loving this conversation. "Food is a bridge, you know?"

Lacey's brown eyes sparkle at me in appreciation for what I've said, and a little heat rushes up the back of my neck.

"I've never heard anyone talk about food that way. I love it." She looks at the bowl of ingredients and then back at me. "Will you teach me how to make these? I want to know how to do it so I can make them at home."

My heart swells. "I would love that."

We share a warm smile, and then I wave her around the island. "You're going to get messy. Are you ready?"

"So ready." She smiles at me, and I notice out of the corner of my eye that it turns into a grin. Smiling to myself, I sink my hands into the messy mixture.

Once everything is evenly mixed and my hands are cold, I nod toward the sheet pan at the far end of the island.

"Bring that over here, and then let's roll." I take a small amount of meat mixture and roll it in my hands, then place it on the tray.

Lacey nods as she watches me, and then reaches in to imitate me, which she does perfectly. It's nice to have the company, I realize.

"This is nice. I don't usually cook with anybody else."

"I'll take that as a compliment."

I chuckle, and we continue our rolling until the tray is full and the bowl is empty.

"Alright," I say after we've washed our hands. "Now, we're going to brown these in the pan."

I bring the tray over to the counter next to the stove, and turn on the burner, but instead of putting the meatballs in myself, I hand Lacey the tongs.

She grins excitedly, and I watch her place each one carefully in the pan.

"Perfect," I comment, and then give the potatoes a stir. "These are almost there, and then we can mash them."

"Oh my gosh, I can't remember the last time I had homemade mashed potatoes," she says, and I'm surprised that she grips my bicep excitedly as she speaks.

"You don't cook much, then?"

She shrugs, releasing my arm. "I honestly don't have time. Or, I didn't, before I was let go. I worked so much, I barely had time to sleep, let alone cook."

Too busy for a boyfriend, too? I wonder, but don't have the gall to ask out loud. It's none of my business.

The meatballs begin to sizzle in front of us, giving off the aroma of Swedish meatballs that makes me feel nostalgic.

"Honestly, being here is making me rethink how I spend my time. My job took up too much of my life. Being with your family today made me realize I'm missing out on the important things."

I take the tongs from her and begin to turn a few meatballs, then hand them back so she can do the rest. "Like salting someone's coffee?"

She laughs, such a sweet sound in my kitchen. "Exactly," she agrees, and I watch her gently take over with the tongs. "Smells good already," she comments as she turns the last one.

"Once they're seared, we'll take them off to make the sauce and put them back in to finish cooking through."

"Yes, chef," she teases, and I can't help but grin at her.

"Alright, let's get the potatoes out." I turn off the burner, grab a couple of pot holders, and drain them in a colander in the sink.

"Potato sauna," Lacey says as she shakes the colander to get the excess water off.

I chuckle and tell her to put them back in the pot I boiled them in. "Will you grab the potato masher? It's in the second drawer." I point, and she dutifully fishes it out. I reach for it, but she moves it away with what looks to me like a very flirtatious smile.

"May I?"

"Think you can handle it?" I wink at her, and again feel like I shouldn't be doing that.

"Oh, I've got some guns, chef. You just watch." She marches over to the pot of potatoes, and I can't take my eyes off of her for more than one reason.

I admire every single thing I've discovered about her. And she's offered me more help than anyone in my family has in months, even though we're strangers. It's impossible for me to not be attracted to that. I might be in trouble here with this woman because if she's really this amazing, I know I'll be thinking about her long after she leaves. Possibly for the rest of my life.

Chapter Seven

Lacey

It smells heavenly in this kitchen right now—like onions and spices I can't identify and buttery mashed potatoes. It smells like someone made this with their heart, and I know firsthand that Will cooks with love.

Love for the recipe and the heritage of his amazing family. Love for the preparations and the hospitality of sharing it with me. I admire that so much.

Food wasn't really like this in my family growing up. We frequented fast food places and very rarely made anything from scratch. My mom loved a good shortcut, which usually meant meals sold in a box with seasoning packets.

But being Will's right hand as he teaches me a family recipe just inspires me to find joy and pride in food like he does. This is just yet another thing I've been missing out on.

"Okay, big guns, you're going to whisk that until it starts to thicken," he instructs with a smile, and it hits me then that his smiles are brightest when he's cooking.

Could he be any cuter?

I'm going to need to call Lindsey tonight and vent about it. If I don't, I might end up turning into a flirtatious mess. Because in one day, I've learned things about Will that make him totally my type.

Cute? Check.

Strong? Check.

Kind? Check.

A good cook? Check.

Loves his family? Check.

Hard worker? Check.

And he's very likely in love with the girl next door or the baker or his high school sweetheart.

Good men like Will don't stay single for long, so I need to keep myself in check here. I don't want to act like a fool, and I certainly don't want to be flirting with someone else's man.

So, I focus on the pan of sauce in front of me and whisk furiously. Maybe I shouldn't be flirting with him, but I can impress him with my tenacity, right?

My arm begins to burn as I whisk and whisk and whisk, not noticing my tongue peeking out the corner of my mouth, and when the sauce made with sour cream and beef broth and love starts to thicken, I let out a hoot of triumph.

I don't notice until then that Will has been standing just to the side, watching me with a very amused expression as I exerted myself.

"You gave that all you had," he praises, and I puff out my chest a bit with pride that I *did* in fact impress him, thank you very much.

"Okay, so now these go back in," I tell myself, and place the seared meatballs into the pan with my perfectly whisked sauce. "Am I or am I not the perfect student?" I gloat, turning towards him.

"Mamma would be proud," he says with that adorable grin.

"Yes!" I raise my hand for a high five, and he doesn't leave me hanging. A satisfying *smack* rings out from between our hands, and then I put my hands on my hips. "Okay, what's next, chef?"

"That nickname is growing on me."

"It's not a nickname if that's who you are, silly," I point out.

A funny expression comes over his face, wrinkling his freckles slightly. "But I'm not a chef. I never went to culinary school or whatever."

My head cocks to the side slightly. "So?"

He blinks at me, thinking over what I've said. "I guess...I've just never thought of myself as a chef."

I glance at our pan of Swedish meatballs and back at him. "I haven't known you long, Will, but it's clear as day that you have the passion of a chef."

"Hmm." He looks at the stove thoughtfully.

My stomach squirms at the way his expression changes from thoughtfulness to something sadder. The last thing I want to do is make him uncomfortable, and it seems like that's what I've done.

"Sorry," I blurt out. "It's none of my business and you didn't ask me for my input." To distract myself from wishing I could melt into the floor and slink away, I start pulling open drawers.

"What are you doing?"

"I'll set the table," I offer, avoiding eye contact. "Aha," I say when I find the silverware drawer. As I go to put the forks and butter knives on the dining room table, Will gets some plates down from the upper cabinet next to the sink. He hands them to me without a word, and I set them on the table. When I turn around, he's facing me with his hands resting on the countertop of the island, just looking at me.

"You like to help," he observes thoughtfully. "You're always asking how you can help, even though you're a guest."

"I'm just grateful I have somewhere to stay while Kia gets fixed, and I like to be useful, I guess." I'm not used to people noticing me helping. Yvette certainly didn't. "Besides, helping is more fun. Don't get me wrong—sitting at the island and watching you cook should totally be a spectator sport."

Oh my gosh, why did I say that?

I clear my throat awkwardly when I notice his eyebrows slowly crawl up his forehead.

"I—I didn't mean like in a weird way." I laugh uncomfortably. "I meant like in a totally normal, not stalkerish way."

Wow, that didn't help. At all.

"Like in an 'I admire you' kind of way. Not like in a creepy way."

Stop talking, Lacey!

You see that thing stuck in my mouth? Yeah, that's my foot. And I think it's going to need to be surgically removed by my own surgeon father.

"Thank you...?" Will asks, a pleased and amused blush warming his cheeks.

I point finger guns at him. "Anytime."

Finger guns? Really, Lacey?

Ugh, kill me now.

So, this isn't awkward at all. Nope, totally fine. Just sitting here at the dining room table with the guy I insinuated was good-looking.

Thankfully, the food is a good distraction, because *oh my gosh* it's delicious. Perfectly savory and my new favorite comfort food. I definitely will be making this at home, even though my kitchen is much less equipped and much smaller. Ooh, I should ask him for the Swedish pancake recipe, too.

"Too bad you can't serve this for breakfast, too," I tell him, chancing a shy glance at him as we eat.

He swirls a meatball through his sauce-covered mashed potatoes with a little smile.

"Seriously, switch the mashed potatoes to hash browns and throw an egg on it. It could totally be breakfast."

He chuckles and brings his fork to his mouth. I take another bite as well.

"That doesn't sound half bad, actually," he says after he's done chewing.

"Right?" I point my fork at him. "Think about it. You can call it the Lacey Special."

Will grins at me. "Has a nice ring to it."

"If you like it, then you shoulda put a—" I break off abruptly, realizing I was about to quote Beyonce's "Single Ladies." I chuckle awkwardly. "I mean, you should, uh, put it on the menu." I take another bite before I embarrass myself even further.

Ah, dang it. Now that song is stuck in my head.

"Yeah, maybe I will."

I'm absolutely certain he said that simply to not make me feel bad, and that's just fine. Commendable, even. I intend on changing the subject anyway.

"So, you run this place all by yourself, you said?"

He nods, the little chandelier hovering above us highlighting the strands of gold in his hair as his head moves.

"Do you like it? Seems like it would be kind of fun."

His fork halts halfway to his mouth when I ask my question, and when he doesn't reply right away, I'm super surprised. He gives a tiny sigh and takes his bite without looking at me, and yeah...remember that foot stuck in my mouth? I think I just crammed my other one in there too. Because apparently, I asked him what I thought was a simple, curious question that he doesn't want to answer because it isn't a positive one.

Maybe I'm psychic but in the worst way. Like I just always know the wrong questions to ask and the wrong things to say. I blame Albie.

"It doesn't really matter whether I like it or not," Will answers finally, looking at his plate. "It's my job."

Oh my gosh. I'm the worst. But how was I supposed to know he doesn't like running the inn? Like I said, it sounds fun. But according to him, it's maybe not so much fun. Why would he be doing this if he didn't like it?

It *doesn't really matter*. Ugh, that's just horrible.

"Of course it matters, Will. Do you like it?" I press because I'm annoying and need answers.

He stirs his fork around in his food for an uncomfortable moment. "Look, I don't know what to say. When my parents retired, they gave it to me to run. It is what it is. "

My shoulders lower as I look at him, wishing I actually was psychic. But I don't need to have psychic abilities to understand that he wasn't given a choice in running this place, and that just breaks my heart.

Back when I graduated high school, my dad tried to talk me into going to medical school. He couldn't understand my love of fashion and textiles and pushed me toward the medical sciences even though the only needle I'm not terrified of is a sewing needle. I've learned that your parents don't always know what's best for you, and it seems to me that Will buckled under the expectations of his family instead of chasing his dream.

And what a crying shame that is because his cooking is amazing. It's more than the recipes he's using because even I can follow a recipe. You can feel his heart in this food, and despite the fact that I'm a perfect stranger who has no influence whatsoever on his life, I know that Will should be sharing his passion.

"You're unhappy, aren't you?" Even though my words come out hushed and full of concern, Will's entire body tenses as I wait for him to admit it. "It's okay," I add gently. "You can admit it. Your unhappiness won't ruin my little travel experience, and I won't say anything to your family if you don't want me to."

For a second, it seems like he's considering being open with me and telling me how he really feels, but then he shakes his head slightly. "There's no point in admitting it," he finally grunts out, sounding much more like Lee than himself. "This is my job whether I like it or not."

I frown and set down my fork. Alright, let's get to the bottom of this.

"But why? Why does it have to be *your* job?"

And then, he finally looks at me. I'm pierced by the unhappiness in his pretty green eyes. "In order for my parents to retire, they needed someone to take this place over. Lee is a police officer, and Svea was too young at the time, and now she has her boutique, which leaves me, who's always helped them here in whatever spare time I had anyway. There was no one else for them to consider."

I don't look away from him even after he finishes speaking. He took on this job whether he wanted to or not, so his parents could retire.

I've never heard of that kind of selflessness. It throws me for a loop because most of the people I worked with at Style by Y had no issues with making a stink over being the one to sacrifice something, even if it meant it was better for the team. I was usually the one to do the extra work on the weekends, mostly because I wanted to prove myself, but also because I had nothing else to do, and I knew it would cause less drama if I just did it.

So for Will to have even a little bit of that kind of dynamic going on within his own family...my heart hurts for him. He deserves a chance to do what he wants to in life; we all do. He should have the choice to do something for a living that makes him happy.

Life is too short to not just go for it.

"I know this is none of my business, Will," I say softly, "but what do you wish you were doing instead of this? What would you be doing if you didn't have to be here?"

His green eyes widen just slightly, and the air in the room seems to shrink as he processes my question. He swallows hard. "No one's ever asked me that before."

I barely manage to restrain my hand from reaching over and touching his. I'm about to burst into tears for this man. No one has ever asked him that? No one?

Mamma, what the hell?

The perfectly quirky family I had a glimpse of today changes slightly in my mind. How could his parents not have asked him what he wanted? How could they put the responsibility of running Larkspur Inn on his shoulders and not wonder if he would be happy doing it?

"Honestly...I'd be doing *this*," he tells me, nodding towards his plate. "I'd be cooking."

My eyes are wet. Shoot.

Keep it together, Lacey.

"Because you love it."

"Yes."

You should, I want to say, but I'm pretty sure I've said more than enough at this point. I don't want to be one of those people who give advice when it's not asked for...but this feels like one of those times where it's a need-to-know kind of thing.

"Do your parents know that?"

He shrugs. "Mamma knows I'm good at it."

"That's not the same thing though."

He nods and sits back slightly. "You're right; it's not."

And then, I lose control of my hand because there it is, covering the warm skin of his knuckles. His eyes cut to mine, and my breathing goes haywire. Despite how out of control I feel right this second, I smile lightly at him.

"You should tell her how much you love it."

Will looks back and forth between my eyes, considering it, and then he gives one short nod. "Yeah, I should," he agrees quietly.

I squeeze his hand, trying not to blush, but at least it's not a bear hug because that's what I'd really like to give him. I force myself to release his hand then, and we finish our food quietly, both of us lost in thought.

I hope I didn't overstep, but even if I did, I think he needed to hear it. And I needed to be reminded, too. I wasn't put on this earth to run the corporate side of fashion. My passion lives within the threads and seams of what I'm creating with my own two hands.

Maybe...maybe I can take inspiration from Svea and think about selling things on Etsy or something. That's how she started, and now look at her—opening her own storefront. If I work as hard for myself as I did for Yvette, there's no doubt in my mind that I could do it.

Will stands up, rousing me from my thoughts, and takes my plate and his into the kitchen. I follow with our glasses and then help him put things away. I can tell that his mind is working. I've really got him thinking about it, and I'm glad. He shouldn't only be cooking for the guests who stay at the inn. He could open a whole restaurant, a Swedish cuisine restaurant, and I'm sure it would be a hit.

But I clamp my lips shut because I'm pretty sure I've unnerved him enough with our conversation at the table.

"Thank you for dinner, Will, and for teaching me," I say, and he straightens up from where he's putting dishes into the dishwasher. He gives me a smile, but it's tight, and I totally get it. "What can I do to make my stay here as pleasant for you as possible?" Yeah, guilt made me ask that.

His smile relaxes. "Pretty sure I'm the one who's supposed to ask that question."

"Right," I say with a chuckle. "Either way, I'm available to help with whatever. It's not like I have any work to do."

It's been weird, actually. I'm used to being able to anticipate the next thing that might be needed by my team or my boss, but now, everything is just radio silent. Thankfully there were a lot of distractions today with meeting his family and helping Svea, but in between that, I've been *bored*.

When was the last time I was bored? I don't like it. I need a hobby.

"That's good if you want to participate in the stuff going on this week." He closes the dishwasher and wipes his hands with the towel hanging on the oven door.

"Oh yeah? Like what?"

"There's the community Christmas Day dinner, the Holly Ball on Friday night, and the Silent Night Vigil on Christmas Eve, and then on Wednesday, there's the city-wide snowball fight, and Thursday the broomball game," he lists off. "And then tomorrow at the library, my dad is doing story time dressed as Santa."

"Oh my gosh, I love it," I say with a laugh.

"You might recognize the elf, actually," he hints as he covers the bowl of mashed potatoes, and then he turns to put them in the fridge.

"Oh, please tell me it's Lee," I beg with a huge smile.

He laughs from his belly, making me feel light, the shadow of our serious conversation gone, and turns back to me. "I wish. Believe me, I've asked him."

"Then who is it? Svea?"

Will sighs and points at himself with an embarrassed smile.

"*You?* You're the elf?"

"That I am," he admits sheepishly.

I giggle because come on...Will has to be over six feet tall. He'd make the tallest, cutest elf ever.

Oh my gosh, I'm so glad I didn't say that out loud.

"Well, I can't miss that, now can I?" I say, still giggling.

He smirks at me, and I honestly can't wait to see some elf ears on this guy. God bless Larkspur. This is going to be the best Christmas I've had in years.

Chapter Eight

Will

The library is bustling with more people than it probably sees on an average day. Poor Emma looks frightened over there behind the checkout counter. I'm pretty sure the usual story time she hosts on Tuesday mornings consists of about seven kids with a parent each, so the thirty-ish people gathered around the plush chair by the window has to be overwhelming for her.

I spot the Gustafsons, who are close friends of my parents, chatting it up with Emma's mom, Silvie, over by the Christmas tree in the corner. She's been wheelchair-bound since she and her husband were in a car accident a few years ago. Her husband, Emma's dad, was killed because a drunk driver hit them head-on. It sent a shockwave through our community, but even though Silvie is paralyzed from the waist down, she's still very active in the community and one of the nicest people I've ever met. Emma clearly takes after her.

The library looks beautiful. Emma strung up white Christmas lights around the two nearly floor-to-ceiling windows and decorated the Christmas tree with literary ornaments. Underneath, she's placed some wrapped books that she sells as Christmas gifts. She calls them "Blind Date Books" because the title and author aren't included on the wrapping. I see a few people standing around holding one, which is awesome.

On the floor is a huge red rug where a few kids are already sitting on their knees, some staring at my dad dressed as Santa and posing for a picture. While Pa usually isn't one for lots of attention, he loves this event. Even with the white beard, which Mamma scoffs at because it hides his handsome face, and Svea snaps when he isn't paying attention.

Storytime is set to start in a few minutes, and I've already donned my custom elf costume. Svea made it for me years ago, and the shade of green is more than a little bright for my liking. Then again, I'm not sure any shade of green would make me feel more dignified in this silly costume. I'm honestly more embarrassed at what I'm willing to do for my family than I am about the costume itself, pointy elf ears and all. A few years too late to put my foot down on this one, I guess.

The whole family is here today, actually. Mamma is wearing a burgundy dress and a Santa hat, and she allows people to call her Mrs. Claus as she walks among the throngs of people with a tray of cookies and bars. Lee disappeared through the rows of bookshelves a few minutes ago, apparently all business even during a special event. Svea is standing over with Lacey toward the back of the assembly, both of them chatting and giggling with coffee in their hands like they've been friends for years.

I see Lars's grandma making her way over towards them, leaning heavily on her walker as she goes. Every small town has a gossiper, and Grandma Janssen is absolutely ours. She has the sweet disposition and elderly bluntness that makes it easy for her to get whatever information she wants. No doubt she's going over to talk to the new woman in town and see what kind of gossip she can glean.

I shake my head slightly when Grandma Janssen introduces herself to Lacey. I know within the hour, information about her will be running far and wide in this town. Hopefully, Lacey doesn't mention Albie because there's no way Grandma J will keep that on the down-low.

She isn't the only community member to notice our new guest. I've spotted a handful of people swiveling their heads in Lacey's direction, no doubt wondering who she is and why she's here. So far, most people are just curious about her and not giving her the stink eye, so it's safe to say that Pa must've said something to his friends this morning. On Tuesday mornings, they get together for coffee at Alma's Diner and gossip more than their wives do. It seems he must have sent out quite the warning to be nice to Lacey, and I'm relieved for her. She already feels bad enough about that whole incident; there's no need for the townspeople to make her feel worse.

"Alright, everybody!" I call out, waving my arms to get everyone to quiet down. I catch Lacey's sparkling brown eyes and try not to think about what she might have to say about my costume after this. "Let's settle in and get ready for story time with Santa!"

The kiddos cheer, and several of them traipse their way to the big rug as Pa takes a seat in the emerald sitting chair Emma usually uses for story time, and opens his book. I take my place beside him, and I always wish I had a chair too because I feel like I stick out just that much more standing, and then he begins to read *The Night Before Christmas* with his best impersonation of Santa's voice.

As he reads, my eyes wander around the crowd. Most of the parents are smiling and watching their own kids on the rug, and for a split second, I feel a pang in my chest. Being a father is something I've always wanted. I love kids, and even though this costume is horrible, I really do like being included in these kids' memories. I like being part of the magic for them, even if it's just for a few years.

"*Merry Christmas to all, and to all a good night,*" Pa projects, and I smile at him as everyone claps, hoping that maybe one day, I'll be the one sitting there playing Santa for the community.

When I look back out at everyone gathered, I see Lee standing off to the side, a library book tucked under one arm. He isn't at all interested in what Pa is doing or who's here. He's steadily gazing across the room at Emma, who's so distracted by the volume of people here that she doesn't notice. And being the annoying younger brother that I am, I take the first opportunity I can to go over and tease him about it.

"Officer," I greet as I move to stand next to him. He rolls his eyes. "Pick out a good one?" I ask, nodding toward the book.

"Yeah."

"Which one?"

His arm clamps down on the book. "None of your business."

I chuckle. "I hope it's *Talking to Women for Dummies*."

Lee finally looks away from Emma to glare at me. "Read that one, have you? Hasn't done you much good apparently."

"Ouch, good one."

He looks away from me again, but this time he makes a show of looking around at everything else. Who does he think he's fooling?

"She looks pretty today," I comment casually, because it's true, Emma always looks pretty, but I say it mostly because I know it'll kill my brother to hear me compliment her.

Something hard hits my arm, and I laugh because it was his hand.

"You think you're so clever, don't you?"

"What? She does." I gesture toward her. She's still standing behind the counter, terrified eyes only partially hidden by her black-framed glasses. "She's single, right? Maybe I should ask her to the Holly Ball."

"Do that and you're a dead man," Lee grinds out, his face as red as Mamma's hat as she shuffles past us to refill her tray of goodies. She stops to offer some to Grandma Janssen, who gives Lacey's hand a squeeze before they go their separate ways.

I don't even bother curbing my laughter at Lee. He needs to get up the courage to ask Emma out. I don't know what's holding him back. She might be a little shy, but I do know that she's a sweetheart who would do anything for anyone.

"Well, hello, Christiansen men," comes Lacey's cheerful voice from the right.

"Merry Christmas," I say, bowing my elf hat at her, and she laughs.

The conversation we had at dinner had me up half the night. Mostly because it caught me off guard how easily she called me out on being unhappy. It felt like whiplash to talk about it, but there's no denying that she's right. I guess Lee isn't the only one who needs to find some courage.

"You look amazing," she says to me, gesturing at my costume. I try not to blush and fail. I can feel Lee's eyes on me, and that doesn't help.

"Courtesy of Svea," I say with a playful eye roll.

"I *thought* the artistry looked familiar." Her smile is sweet but also teasing, and I can't help how much I like it.

"I hope you didn't tell all your secrets to Grandma Janssen," I tell her. "She's Lars's grandma and the biggest gossip in Larkspur."

Lacey's jaw drops open a little. "What? But she was so nice."

"She is nice, but she's also a snoop. She uses her age to get whatever she wants."

She looks in the direction of where Grandma Janssen is shuffling off to. "Sheesh. I guess I need to watch my mouth."

"You going to the Holly Ball?" Lee throws out gruffly.

She and I both look at him, startled by his sudden interjection.

"The Holly Ball? I'm not sure...I don't really know the details," she answers. I keep my eyes on my brother because I have a feeling he's up to something. When his dark eyes meet mine, I catch a glint of something mischievous that reminds me of our little sister.

"Elf boy knows all about it." He pats me hard on the shoulder, enough to push it down, so I shove him lightly.

"More like elf *man*," Lacey blurts out suggestively, and then her previously carefree face goes slack, her brown eyes wide.

Lee coughs out just one surprised huff of laughter, but it's enough to immediately send her into explanation mode.

"I mean obviously he's a *man*, Lee, and not a boy. That's...obviously obvious." She laughs nervously like she did last night when she said watching me cook should be a spectator's sport. This time, she's blushing even more, and I'm trying even harder not to laugh than I was last night. "Anyway...uh, what's the deal with the Holly Ball?"

"It's a dance," Lee answers, his deep voice wavering just slightly like he's also trying not to laugh. "People dress up and all that."

"Sounds fun."

"Elf *man* here usually goes stag."

I narrow my eyes at Lee, but he ignores me. "So do *you*."

"By choice," he clarifies irritably.

"Right. It's your *choice* not to ask—"

"*God Jul!*" Mamma interrupts, suddenly standing in front of me with a full tray of treats.

"Sorry?" Lacey asks, puzzled.

"That's 'Merry Christmas' in Swedish," I translate, and she brightens.

"Oh, *God Jul* to you, too!" she replies to Mamma, who gives her a very approving nod.

"So good to see you again, dear," Mamma tells her genuinely, and I suddenly remember that Lacey's mom died. No wonder they're hitting it off so well. Now there's no way she isn't spending Christmas with us.

"You, too. We were just talking about the Holly Ball," she tells Mamma.

"Oh, the Holly Ball is so much fun. It's the one night of the year that Freddie and I dance the night away."

I smile at her and glance over to where Pappa and Svea are talking with Lars's dad.

"That sounds so fun," Lacey says warmly. "I'd love to go, but I don't have a dress."

I elbow her gently. "Weren't you the one helping Svea with sewing yesterday? You have a couple days to make one. Otherwise, you could buy one from her that's already made."

She gives me a little sheepish grin. "Duh," she says with a chuckle. "Of course."

"Great, so you two can go together then," Lee concludes with a clap on my back that wobbles my elf ears.

"What a lovely idea," Mamma gasps.

Honestly, yes. It's a lovely idea. But only if it doesn't exist in this situation where I kind of already like this girl, and she's from Minneapolis. And I'm busy.

"Yeah, but I'll be a miserable date. There's always so much to do that I don't even get to enjoy it," I point out, and even though it comes off sounding like an excuse, I realize it's absolutely the truth. That's kind of depressing.

"Too busy chaperoning those teenagers, huh?" Lacey asks with a big smile and nudges my arm. Her levity is deeply appreciated, and I return her smile instantly.

"Something like that."

"Oh, well, maybe you and Lee, then," Mamma suggests, looking at her firstborn. His brown eyes widen slightly as he glances between her and Lacey. I bite my tongue to keep from laughing because he's caught in the classic dilemma that I usually am—you can't say no to Mamma.

But Lacey laughs good-naturedly. "Me and this guy?" She thumbs toward Lee. "No offense, buddy, but I can't imagine you dancing."

Lee relaxes slightly and just nods in agreement.

"Svea can be my date," she decides, looking over her shoulder for my sister, who's attempting to snap Pappa's Santa beard while his head is turned away from her.

When I look back at Mamma, she has a scrunchy frown on her face that she aims at both me and Lee, but she drops it when Lacey turns back to face our little group again.

"Well, I better get back to mingling. Will, grab a tray, too. We need our elf making the rounds as well," she instructs, and then heads towards Pa, who's scowling playfully at Svea while she slinks away from him, apparently successful in snapping his beard.

"Duty calls," I tell Lacey with a sigh. "You're going with Svea to finish up her inventory, right?"

"Yeah, she and I are going straight over after this."

"Let me know if you need a ride back to the inn. I'll be around."

"Thanks, Will."

I give her one last smile and then turn towards my brother. "Officer," I mutter in farewell, and give him a nod.

He gives me an unimpressed look. "Idiot."

I smirk and shake my head, then make my way to the folding table across the space where I load up a tray of treats.

As much as Lee just tried to put me on the spot, I realize it doesn't matter. I know it would be really fun to go to the Holly Ball with Lacey, but what I said was true. I'm usually the one refilling the punch bowl and making sure no one has spiked it, or the one serving snacks or cleaning up spills. I don't usually mind it that much because I get to watch my parents dance, but this year, I realize it would be nice to actually attend for the fun of it.

I sigh and bring my tray around to the slowly dissipating crowd. Lars's dad claps me on the shoulder as I go by, and others joke about me being the biggest elf in the county, and by the time my tray is empty, the crowd is clearing out, and Mamma instructs me to start cleaning up.

I empty the garbage pails, put the leftover treats into the containers Mamma brought them in, and then break down the folding table. When I look up, I see Svea and Lacey heading out the front door, and Mamma and Pappa getting their coats on. Silvie Mackenzie is being wheeled out by her oldest daughter, Caitlin, and Grandma Janssen is holding her hand as they go. I spy Lee over at the counter, checking out his book at the last possible moment, I realize, and head over that way too with a container of cookies to give to Emma.

Their exchange is brief, probably just simple pleasantries, but I walk slowly to see if maybe my brother will actually ask her to the ball. But all he does is take his book and give her his friendliest nod. He catches my eyes as he turns away from the counter, and his eyebrows immediately lower.

"Hey, Emma," I greet with a smile as I approach the counter.

"Hi," she replies quietly, a shy but genuine smile on her face as usual.

"Thanks for putting this on again this year. The kids love it almost as much as my dad does."

She snickers and tucks a few strands of jet-black hair behind her ear. Lee lingers slightly behind me, and it gives me so much joy that he doesn't trust me to talk to her alone.

"Yeah, you always do a great job," Lee adds, to my surprise.

Emma glances at him and blushes a tiny bit more behind her glasses.

"Here, these are for you." I hand her the cookies. "If you don't want to share them with your family, I won't tell anyone." I wink at her, and she chuckles again, so quietly I almost don't hear it.

"Thanks."

"Merry Christmas, Emma," Lee says, his hand coming down on my shoulder as if to say I better be done speaking to her.

"Merry Christmas." She gives Lee the sweetest little smile, and I watch him return it.

I don't know what he's doing. He's crazy about this girl, and yet he won't do anything about it. Is he really just that stubborn?

"Thanks again," I say, and then head towards the door where I left my coat. Lee follows, and as we go outside, I can't help but give him a little guff. Before I can open my mouth though, he speaks.

"Didn't realize you were such a flirt," he grumbles, and I stop to look at him. He stops too, still blushing slightly from his interaction with Emma.

"I wasn't flirting, Lee. I was being friendly. You should try it some-time," I hint, nodding towards the library behind us. He instantly frowns at me.

"I'm friendly enough."

A laugh erupts from me. "Right. Well, if you want to get the girl, I suggest you amp up the friendliness a bit more." I pat his shoulder and turn towards where my truck is parked down the street a ways. He falls in line with me.

"Who says I want to get the girl?" he scoffs like that's the most ridiculous thing he's ever heard.

"Uh, the hearts in your eyes every time you look at her?"

Lee elbows me hard enough to nearly knock me over, but I laugh anyway.

"I'm not going after her, alright?"

I shake my head as we near my truck. "You're an idiot if you don't."

"Why?"

"Because I think she likes you, too. So if you don't ask her out, that definitely makes you an idiot. Especially because we both know she's too shy to ask you."

He stops and stares at me like he isn't sure whether I'm messing with him or not. I wait for him to ask if I really think so, but his mouth presses into a firm line instead. His mind processes what I said for so long that I have to purposely focus on keeping my eyebrows from raising in amusement.

After a moment, he huffs, which could mean anything from irritation to acceptance of what I've said, and then stalks off towards his police cruiser.

"Just think about it!" I call after him, but he ignores me and gets in his car. He honks at me as I get in the truck, and despite the annoying little brother in me, I really do want to see him happy.

He's always been the quiet, serious one, but I think deep down, he has a soft heart. I know he would make a loyal husband and good father, but for whatever reason, he's never put himself out there to anyone, including Emma. I think maybe he just wants to make sure he gets it right and that he doesn't get hurt, but at the rate he's going, he'll end up watching some other guy sweep Emma off her feet and then hate himself for the rest of his life because he never took the chance.

Chances are funny like that. There's always some element of risk involved that makes the outcome feel so improbable. But what Lee, and myself if I'm honest, forgets, is that taking a chance is always worth it. Because then, at least you know for certain what is meant for you to keep and what was meant for you to lose.

But that doesn't mean that I'm going to take a chance and ask Lacey to the Holly Ball. Some chances are more like calculated risks...and Lacey is a risk that really only has one possible outcome, which is me alone in Larkspur while she goes back to her life in Minneapolis. It doesn't matter how well she gets along with my family or how good a person she is because when her car is fixed, she'll be gone.

So don't get attached, Will.

But deep down, I worry it's already too late for that.

Chapter Nine

Lacey

I can't stop the mental image of Will in his elf costume from living rent-free in my mind as I sew in Svea's office. It was just...perfect. Big-shouldered, tall bright green elf with the hat and ears and everything. And honestly, the guy wasn't even embarrassed. He *owned* that costume, and I had the hardest time keeping my eyes off him at the library.

"So, I assume you're going to the Holly Ball?" I ask Svea, who's bent over pinning some fabric at her desk while I work away at the sewing machine.

She gives a little wistful sigh. "Ah, the Holly Ball. What better place to let love unfold?" Then she cackles. "What better place to play pranks on your brothers?"

I laugh with her at that.

"One year, Lee was standing so still all night that he didn't notice I'd tied his shoelaces together for nearly an hour." Svea stands upright as she laughs some more. "Oh, the poor soul went down like a sack of potatoes."

I shouldn't laugh, but I do. "Oh my gosh, I bet he was super angry."

"Wouldn't speak to me for two weeks after that, but it was totally worth it."

I feed the fabric through to the end and then lift the foot so I can take it out and cut the thread. Then, I flip it over and begin sewing the other side, taking pins out as I go.

"And then Will—" Svea stops her sentence to laugh, "Will couldn't figure out why he smelled so bad until he finally reached into his jacket pocket and found the pickled herring I left in it." She's gasping now and wipes at her eyes as I laugh, too.

"You're the worst, Svea," I say through my laughter, but she just eats it up.

"Oh, they know it's all in good fun." She takes a deep breath as her laughter dies down, and she returns to her work with a big smile on her face.

I think of how she salted Will's coffee and how I said I would help him retaliate. Hmm, we need to get on that.

"Do they ever get you back?"

"Pssh. They're too scared. They know I'll get them back even worse."

I chuckle, knowing full well that she absolutely would.

"But to answer your question, yes, I'm going." She gasps and stands upright again. "You need a dress!"

I lift my foot off the pedal. "Yes, I do."

Svea's green eyes sparkle with excitement. "Oh my gosh, I have just the one—" Then she sprints out of the office and returns a moment later holding a glittery green dress. "Look at it. It's glamorous and sparkly, and it would look dynamite on you!"

I cut the thread and stand up, then put the shirt I was working on down on my chair so I can take a closer look at this beauty.

The fabric is smooth and iridescent in my hand. It's floor length with a slit up one side and a sweetheart neckline held up by black spaghetti straps.

"Wow," I whisper. "You made this, Svea?"

She grins with satisfaction. "I did, and it would look perfect on you. Try it on! If it doesn't fit, we can make alterations." She puts the dress in my hands, and I only hesitate for two seconds before I oblige. I take it into the bathroom across the hall, and the second the fabric touches my skin, I feel beautiful. The middle section is a little big on me, but I actually don't mind that it isn't skin-tight. It'll be easier to dance in.

"So?" Svea calls through the door. "It's perfect, isn't it? I knew it!"

I smile and open the door to an ecstatic Svea, who insists that I twirl and walk up and down the hallway to see how it fits.

"I love it," I tell her. "You have such a gift when it comes to creating."

My heart clenches as I look down at myself. *This* is what I should be doing. This one-on-one with a garment until it's perfect, and then selling it to a woman whom I actually meet in person. I shouldn't be up in some office, deliberating over swatches and trends, far away from the client and the fabric. *This* is the experience I should be chasing.

"It's yours, girl. You're going to drop some jaws at the Holly Ball, that's for sure."

"I'll pay you for it. How much is it?" I search around on the dress for a price tag, but there isn't one.

"Lace, you've helped me so much by donating your time and talent. It's on the house, okay? You won't talk me out of it, so just say yes." She beams at me and claps her hands in excitement. "Ooh, I can't wait. I'll totally be your wingman. Any guy you want at the Holly Ball, okay? I know everyone. I can help you snag a good dancer."

I laugh softly. "Oh, good. Lee was trying to set me up with Will, and then Mamma was trying to set me up with Lee." I shake my head as Svea laughs.

"With *Lee*?"

"I know." I cackle. "I told her that you were my date, so I hope you aren't already going with someone. If you are, that's totally fine though. I'll still have fun."

"Ha, good one. I don't have time for dating," she replies with a sigh, though she keeps the smile on her face as she lovingly lifts the skirt of my dress. "Besides, the guy I like is sort of off limits, so I'm all about going with you."

"Off limits? What do you mean?"

She rolls her eyes up to the ceiling. "It's so dumb, okay? I *know* it's dumb." She heaves a heavy sigh and looks back at me. "But I can't help it."

I'm not one of those gossipy people, but I have never wanted to know more about something than I do right now. I try to keep my excitement in check because Svea's expression is less than happy, and I need to be good to my new friend.

"Here, let me change out of this, and then you can tell me all about it, okay?"

"Sounds good." She gives me a little nod and ducks back into the office, and I quickly head back into the bathroom to change out of my gorgeous new dress. Part of me wishes I had someone to wear that for, but I realize as I bring it back out with me that I can wear it for *me*. That can be enough.

"Alright," I say, placing the dress near my coat. "Let's hear it. I'm all ears."

Svea's sitting in the desk chair behind her desk, and when I take my seat at the sewing machine, she slowly spins in circles as she starts talking.

"You know that guy who just always knows how to make you feel validated? Like the really supportive guy who can't see a single one of your flaws? He's that guy. He's...sweet, and funny, and just an all-around good guy."

"He sounds great," I agree, as she continues to spin slowly in her chair.

"So great. And he's cute, and his family is amazing." Svea sighs again, sounding truly lovesick. "But the problem is, he's kind of my brother's best friend." She winces up at the ceiling.

Her brother? Which one?

"So, my stupid feelings don't matter because he's always just seen me as a little sister. And even if maybe somewhere deep down he *does* like me, he'd never do anything about it because Lee would kill him."

"Oh, he's *Lee's* best friend?" I blurt out. "Yikes."

Now, I get it. Wait—her brother's best friend? Isn't that what she said when we were talking about how Lars can't keep a secret to save his life?

"Exactly," Svea says, finally slowing to a stop. "So, it can never be. What a shame, right?"

"Are you sure there's no way to even just see if he feels the same?" I ask gently.

She shrugs, and I hate to see how bummed out she looks. I can't imagine how horrible it would be to want somebody you feel like you can't have.

"I'm just saying. If he doesn't, then you know for sure, and you can try to move on." Ugh, there I go again, giving unsolicited advice. I open my mouth to apologize, but Svea speaks first.

"But what if he *does* feel the same? What do we do then? Lee would never be cool with him dating me."

I scoot my chair closer and put my hand on hers. "It really isn't up to Lee. What's he going to do? Arrest you?"

Svea giggles at that. "I'd like to see him try."

I chuckle and squeeze her hand. "I know I'm a complete outsider here, but if you really think it could be a forever thing, then screw what Lee thinks."

She smiles at me appreciatively. "I can't tell whether you're the angel or the devil on my shoulder."

I laugh. "Maybe I'm a little bit of both." I grin at her and then pull her into a hug that she doesn't shy away from.

"I'll think about it," she says as she pulls back.

I smile, and I'm struck by how quickly I've bonded with Svea and her family. Being around them makes me feel happier than I have in years.

Who would've thought? I'm jobless and stranded in a small town I've never been to before, and I'm...*happy*? Who knew I needed so little to feel so content? Maybe I should be *thanking* Albie. It's because of him that I ended up here.

It's becoming more and more apparent to me that I should be making some life changes. Maybe I need to move out of the Twin Cities where it's cheaper to rent a storefront. Maybe I can have a little boutique just like this. Maybe I could get on a dating website or try speed dating or something.

All I know is, I like what Larkspur has to offer, especially because the Christiansens live here. I already hate the idea of leaving next week and never speaking to any of them again. I decide right then that I'll keep in touch with them, especially Svea. I'm not dumb enough to let good people slip out of my life.

I spent the afternoon with Svea finishing up her inventory, and then Will picked me up on his way back to the inn after he was done grocery shopping. Being back in the kitchen with him only reminded me of last night's awkward fest, but I still had dinner with him and helped him clean up afterward.

And as I was wiping down the dining room table, I happened to notice a small glass front cabinet with all the classic board games inside it. Monopoly, Battleship, Jenga, Yahtzee, all of them. But the one that caught my eye was Scrabble. My mom and I used to play Scrabble when I was a teenager. It was our rainy day game, and I loved playing it with her, even though she nearly always won.

So, basically, I begged Will to play with me.

I don't know if he had other plans for the evening, but too bad. We're playing Scrabble so I can feel a little closer to my mom.

"So, be honest with me about something," I say to Will as we take turns picking Scrabble tiles.

"Uh, okay," he agrees skeptically.

"How many times a year do you wear that elf costume just for the hell of it?" Maybe I shouldn't make fun of him, but I can't help myself.

He chuckles. "Oh, a dozen, at least," he answers with sarcasm.

"Halloween, birthdays, etc," I tack on as we laugh.

"Yeah, people hire me for special appearances, all of that."

I snort and choose my tiles, setting them on the little wooden holder. I start to rearrange them. "You're basically the town mascot."

"Oh, no, that was Albie." He grimaces at me but then winks, and my little heart goes pitter-patter. He nods toward my letters. "Ladies first."

"Such a gentleman."

"I try."

I eye him for a moment, observing the easy-going expression on his lightly freckled face as he moves his tiles around on his holder. He really is a gentleman. It's probably because he's in the hospitality business and being polite is sort of part of the job, but I also get the sense that Will is a genuinely good person. The fact that he doesn't enjoy his job, but still continues to do it for his parents, says a lot about his character.

"You really are. You're a good guy," I say softly, and his green eyes look up at me. I smile at him. "Not many of those around in the Twin Cities, at least not that I've stumbled upon."

"Hmm," he says, and I decide on the word I'm going to put down on the board to get this game rolling. "You'd think there would be more people to pick from with a higher population there. Here, dating prospects are pretty limited. Everyone knows everyone, you know?"

I place my word down tile by tile. "I suppose, yeah." I pick out four more letters to replace the ones I used and put them with the others, trying to figure out how best to use them all together.

"Not that people don't get married here, because obviously they do, but it's pretty rare to find your soulmate in a small town. The exception is probably Lee, but he'll never do anything about it."

Ooh, more gossip. About *Lee*? Call me Grandma Janssen, because wow, I'm getting all the stories today.

"Lee has a soulmate?"

He smiles in amusement and puts down his word, working off of the one I put down. "He won't admit it, but he does. I don't get why he doesn't go for it. If I was in love with someone, I couldn't just ignore it like he does."

Aha, so Will is definitely single. Why that matters, I don't know, but it's definitely noted. "Yeah? There's no lucky woman you have your eye on?"

Will replenishes his holder with new letters as a laugh catches in his throat. "Nope. Believe me, Mamma isn't happy about that. She's been asking me and my siblings for grandchildren for years."

The thought of Mamma being a grandma is such a warm thought. His parents will make fantastic grandparents. I can't imagine them being anything but completely involved in their lives as they grow up in this town. A new generation of Christiansens.

"Besides, I'm too busy for dating. I don't have the time to devote to a relationship. It wouldn't be fair," he adds, and I put down two tiles to work off of the word he put down.

A bit of guilt creeps in. That's exactly the issue I had with the last guy I dated. I wasn't available enough and never saw him.

"I hear that," I agree. "Work has consumed my life so much that I haven't had time for love either. Now, I'm realizing how much I regret that." I fidget with an E tile. "There's more to life than work, and being here in Larkspur is teaching me that."

Will smiles at me. "That's good."

I nod and thoughtfully watch him place his letters on the board. "I don't know how I got it so wrong, you know? Now that my job isn't filling up every spare bit of my life, and I'm here, I see how much I've missed out on. Family. Friends. Love." I sigh heavily, reminding me of Svea's lovesickness. "I want what your family has. I—I want what my parents had before she died." My eyes stay on the tiles in front of me, but I don't really see them. "It's kind of crazy that I never realized how lonely I am until I showed up here."

"Nothing like a little car accident to shake things up, I guess."

I smile at him. "I guess."

We each play a turn in comfortable silence, both of us in our own heads, and then he plays the word HEJ, which is definitely not a word.

"Challenge," I say, nodding at his tiles.

"It's Swedish," he explains. "It means 'hey.'"

I narrow my eyes at him slightly. "Oh, we're using words from other languages, too?"

One side of his mouth curves up. "That's how my family plays it."

"Mhm. And this non-Swedish speaker is just supposed to trust you?"
He chuckles and shrugs.

I make a show of dramatically conceding. "Fine. But only because
you're cute." A gasp escapes me that those words just came out of my
mouth. I swear, I'm not trying to flirt with him. But apparently, I can't
stop flirting and then mortally embarrassing myself. "Uh—I mean, uh—"
I cough and feel my cheeks heat up. "Only because—because you're a
cute elf."

Nope, that's not much better.

I laugh nervously and avoid his eyes. "So, Swedish words are fine.
Yup. Let's move on." I put down two tiles. "There. Your turn, elf man."

Oh, wow. I need to just duct tape my mouth shut. Or confine myself
to my room. Will is grinning so wide now that I can see it out of my
peripheral vision.

"Sorry," I whisper. "You're probably used to being flirted with or
whatever."

His grin slips, and his eyes move up to the ceiling as he considers
what I said. "Actually, no. I can't think of the last time a woman flirted
with me."

"Oh." That just makes it worse, right? Sigh. "Well, I'm not trying to
make you uncomfortable. I can't get myself to stop putting my foot in
my mouth, apparently."

His smile returns. "You're fine, Lacey. I'm...flattered."

My cheeks feel even warmer.

"And honestly, I can't remember the last time I got to know anyone
new. Being around you is exciting." He rakes his fingers through his
reddish-brown hair and shoots me a friendly smile.

My shoulders relax a little as my embarrassment eases.

"Even if you think I'm hot stuff," he adds with a smirk.

I scoff. "Okay, Mr. Cocky. I never said that."

"Didn't have to." He chuckles and winks at me.

He really is cute, dang it. And kind of sweet, and nice, and funny. I
don't buy it for a second that no one flirts with him. Who wouldn't?
The guy's a catch. Too bad he's too busy for a relationship, because—

Because what? I'd be interested?

Hooo, no. No, no. That's just...not a good idea. I barely know this guy, so even if we wanted to date or whatever, it would be long distance—I would be *getting to know him* long distance. I mean, that's not impossible to do, but... No. He lives here where he's too busy running the inn. I live in Minneapolis, where I'm too...unemployed and lost about what I should do next.

Well, kind of lost. Sewing with Svea has certainly helped clarify what I want to do with my career going forward. But I still am probably going to have to move out of my apartment and into a cheaper part of the Twin Cities and probably get a roommate so I can try to start my own business...

All of that sounds truly overwhelming. No wonder I haven't done it yet. No wonder I've stayed working at the same company even though it was sucking the life out of me. It was...safe.

And from where I'm sitting, the future looks pretty scary and uncertain. Can I really do what Svea is doing and be successful? Can I really get myself to take that kind of risk?

I frown down at my Scrabble tiles as Will takes his turn.

What is life without a little risk...right? Sometimes you have to do things that scare you to get where you want in life. Quit that job. Say yes to that date. Make that move. I've spent years being stuck in a holding pattern that benefitted somebody else. And the second that changed, I ended up *here*. In a place that has opened my eyes to all the other things in life that I want and have been too busy to pursue.

That has to be for a reason somehow. Right?

I better make sure Albie's death wasn't in vain.

Chapter Ten

Will

S he's lost in thought over there, and I'm not sure whether to intrude or not. The flirtatious, teasing moment we just had has passed, and I don't know what she's thinking about now.

Her flirting really is flattering. I've never had a woman so blatantly say things to me like that, and every time she does, it makes me feel lightheaded. And the little blush that steals across her face, and the way her brown eyes always widen...it's quickly becoming my favorite thing. It shouldn't, but it is.

That's not the only reason I like being around her though. She's something new and different, and yet she has moments like these where she's thoughtful and introspective. She's a perfect mixture of fun and depth, and if things were different, if she lived here and I knew how to say no to my parents, I wouldn't hesitate to ask her out.

"So, you up for the Annual Snowball Fight tomorrow?"

Lacey looks up at me with bright eyes. "Oh, that's right! I don't have any snow pants or anything."

"No worries. People come and just watch, too. It's not as intense as the Broomball Tournament. That's Thursday."

She smiles at me. "Do you play in the tournament?"

"I do," I answer. "If you come watch, you'll get to see me participate in an actual spectator's sport."

She blushes and laughs nervously. "Never going to live that down, am I?"

I just chuckle. I shouldn't tease her, but I can't help it.

"Svea had a dress for me to wear to the Holly Ball," she informs me excitedly. "It's beautiful. I can't wait to wear it."

I smile at her and put down my word on the board.

"It's green, just like your elf costume," she adds with a snicker and a flash of brown eyes behind her dark eyelashes. "You could wear it, and we'd totally be matchy-matchy." She barely gets the words out before her snickering turns into a full-on laugh.

"Matchy-matchy," I mutter thoughtfully. "Challenge."

She beams at me and then shrugs. "I'm just saying, Will."

"Mhm." I can't stop smiling at her. "Tempting, but no."

"Well, what are you wearing then? You have a tux in the back of your closet for special occasions?" I watch her slender fingers put down two letters around my word.

"Would you believe me if I said I did?"

"Well, I know for a fact you have that elf costume in there, so at this point, I wouldn't be surprised by what else is in your closet."

I smirk. "No skeletons, I promise."

Lacey's smile relaxes a little. "None? I'm sure you all are on your best behavior around Mamma, but I can't imagine you and your siblings haven't gotten into at least a little trouble growing up."

I move a couple of tiles around on my holder, avoiding her eyes. "Well, we had to have a little fun, didn't we?"

She claps, getting my attention. "I knew it! Tell me. Tell me all the things!" she pleads with such an exuberant expression that I can't help but laugh and feel my heart warm for her just a little more. I can't deny her.

"Well, you already know that Svea has always been the prankster in the family, so obviously she's gotten up to quite a bit of things over the years, but the best story I have of all three of us is when—" I pause, narrowing my eyes on her anticipating expression. "How good are you with secrets?"

"Oh, the best. I'm the *best* with secrets. I swear I won't tell a soul," she assures me vehemently, even raising her right hand like she's taking an oath.

"Alright. I'll tell you, but it stays in this room, understood?"

Lacey nods vigorously. "I promise."

I lean forward slightly, forgetting about our Scrabble game for the moment. "So, Lee was fifteen, I was thirteen, and Svea was ten, and my parents had gone to the Gustavsons for card night or something, so it was the three of us at home."

"Uh huh," Lacey urges me on, hanging on my every word and making me feel stupidly lucky to have so much of her attention.

"Lee was supposed to be in charge of us, and he was taking that job very seriously, as you can imagine, pretty much being a demanding tyrant about us not playing around or literally having any fun. Naturally, that got on my nerves and egged Svea on all the more to be rambunctious." Lacey links her hands together in front of her and brings them below her chin, eyes intent on me as she listens. "I think Svea said something about tattling on Lee for saying a bad word, but said she wouldn't if he kissed Mamma's favorite *tomte*." Her eyes go round. "And, well, obviously he wouldn't do that, so Svea started chasing him around the house with it. Lee started yelling at her that she was going to end up breaking it, so she threw it to me, and we started playing catch with it."

"Oh my gosh," Lacey whispers in anticipation, her eyes wide but her grin just barely held back.

"So, then Lee tried to get it back from us, and we were playing keep away. He's boiling mad, and me and Svea are having the best time of our life, but then—" She gives a little gasp like she can see into my brain. "Lee reaches for it midair and instead of catching it...knocks it to the ground."

"Did it break?" she blurts out. I nod, grimacing.

"It broke clean in two. And all three of us went completely silent for about thirty seconds before the blame game started." Lacey giggles. "It was a combined effort, but no one would own up to it. We did agree though that we needed to fix that thing before our parents got home because we all knew Mamma would never forgive us."

"And did you? Did you fix it before they got home?"

"The glue was still wet when they pulled in the driveway," I answer, still remembering how terrified we were that she would happen to touch it that night. "But the worst part is that even after the glue set and we all agreed to never speak of that night, we also knew that there was a really big chance she would notice the crack when she did the dusting or whatever. So we lived in fear for months, never knowing if today was going to be the day we all got caught."

"Did she notice? Did she whoop your butts?"

I chuckle. "No. Thankfully, she's farsighted."

Lacey lets out the cutest little cackle. "You were such naughty kids," she teases, and I shrug because, yeah, we were. Man, I haven't thought about that memory in a long time.

"So now you know, and you promised not to tell a soul, remember?" I warn, raising one eyebrow at her.

"Right. Not a soul. I swear." She holds her hand out to shake across the table, and I take it with a smile. The strange notion to kiss her hand zips through me, alarming me slightly, and I clear my throat.

She sighs as I bring my tingling hand back to my tiles. "I always thought it would be fun to have a sister."

"It's overrated," I claim with a wink that makes her snicker.

"Especially when she salts your coffee."

"Don't remind me."

Our light laughter mingles together, and the way it sounds echoing around the house has my heart beating a little harder. She's something special; I can feel it. I don't know why it's so easy to talk and joke with her, but I can't ignore how much I like being around her. And every time I remind myself that she isn't staying, that she's just stuck here temporarily, I find myself more and more disappointed.

"So, have you heard any news about your car?"

She shakes her head and moves a tile from one side of her holder to the other. She says nothing for a moment but opens her mouth and closes it twice.

"What?" I prompt.

Lacey glances up at me, biting her lip. I slide my foot forward and bump hers under the table. She looks up again, and this time, her brown eyes stay on mine.

"What is it?"

She taps the tile in her fingers on the table a couple times before she speaks. "Do you believe in fate or destiny—or just...things happening for a reason?"

My head cocks to the side, not expecting her to say that. "I don't know. I guess I haven't thought about it before."

She nods to acknowledge what I said.

"Do you?"

She bites her lip again, and I hate how it makes my attention zero in on her lips. "I didn't. But, after ending up here...I think I might," she explains quietly, her eyes dropping again. I wait for her to say more and am grateful when she goes on. "Things here are just so different from my normal life, but in a really good way. In a way that makes me realize I have the opportunity to start completely over and...reorganize my priorities." She gives a thoughtful sigh. "If it hadn't been for Albie, I would've driven right past this sweet little town and your amazing family and never realized what I was missing." Her eyes finally lift to mine, and the vulnerability in them slices me clean through. "So, yes. I think it happened for a reason."

I can't look away from her, my heart pounding as I wonder...*what reason?*

And the selfish part of me that doesn't make an appearance all that often desperately wants to be that reason. I want to be the reason she's here. I want to mean something to her. But that's ridiculous. I'm not anybody to her. The things she's talking about—the things she's missing—those don't involve me. I'm not an important person in her world, and I won't become one either. There isn't time. She'll go back to her life and make it something she loves. She'll go back knowing what she's looking for.

I'll be here like I always have been. Carrying on in the same way I always do. Without her and without anyone even like her. While she makes good on her epiphany, I'll continue to plod along in this inn, endlessly working to take care of everyone and everything else.

Where's *my* epiphany? Where's the thing that puts it all in perspective?

And those beautiful coffee-colored eyes, filled with such transparency and openness, will be burned into my brain for the rest of my life. I just know it. That's all I'll have of her to hold onto as her life moves forward and mine stands still.

If she's here for a reason, it's to give me a tiny glimpse of something I can never have. And that just seems...cruel.

The Annual Snowball Fight is supposed to be fun.

It's a family event, where kids and adults alike gather at Larkspur Park to lob snowballs at each other for the sake of doing something fun. There's only one rule, and that's don't throw snowballs at anyone's face. Simple. All play, no seriousness.

But apparently, I didn't get the memo because it's only been twenty minutes, and it's already become an all-out war. Svea and I are ducked behind a park bench and making plans to annihilate Lee and Lars, who are holed up behind the statue of Larkspur's founder, Charles Larkspur, about thirty feet away.

Kids are weaving in and out of our battleground, some chased by their parents, so beaning my brother and his best friend has been incredibly tricky. Thankfully, they're having the same problem, and we've only been hit a couple of times by their snowy projectiles.

"Okay, I think if I can lob it just right, I can drop a snowball right down on them from above," Svea says conspiratorially, her mittened hands pressing snow into a ball.

"Yeah, up and over," I agree, forming snowballs, too. We have about a dozen stockpiled between us. I peek up over the top of the bench and almost immediately see Lee send a snowball at my face. I quickly duck down, and it sails over my head. "Ooh, he aimed right for my face, Svee. All rules are out the window."

"Yes!" she hisses, his eyebrows dipped low as she smiles in an evil way. It would scare me if I wasn't on her team.

"Ah, I wish I had my slingshot. Oh well—you chuck one up and over. You can do it."

"I got this." She packs the snowball in her hands together one more time and then peeks around the side of the bench to guess the distance. She looks back at me seriously and nods.

I proudly watch my little sister take a steadying breath and heave a snowball up in the air, over the park bench. I look over the top just in time to see Lee about to hurl another snowball at me but instead gets hit from above with the snowball Svea perfectly aimed.

"Åh nej!" he exclaims in surprise and dismay as he stumbles back.

"What the—?" Lars starts to say, appearing just next to my brother, but Svea has already aimed another and gets him, too. "Ah! I've been hit!"

Svea cackles as we both stand up and chuck the remaining snowballs we have at them. We land two hits each before they scramble back behind the cover of Charles, and we drop back down to replenish our snowball stockpile.

"Svea, you rule!" I shout, and high-five her.

"I was born for this, bro!"

We quickly pack and roll more snow into ammo, and Svea's evil mind keeps turning.

"Okay, they're onto us now. They're likely going to try and get us from above, too. So, we should switch our strategy."

"Right. Yeah." I look around us, becoming aware of the small throng of people collected along the edge of Larkspur Park. I see the familiar puffy black coat and lavender beanie, and I get an idea. "We need a diversion," I say.

"Yes. Love that idea. What do we—" She sees where I'm looking, and I can feel her grin warming the side of my periphery.

"We get Lacey to join the fight," I suggest. "She can go over and join their ranks to find out their plans, and then we'll cover her while she abandons them and joins us."

"A spy!" Svea cheers, but then she frowns. "Wait—there's no way Lee is going to fall for that. He isn't going to let her just stroll up and join them."

I look over the park bench and another snowball whizzes by my head. I duck down again. "I don't know; they might be desperate enough."

Svea shakes her head. "Think about who we're talking about here, Will. It's Lee. He doesn't trust anyone, much less the out-of-towner who ran over Albie." She tosses a snowball up and catches it. "But we do know that he'll do anything to protect anyone, right? That's his job. So, I say Lacey plays the damsel in distress card to lure him out, and then we go avalanche on his butt."

I stare at my sister in wonder and a little fear. "Remind me to never cross you."

She grins. "It would be wise. Do you have your phone on you?"

I bite the fingers of my glove and pull to get it off, then dig underneath my snow pants to get to the pocket of my jeans. I quickly dial Lacey's number as Svea makes more snowballs.

"Hello?" Lacey answers, sounding a little confused.

"Hey, we need you," I say without pretense. "Can you fake an injury?"

"*What*? You want me to fake an injury? Why?"

"To distract Lee and Lars, then me and Svea can go in for the kill," I explain, watching her from the distance between us. I can just barely make out the surprised expression on her face from here.

"I thought this was supposed to be just a fun thing."

"We're way past that. Will you help us?"

She laughs awkwardly for just a second and then sighs, full of uncertainty. Svea holds out her hand towards me.

"Gimme," she demands, and I hand the phone over. "Girl, listen. It's all down to you. We want to take down these bozos, and we need you to help us. All you have to do is come closer and throw a snowball at a passing kid or someone, and then pretend to trip and fall. Do it right in front of our park bench, okay? Then, when Lee comes out to check on you, get the hell out of the way."

I grin at my sister as she speaks, all business. She listens for a second, and then her eyes meet mine as a triumphant smile comes over her face.

"Lacey, you're the best! Alright, we'll wait for your cue. Thanks, Lace." She hangs up and gives my phone back. "She's in."

I turn my grin towards Lacey as she pockets her phone and then makes her way forward. With one furtive glance in my direction, she squats down and forms a snowball with bare hands. She disappears from view as she straightens up and moves closer to where a group of kids are chasing each other and shrieking.

"Alright, bro. Let's do this," Svea says seriously, handing me a snowball.

"I have a better idea." I grab four of the snowballs she's made and press them into one giant one. "You can throw smaller ones faster," I explain, "so you take the rest of those. I'll make another big one." I gather an armful of snow and pack it together. "That way if Lars comes out, too, I can get them both with snow boulders while you pelt them with the small ones."

"Got it."

Only a moment later and I hear Lacey let out a very convincing cry. "Ow! Ah, my ankle!" she shouts in pain. "Medic! I'm down!"

I nearly chuckle at that but forget about her theatrics when I hear Lee's growly voice.

"Don't move—let me see it."

Svea holds eye contact with me, both of us waiting.

"Ah man, Lacey. First your car and now your ankle?" comes Lars's voice, and then Svea grins, nods, and we follow through with our plan.

They never stood a chance, the idiots.

Lee is kneeling on the ground next to where Lacey sits, attempting to take her boot off as I haul the huge snowball up and dump it down on his shoulders.

"Ah! Will—time out! Lacey's hurt—"

As I bend down for the second snowball bomb, Svea unloads on Lars.

"Svea! Ah, dang it!"

I reappear with my ammo to see Lacey sprinting away toward the onlookers. "Sorry, Lee!" she calls out as she runs.

"What the hell?" he says, as Svea switches to pelting him, and I heave mine at Lars. He goes down, snow covering his upper body.

"Uncle!" Lars cries, waving his arms.

"Quitter!" Lee growls, but he's been knocked back to the ground as well.

"Say we won," I demand, my arm cocked up with a snowball aimed down at my older brother. Both of us exchange a death glare as Svea helps Lars up.

"Just say it," Lars groans out, dusting off his snow pants.

"You cheated," he says through gritted teeth.

I shrug. "No one said we couldn't call in reinforcements."

Lee's brown eyes narrow. "You won. *This* time."

I smirk and let the snowball in my hand drop to the ground.

Ah, victory.

It never gets old beating your brother. Especially Lee. He's so competitive and thinks he's the best at everything. His pride is wounded, and it feels fantastic. He probably won't speak to me until Christmas over this, but it was worth it.

Lee gets to his feet with a huff and casts me one more glare before he stalks off.

"Don't be a sore loser!" I call out after him, and I'm sure if there weren't kids and half the town present, he'd be flipping me the bird over his shoulder.

"Man, next year, I want to be on your team," Lars says to my sister, who beams like the sun itself. "Don't tell Lee I said that."

She chuckles and reaches up to knock some snow off his shoulder. "No promises."

"You've got a good arm, Svea," he compliments, and rubs his gloved hand in her hair. When he removes it, Svea has a flat look on her face, like she didn't appreciate the noogie he just gave her.

"We're still on for broomball tomorrow, right?" I ask him, and he reaches a fist out to tap mine.

"I'll be there. Good luck getting Lee to be a team player though."

"Ah, he'll get over it," I claim lightly, though I know he won't. But I'm more than confident that he won't sacrifice a broomball win just to get back at me and Svea.

Lars gives me a doubtful look but then shrugs. "Tomorrow, then. Later, Svea."

"See ya," she says, her voice sounding strangely small. I put my arm around her shoulders and steer her over to the sidewalk where the others are gathered. Lars goes over and hugs Grandma Janssen, who's sitting on a park bench nearby and piled with blankets to keep her frail little body warm.

I spot Lacey standing next to Mamma and grin at her. She rolls her eyes at me playfully as we approach.

"There she is," I say, dropping my arm from around my sister. "We couldn't have done it without you."

She laughs softly. "I'm probably going to hell for that."

"*Stygga barn*," Mamma mutters, which means "naughty children," but I can see the sparkle of delight in her eyes. She pulls down her blue wool scarf further over her head like she's embarrassed by us.

"It's my fault. They get it from me," Pa pipes up, and kisses Mamma's cheek.

"They absolutely do," she agrees, still pretending to be disappointed in us.

"It was Svea's idea—" I start to say, but when I turn to where Svea was standing next to me, I spot her walking away from us toward the street. Just from the tightness of her stride and shoulders, I can tell she's upset.

"Svea!" Lacey calls out and follows her. I watch her stop my sister, and then I see the anger and maybe even embarrassment on Svea's face. They speak to each other briefly, and then she departs after giving Lacey a quick hug.

What happened? She should be happy we won. She *was* happy about it, but now she's not? It isn't like my sister to be anything but bubbly or scheming.

When Lacey rejoins us, I can't help but ask, "What was that about?"

Lacey's brown eyes are concerned as she shrugs. "She wouldn't tell me. She said she just wanted to go home."

Mamma looks over her shoulder in the direction she went and then turns back to us, her features just as confused and worried as mine. "Go home and change out of your wet things," she says to me. "Then go see what has your sister upset."

I'm already nodding, but Lacey speaks up.

"I actually think she might need a little space. She said she didn't want to talk about it."

Pa's face scrunches into a frown. "You're right, dear. I know a certain someone who needs space when she's upset, too." He raises his eyebrows at Mamma, who frowns at him in return, though she doesn't deny what he said. Pa looks back to Lacey. "Everything hunky dory over there at the inn? Will is taking care of you?"

A streak of irritation sizzles through me. It's been years since I took over the inn, but both of my parents still express their doubts in what I'm doing. I realize they have high standards because the hospitality industry can be tough to navigate when it comes to travelers' expectations, but it stings that they still don't seem to trust that I know what I'm doing.

"Oh, of course," Lacey chirps. "I feel right at home. He even taught me how to make your meatballs, Mamma."

Mamma looks over at me in surprise. "You did?"

I nod and rub my damp gloved hands together.

Lacey gasps. "And those *curtains*! I can't believe they were handmade."

Mamma's previously surprised face splits into a wide grin filled with pride. The irritation I felt melts away as they both fall into a warm conversation about needlework, lace, and quilting.

It feels like a knife is twisting in my heart to see how easily she gets along with Mamma. Not that it's difficult—my mom is one of the friendliest people in our community. But I can always tell when Mamma speaks to someone she really doesn't care for, and that's definitely not the way she's speaking to Lacey. Mamma is being more than just polite with her—more than just the typical welcoming manner of conversing. Mamma adores this woman. And I'd be lying if I said I didn't adore her, too.

Chapter Eleven

Lacey

I wasn't sure what to expect from the snowball fight, and I definitely didn't plan on participating. But I couldn't let Will and Svea down. They were so serious about it. I had to help them out, even if it means I'm a terrible person.

Poor, sweet Lee, coming to see if I was okay... Despite his usual cloudy disposition, he really is a good man. Though I could say the same for Will, whose selflessness rivals a saint. And then Svea, so spunky and hardworking. All three of them have wiggled their way into my heart, and I feel incredibly grateful to know them.

They're so different from the people I'm used to being around. My coworkers were nothing like the Christiansens. The environment at work was cutthroat and gossipy. I could never really tell if I could trust my coworkers. I'm sure more than a few of them were glad to see me go because it meant better opportunities for them. I haven't heard from a single one of them since I was let go, not even a "thinking of you" or "wishing you the best" text. I don't miss the people I spent almost every day with for years.

But *these* people? The Christiansons? I can already tell that I'm going to miss them like crazy when I leave. Because they're people who live their lives based around family and community, not around what's best for themselves or their interests. I want to be everything they are and have everything they have.

As Will drives us back to the inn, I feel the urge to tell him these things. I want him to know how special I think his family is. I want him to understand how much of an honor it is to know them.

But he's been a little quiet today, and I'm not sure why. He could be tired. He could be tired of *me*. I don't want him to feel like he needs to entertain me or drive me anywhere I want to go. I don't want to be a burden on him, especially when he's unhappily running the inn alone.

So, when we arrive, I disappear upstairs and try to give him space. I consider Will and I to be friends, but maybe he doesn't. Maybe I'm just a guest, even if we've talked about important things. It's been a long time since I've made any new friends, and I realize I feel a little insecure about it. Will and Svea have both opened up to me about personal things, but today they both seem to have drawn back from me a bit. Will has been quiet, and Svea left the snowball fight earlier without saying much to me. I'm not sure how to gauge those things, so I'll err on the side of caution by sticking to my room for the afternoon.

The only problem is that I'm incredibly bored. I putter around my room, tidying things and reorganizing what's in my suitcase. Then, I decide to just unpack it all since I'll be here for at least another five days. After my things are tucked into the dresser, I unnecessarily wipe down the surfaces in the bathroom with a washcloth.

I'm wringing it out in the bathtub when I hear my phone ringing. I dry my hands quickly and retrieve my buzzing phone from the nightstand where I left it to charge. Lindsey's name is displayed on my screen, and I pick up with a smile.

"Hey, Linz."

"Hey, wayward soul. Any news about Kia?"

I sigh. "No, ma'am. Still waiting on the new part." Lars didn't say anything to me at the snowball fight, so it's pretty safe to say nothing has changed.

"Booo. I was so excited to have you for Christmas."

"I know; I was, too." With how much I've been working, we haven't been able to see each other much at all, and I feel horrible that we both were so excited to spend the holidays together, and now we aren't.

"It's so lame that you're stuck in some little town in the middle of nowhere. You're going to be alone for Christmas, Lacey. That just sucks."

I unplug my phone from the charger and swivel to glance around my home away from home. The charm of it still makes me feel content here. There's a coziness to this room and this house that make me feel less lonely. It must be all the family artifacts and charming gnomes everywhere.

"Maybe it'll be good for me," I suggest with a shrug. "You and I both know a low-key Christmas could totally be a blessing in disguise after how much I've worked all these years."

"Well, yeah, but where's the fun in it? Spending Christmas alone is legit depressing."

I chuckle at that, even though she's not wrong. But this wouldn't be the first Christmas I've spent alone. At least this year, I'm not working. I'm only slightly grateful for that, to be honest, but I can't do much about it.

"I guess you could video chat with your dad or something."

Lindsey's suggestion settles heavily in my stomach as I sit on the bed and lay down on my back. "He doesn't even know I'm here or that I was let go." I sigh. "I should probably call him, I just..."

"Hate talking to him?" she finishes for me.

It's been two years since I spent Christmas with him and Mariah, and probably a year since I've seen him in person. Our usual interactions are over the phone, but they're brief, strained, and occur every two or three months.

"Yeah, I guess. Mostly because it's never just him I get to talk to. Mariah is always there, too." I frown up at the white ceiling, thinking of all the times she's gotten him off the phone while we were talking because she apparently needed something.

"Ugh, Mariah. I never thought you would have an evil stepmother."

I laugh softly. "She's not evil...she's just...not that fond of me. And I don't think of her as my stepmother. She's just my dad's wife." She definitely isn't anything maternal to me. I think she considers me family just as much as I consider her family. Not at all.

"When you have to explain what she is to you, that's sort of a red flag. I've told you before, if she starts beef with you, I'll be there with every ring I own on my fingers so I can put her in her place."

I love my best friend, but even with her fierce fighting spirit, she wouldn't hurt a fly. She's all talk. Her bark is worse than her bite.

"Thanks, Linz," I say, stifling my laughter.

"I'm serious. I may be small but I know things. Fighting things."

"I know." She's always had my back, even in apparently hypothetical situations, and I love her for it. "How's Jack?" I ask, changing the subject.

"He's good. Excited to be off for the holidays."

"I bet." Her fiancé works for the state of South Dakota as a contractor, and he's been busy drawing up plans for some big new stadium they're set to break ground on in the spring. "Is he still worshiping your very existence?"

Lindsey snorts. "Of course. He tells me almost every day how he can't wait to marry me next summer."

I grin up at the ceiling, knowing she isn't exaggerating. He's madly in love with her and has been since they were kids. Luckily for his shy personality, she took the first step and kissed him one day totally out of the blue. They've been inseparable ever since.

"You know, his brother is really nice. I could set you up with him," she offers, with only the tiniest bit of hesitation. This isn't the first time she's tried to set me up with Jordan.

"I thought he was dating somebody."

"So?"

I burst out laughing. "What do you mean so? You really think I want to date someone who's already dating someone else?"

"Hey, don't sell yourself short," she chastises. "The girl he's dating is totally a placeholder, I can tell. He's not that hung up on her."

I shake my head slowly. "Lindsey, I appreciate the offer, really, but I'll pass."

She scoffs. "I'm just trying to make us related! If you married Jordan, we would be sisters-in-law!"

I snicker at her crazy ideas. "I love you, Linz, but not enough to go out with someone who's already taken."

"Ugh. *Fine*. But when he breaks up with her, I'm giving him your number."

I shake my head again. "Fine."

"Thank you."

"You're ridiculous, you know that right?"

"Ridiculously hellbent on finding you the love of your life," she corrects me.

I normally would laugh at her when she says something like that, but this time, the last five words in her sentence stand out to me.

The love of my life.

That really does sound nice.

"I'll keep my eyes open," I tell her gently. "Having all this time off has given me time to think and...yeah, I definitely do want to find the one."

Lindsey squeals loudly in my ear. "Yes! We need to sign you up for all the dating sites and—"

"Whoa, whoa," I interrupt. "Not *all* the dating sites, okay? Let's start with one and go from there."

"Oh my gosh, Lacey. You have no idea how much you need my help. You *have* to do all of them, that way you can see if the guy you're talking to on one is also talking to other people on the other sites."

"Ew," I mutter.

"Believe me, it's important."

"Or I could just skip the dating sites and try to get a hobby where I can meet someone."

"Ooh. Yes. Like a cooking class or something."

Her suggestion reminds me of Will and how he taught me how to make Swedish meatballs. I can't help but smile. But that smile fades when I imagine myself cooking with someone else. The activity loses its charm when Will isn't involved. I swallow hard.

"Linz?" I ask softly.

"Yeah?"

I bite my lip, uncomfortable with the squirming sensation in my stomach. "There's this guy here who—well, he's really nice. And—"

"A *guy*?!" she screeches. "Lacey! You met a guy in Nowheresville?"

"Well, he's the owner of the place I'm staying at, so I've been seeing a lot of him. And his family is super great—"

"You met his *family*?"

With a sigh, I realize I have to start from the beginning.

I tell her everything I can think of, including the ways I've embarrassed myself with the things I've blurted out. When I'm finished, Lindsey is quiet. I wish I could see her face so I would know the reason behind her silence. Is she shocked? Nervous for me? Thinking I'm a moron? Probably that I'm a moron.

"Oh my gosh," she whispers finally. "You're in a Hallmark movie."

I laugh, but she doesn't join in.

"Lacey, this could be awesome. I can tell. Just from the way you talk about him, I know he's something special."

"Yeah, he's great. But I'm not sure what he thinks of me. I'm just some out-of-towner stranger who loves his family and helped his sister. And I'll be leaving next week, so obviously nothing can happen."

"Why *obviously*?"

I sit up on the bed, and my eyes go to the little yellow gnome on the dresser. "Because I'm not staying, Linz."

"Have you ever heard of long-distance relationships?" she asks like I'm an idiot. "Besides, you're stranded only a few hours from the Twin Cities, right? That's not even far. If you really like him, you should at least see where it goes."

My thoughts return to the changes I want to make in my life. How I want to have new priorities that reflect the life I want—the life that looks like what Mamma and Pappa Christiansen have. I want a love like my parents had before Mom died. I want a partner in crime. Someone I can rely on when I'm unsure about myself. Why should it matter if I met him by chance in a small town? Why should I let distance get in the way of being happy with someone like Will?

"I don't know," I answer softly.

"Babe, listen. You've had your life turned upside down by that witch boss of yours, but look where it led you. You would've never met this guy, right? That just seems too perfect to be an accident."

I close my eyes. "That's what I've been thinking."

"Right, so...you're going to go for it?"

I groan. "Aren't you supposed to tell me that I barely know him and I'm crazy to like him or something?"

She chuckles. "Oh, Lacey. Don't be a chicken. I'd bet my future firstborn that he's into you, too."

"I'll...think about it."

"You're going to think about it and agree with me."

"We'll see. I gotta go. I'll talk to you later."

"Alright, later girl."

We hang up, and I toss my phone on the bed behind me, feeling unsettled. It's been a really long time since I've been interested in a guy. And to admit it out loud felt...foolish. Will hasn't given me any indication that he thinks of me as anything other than a guest at his inn. If anything, he's been extra kind and gracious, especially when I embarrass myself by blatantly telling him he's cute. Multiple times.

No, my feelings are dumb. It'll be far less humiliating if I say nothing than if I tell him I like him and he doesn't feel the same way. Because then I'm stuck in this house with him for another five days while my unrequited feelings hover between us. Talk about *awkward*.

But there is a tiny little romantic part of me that wants to take the chance. Because...just *maybe* it could be the real thing.

Downstairs, I hear the front door open and close. Thinking Will probably left to go do something, I let out a sigh. But then the stairs creak with footsteps, and I hear his voice sound out from somewhere else on the lower level.

"I'm not here for you!" comes Svea's shouting voice.

I perk up and quickly go to open the door. "Hey, Svea."

She finishes the steps and barely looks up at me when she brushes past me into my room. Her face is set and serious, and I instantly wonder what's wrong.

Damn, I wish I had more creme pies; I'd give her one. Debbie makes everything better.

"Close the door," she orders softly, and I do as she says. When I turn back around, she's flinging herself back on the bed, her arms and legs star-fishing out.

"What's wrong?" I ask, coming to her side.

She stares at the ceiling, much like I just was, and heaves out a depressed sigh so huge it seems to fill the room.

"He gave me a noogie," she grinds out through clenched teeth. "A freaking *noogie*. Like I'm a child." She throws one arm over her eyes.

I grimace at that and pat her leg. "Lars did?"

She nods beneath her arm. "Not even my brothers give me noogies. Ugh," she laments in humiliation.

"I'm sorry, Svea."

Her arm moves off her face, flopping back onto the bed beside her. "I'm so stupid. I don't know why I can't just get over him, you know? It sucks so much."

I sit down on the edge of the bed, my hand still resting on her leg. "It's hard to get over a good man," I murmur, unwillingly thinking of Will.

"I just wish he would open his eyes and really *see* me."

"Maybe he needs glasses," I attempt to joke. She finally looks over at me, seeming only vaguely appreciative of my comment.

"Maybe I need a brain," she adds, though she doesn't sound at all like she's joking.

I shake my head slightly, and she turns her green eyes, so like Will's, back to the ceiling.

"I don't know what to do," she admits, her usually cheerful voice so soft and broken that my heart breaks for her.

"Well, what have you tried?"

One brow crinkles when she looks back at me. "What do you mean? I can't *try* anything. He's my brother's best friend."

I give her a comforting smile. "I know, but...so what?"

The words out of my mouth instantly remind me of what Lindsey said in reference to Jordan, and I nearly snort. But then I remember how she and Jack started out. *Hmm.*

"What do you think would happen if you just kissed him without warning?"

Svea's eyes nearly bug out of her head, and she sits up straight. "What? You think I should *kiss* him?" she chokes out in surprise.

I shrug. "Worked for my best friend. She's marrying the guy this summer."

She blinks at me twice, her features drawn and pale. "But...what if he's disgusted?"

I laugh at her. "I'm sure that won't be the case."

Svea stews on my suggestion for a moment, and I watch her expression gradually crunch into a tight frown. "I would die if he didn't kiss me back. And then it would be so awkward. Forever. I mean, I can't avoid him in this little town."

I shrug again. "But what if he *does* kiss you back, Svea? Then, you get the happily ever after."

The color starts pumping back into her face again, and I'm sure it's because she's imagining what it would feel like for Lars to kiss her back. Her eyes dart around the room and then land back on me.

"I don't know, Lace. It's a pretty ballsy thing to do."

I grin at her. "I don't know anyone ballsier than you."

She smiles at that and chuckles. "You're such a bad influence."

I wink. "I'll take that as a compliment."

She chuckles and then her expression softens. "Thanks. I feel like I have no one to talk to about this because everyone knows everyone. It's nice to have a friend who's sort of outside of things. You're probably the only one who can be objective."

I brush my knuckles on my shoulder. "Anytime, Svea."

Chapter Twelve

Will

I spend the afternoon getting caught up on chores around the inn. Sweeping, dusting, laundry. All the while, my brain whirs through what's left to be done this week before Christmas.

Thankfully I don't have to help out much for the Broomball Tournament tomorrow, but I usually help set up for the Holly Ball and the Christmas Day Dinner, which both take place at the community center on different days. It's a whole lot of setup and tear down and then setup again in a short amount of time. All of those things weigh down on my shoulders, but there's no doubt in my mind that it's all worth it. I love my community, and even though I wish there were more people jumping to help do all those things, I still do my best to remember how blessed I am to have grown up in a small town like Larkspur.

I have memories down every back road and up every sidewalk. The smell of the cornfields in the summer and the huge blue sky are things I would miss if I lived anywhere else. I can't imagine living in Minneapolis like Lacey, where she's just one person lost in a current of busy people. The anonymity would be crushing to me. I wonder if she likes the hustle and bustle of the city.

When I was about ten years old, I watched a cooking competition show on TV, and I still remember how I felt the whole world open up. Like I had never considered how many more opportunities there are outside of our small town. Not that it matters because this is where I am, and I have no plans to go elsewhere, and I truly never have. I'm happy being a small-town man. Besides, I could never be far from my family. No matter how much extra stuff Mamma puts on my shoulders, or how many pranks Svea pulls on me, I wouldn't trade them for the world.

There may be more opportunities in bigger cities or in other parts of the world, but this little rural town is where I choose to put down my roots. That is, if I ever get the chance to settle down...

After Svea stopped by unexpectedly and left the inn with a woeful "later, buttface," I've been wondering what she and Lacey talked about upstairs. I can't think of a single thing that Svea hasn't talked to me about over the years. Everything from periods, bras, and pooping to things like goals, life, and disappointment. We've always been close. So, for her to seek out Lacey instead of me is a valid reason for me to be worried. And maybe just a tiny part of me is wounded.

But I shouldn't feel that way. I'm more than confident that my sister knows she can talk to me about anything, and I shouldn't take it personally that she confided something to someone who hasn't been around since her birth and won't be around in the future either. That says more about Lacey than it does about me.

But that doesn't mean I shy away from asking Lacey what the hell they talked about when I bring up some clean bath towels for her later. I shift the little stack of towels to my left hand so that I can knock with the other.

She swings the door open a moment later with a smile already on her pretty face, which makes my heart beat in a rhythm I don't appreciate. I haven't really seen her since the Snowball Fight this morning, and for just a second, the thought hits me that any time spent without her is time wasted.

"Well, hello there, towel boy," she blurts out, and then slaps her hand over her mouth with wide eyes.

I don't bother holding back my chuckle. "At your service," I tease, and bow my head. I hand her the towels, trying not to let her notice how adorable I think it is when her true thoughts spill out of her mouth without her permission.

"Thank you," she says, and I stay in the doorway while she takes them into the bathroom.

"Did you need anything else? More shampoo or anything?" I glance around her room, taking a quick inventory of tissue boxes and the wastebasket in the corner. Usually when I have guests stay, I clean daily, but with Lacey, I've tried to stay out of her space. I want her to feel like she has her privacy, but I also need to do my job.

"Nope, I'm good," she says as she reappears. "I'm probably the most low-maintenance guest ever."

I smile at her and lean my shoulder against the doorframe. "So, what did Svea want?" I ask her casually, and she instantly does her best impression of not knowing what I mean. She even looks up at the ceiling to avoid eye contact. Something about it is unbelievably adorable.

"Nothing," she claims, her brown eyes still pointed upward.

I smirk at the way she feigns an innocent expression. "Mhm."

"Unlike Lars, I know how to keep a secret."

I chuckle. "That's good to know."

"I'm serious. I'm not saying a word," she insists, but I can tell by the shallow way she's breathing and the tension in her shoulders that she really wants to.

"Okay."

But she looks back down at me, her mouth pressed tightly together like she's afraid she might just blurt out a bunch of word vomit against her own will. I try not to laugh, but it comes out stifled.

"It has nothing to do with Lars," she rushes out, and then her brown eyes get wide. "Nope, nothing at all," she adds like that's going to cover her terrible lying.

I raise one eyebrow at her, wondering what in the world would be going on between Lars and my sister that would have Svea acting the way she did before she left. The protective big brother switch engages in my brain.

"What happened?" I demand, which causes Lacey to go into panic explanation mode.

"Nothing! Nothing, honestly. Lars gave her a noogie, and she just hated it. She already has two big brothers, you know, she doesn't need another one... That's all. It's nothing more complicated than that."

I instantly pull my phone out of my pocket.

"What are you doing?" she gasps out as I unlock my phone.

"Obviously something more happened. I'm going to find out what," I explain in a low, calm voice that belies how amped up I feel at someone hurting Svea, especially Lars.

"No!" Lacey snatches my phone out of my hand.

"Hey!" I reach for it, but she hides it behind her back. She's looking at me wide-eyed, like she can't quite believe she just did that.

"Will, you can't call anybody, okay? Svea is a big girl, and she's going to work it all out. She'll be upset if you get involved."

"*Involved*? I'm trying to look out for her."

"Which is very sweet," she replies gently. "But there's a lot you don't know, so maybe, just...trust your sister, and wait for her to come to you if she needs something."

I take a step closer and hold out my hand. "Give me my phone back."

She bites her lip and slowly shakes her head like she's uncertain about what lengths I might go to. But that little tug on her bottom lip has my eyes zeroing in on her mouth, and the big brother instinct evaporates instantly. Instead, I realize I'm standing much closer to her than I realized, and I can smell the floral scent of her perfume. It makes my heart beat strangely.

I force my eyes back to hers, realizing as I do that she's blushing. I feel my cheeks heat a little too as the moment continues. The only sound in the inn is the little crackle of the wood stove downstairs. There's a buzz between us that sharpens each of my senses and has me wanting to do things I shouldn't, like move in even closer. Touch her cheek. Bend down and kiss her lips.

But I don't.

These wants don't change the fact that she's here temporarily. Touching or kissing her would feel amazing, I have no doubt, but then what? No one's heart deserves to be played with—hers or mine.

Showing or admitting feelings for Lacey would only make it worse when she has to say goodbye.

So, when I can't stand it any longer, I take a breath and reach around her to where she's still hiding my phone. Her eyes stay on mine, but she lets me take it slowly out of her grasp.

"Will, please don't say anything," she begs. "I promise, nothing bad happened. You have to trust me."

Do I trust her? I certainly trust that she isn't asking for my inaction to save her own butt. She wants me to do nothing for the sake of my sister. And...damn it, I'll do anything for the sake of my sister.

I give a little sigh through my nose. "Alright."

Relief floods through her expression as her shoulders drop.

"I won't call either of them," I concede. "But you have to tell me what happened."

"I did."

I pocket my phone. "You told me he gave her a noogie. What else don't I know?"

She closes her eyes tightly, and in doing so, her entire face scrunches up. It's possibly the most endearing thing I've ever seen. "I shouldn't. It's not my business."

Despite how badly I want to know the details about whatever is going on with Svea and Lars, I have to say I respect her answer. There are way too many gossipers and loose lips in this town. It has my heart softening toward Lacey even more, which is the only reason I can blame for why I reach out and touch her hand.

She opens her eyes, surprised, but I remove my touch quickly.

"Okay," I murmur, and then clear my throat. "Thanks for looking out for Svea."

Lacey's surprise drops away, and she smiles warmly at me, that smile that I can feel in every extremity. "You know, you tease about having a sister a lot, but I can tell how much you love her."

I shrug, my fingertips tingling from touching her soft skin moments before. "She's my baby sister."

She hums and grins. "Such a family man. I like it." Then, she blushes again, and damn, I'm smitten. The urge to kiss her comes back full force, and all I can think is what a shame it is that this woman isn't from here. What a shame that I won't get to find out every little thing about her. What a shame that next week, we'll go our separate ways and never see each other again.

"So, hear anything about your car yet?" I ask to change the subject, willing myself to put Svea and Lars to the back of my mind until later.

Lacey sighs. "No, still looks like I'll be around for a while." She says this with a tinge of disappointment, but then she glances around her room and smiles. "I'm kind of okay with that though. Larkspur is something special."

I smile, too. "Yeah? You like it here?"

"I love it here. I'll be sad to leave, actually."

My lungs squeeze. Does she love it here enough to come back someday? Does she love it enough to *stay*? Am I fool enough to hope she'll miss me when she goes back to her life in the cities?

"Well, you're always welcome back."

"I would actually like to see what Larkspur is like in the summer. Is it just as magical here during the other seasons as it is in the winter?"

Her answer has me longing to convince her that *yes*, Larkspur is magical all year long. I want to tell her it's the perfect place to grow up. The perfect place to fall in love and start a new life. The perfect place to settle down and raise a family.

"You'll just have to find out for yourself," I hint, and leave it at that.

"Playing your cards close to the chest," she teases. "I see how it is."

No, I think, I *just want you to come back.*

It's after nine o'clock when I hear a loud *thump* upstairs that has me curious as to what Lacey's up to. After dinner, in which the conversation was polite and friendly, she went up to her room, and I finished the laundry and dusted the main level. I would be lying if I said my thoughts hadn't strayed to her while I completed my tasks. Just the slightest chance that she might come back someday is enough for me to wonder if she's fighting this, too.

Lacey's door opens, and my heart pounds as she races down the groaning staircase.

"Everything okay?" I ask from where I'm wiping the counters in the kitchen. As she turns away from the stairs and makes her way toward me in a hurry, I'm surprised to see that she's smiling. The glint in her eyes only gets more pronounced the closer she gets to me until she's standing in front of me.

"Stop what you're doing," she demands, but her voice is full of suppressed excitement.

I toss my cloth in the sink and give her my full attention. My curiosity is piqued for sure, but I also feel a warmth flood my body at seeing her nearly bouncing out of her skin.

"I need a piece of paper and a pen," she says next, and I fetch her a notebook and a pen from a drawer in the dining room cabinet. When I hand it to her, she slaps it down on the kitchen island and poises the pen over the paper.

"What's this all—?"

"The Swedish Chef," she interrupts, her brown eyes blazing at me. Then she repeats it, like I didn't hear her, and writes the words down at the top of the page. "*The Swedish Chef,*" she says for the third time, and shakes my biceps as she speaks through a huge smile. "That's *you*, Will. *You're* The Swedish Chef."

"Uh..." I mutter, glancing between her jubilant expression and the page she's written on. "You mean like, from *The Muppets*?"

She beams. "Yes! But in real life!"

I squint at her slightly, not following. When she realizes I'm not going to say anything else because I have no idea what to say, she sighs in exasperation cloaked in enthusiasm.

"Will, *you're a chef.*" She narrows her eyes at me when I give her an uncertain look. "You *are.* Food is your passion. Cooking is what you want to be doing, right?"

My chest squeezes uncomfortably, but the answer is clear. "Yes."

Lacey's smile broadens even more, and she hands me the pen. "Then dream with me. For just a little while, dream with me about what could be." She points at the page. "Write down your menu. Put down all the things you love and forget for just a second that Larkspur Inn is your responsibility." Her coffee-colored eyes are so bright and so full of hope for me that despite how I feel like maybe it isn't a good idea, I can't tell her no.

I take a deep breath and try to do what she's asking me: forget the to-do lists and errands and everything that's been put on my shoulders.

Dream with me.

I focus in on the page and smile a little at *The Swedish Chef* scrawled in loopy handwriting at the top.

"Come on," she encourages me, and pulls me closer to the counter by the arm. "And don't forget The Lacey Special." Her grin is contagious, and as soon as I write it down, it's like a floodgate is opened. Ideas pour out of me.

Swedish Meatballs.

Pannkaka.

Mamma's *Semmeltarta.*

Pyttipanna.

Kanelbullar.

I write down everything I can think of, and each word written feels like a weight lifting off my shoulders. The page fills up and then another when Lacey brings up marketing ideas like putting up billboards on the highway to draw more traffic to Larkspur, making an internet presence, and hosting parties or club meetings.

My heart swells and swells until I think it might burst. This is me on a page. My heart and soul in ink. This is everything I want, everything that fulfills me and makes me feel strong and confident and *right*. This is what I've been missing while my head has been buried in the business my parents left for me to run. I'm energized in a way I haven't experienced since I was kid.

"Can you imagine the kind of business you could do with your restaurant being part of the inn?" Lacey says then, gripping my wrist as she grins up at me. "People come here to eat and see how amazing it is, and then they book a room!"

The wheels turn instantly at that thought.

Could I really run a restaurant out of this kitchen? Would it be possible for me to bring in more revenue for the inn this way? Larkspur Inn has the most business in the summer months, but maybe having a restaurant would help bridge the gap between the seasons. Instead of relying on the snowmobilers and church retreats, the restaurant could open up more opportunities for people to find us in the winter months.

Suddenly, this seems less like a dream and more like a possibility.

I grip Lacey's hand with my free one. "Lacey, you're a genius."

She beams and bounces up and down on the balls of her feet. "It would be amazing, Will. And eventually, you could hire someone to run the inn for you, so then you'll be able to focus on the restaurant."

The breath rushes out of me in relief at that thought. Just the idea of not being responsible for the inn has me feeling a strange sense of freedom that I didn't realize I craved so deeply.

"Wow," I whisper.

Her hand rests on mine, sandwiching it between her other hand that's still covering my wrist. "None of this is my business, Will. I know that," she murmurs. "But I've lived the last three years of my life being unhappy in my work life and going in the completely wrong direction." The kitchen around us disappears as she speaks, her beautiful eyes connected with mine. "I don't want that to happen to you, too."

I just barely stop myself from leaning my head down to rest against her forehead. What wouldn't I give to forget the reality we're in and just dream with her about *us*? Because I have dreams of us. I can see her in this restaurant dream of mine. I can see her helping me with marketing and running the business end. I can see myself kissing her goodnight *every* night.

But even though I can see her being a part of my everyday life, that doesn't mean it's possible. She doesn't live here and has plans to go back to Minneapolis as soon as she's able to. My dreams of us will only ever be dreams.

"What's wrong?" she asks, alerting me to how I've let the disappoint-ment show on my face.

"Nothing." I remove my hand from her warm grasp and take a step back. I turn toward the pages I've written my life's purpose on and sigh. Suddenly, those words don't seem quite as buoyant, not when she won't be here to see those ideas come to life.

"Will, I was just trying to help," Lacey explains, sounding as crestfall-en as I feel. "I didn't mean to—"

"You did help, Lacey." I collect the notebook and pen, then turn to leave the kitchen so I can hide in the back office. "It was fun dreaming with you," I say over my shoulder as I go.

Chapter Thirteen

Lacey

It's a nice mid-morning for a Broomball Tournament, or so Will told me when we arrived at the Community Center fifteen minutes ago. Cars are parked all the way down the street, and there's a crowd of people sitting in camping chairs surrounding a mostly flat rectangle of ice just next to the parking lot. For some reason, I had been expecting something enclosed, at least with some sort of barrier, but it's just ice and snow and people. Two soccer goals are set up on each end of the ice and someone spray-painted a blue line halfway across for the centerline.

I have no idea how to play Broomball, but Will summarized it on the way over. It's basically hockey without skates, and instead of hockey sticks, you use broomsticks, and instead of a puck, you use a little round ball. Honestly, I didn't pay that much attention to the rules he described because my mind has been constantly thinking about his quick exit from our little meeting in the kitchen last night.

Ugh, I'm the worst.

You'd think by now I'd learn to not open my big mouth and tell people what I think. Who do I think I am, going around telling Svea to kiss Lars and Will to pursue cooking? Just because I'm an objective outsider doesn't mean it's okay for me to wag my tongue.

But come on. The Swedish Chef. It's just too perfect to pass up. Before I could think twice, I stumbled downstairs like a bat out of hell to reveal my amazing idea, which Will so sweetly went along with...until he didn't.

Will was totally normal at breakfast this morning. He joked about needing me to tap in at the Broomball Tournament if he gets tired while we ate one of the things he wrote down last night during our brainstorming sesh. *Pyttipanna*, he said it was called. It was some kind of delicious hash made from potatoes and sausage, and I ate more of it than was ladylike.

But I was awake half the night wondering what happened to make him switch off so suddenly. We went from throwing around ideas and dreaming out loud to him hoofing it out of the kitchen before I could fully understand that maybe I had done something to cause it. Apparently, I'm more oblivious than I realized. I guess I can't help putting my foot in my mouth every time I open it.

Even now as I sit in a camping chair next to Mamma and Pappa Christiansen outside the community center, my mind isn't at all on the match about to begin. Svea, Lars, Will, and Lee are set to play after the current game, and they're all gathered around the edge of the ice. Lee shot me an unimpressed look when I greeted him, so he hasn't gotten over my little fake injury. Hopefully, I'll win him over again, that is, if I ever actually did win him over to begin with.

Svea also gave me a look while Will exchanged fist bumps with Lars, and I smiled back in a way I hoped she took to mean loyalty. I'm so glad Will didn't force me to spill the beans about her crush on Lars because I would have hated for Svea to be angry at me. I may not be sticking around here long, but I don't like to be in the business of hurting people.

"They're going to wipe the floor with the Wilsons," Fredrik says on the other side of his wife. "No one likes to go up against Lee," he adds, leaning forward to look over at me. "He's a police officer, so everyone is afraid of him."

I nod, but I have a hunch that most people would be afraid of him even if he wasn't a police officer.

"Ah, that's just rubbish. He's a sweetheart," Elsie disagrees sternly, and sips from the travel mug she brought along. I secretly hope Svea didn't salt it.

I smile at what she said and look over at the big brute. He's wearing a navy blue sweatshirt with snow pants tucked into his boots. His arms are folded over his broad chest, and even though Lars says something to him with a lighthearted nudge, he remains still and serious as always. And yet, I remember the night I skidded into the picture and how he spoke of Mamma in a reverent way, how he found me a place to stay without me even asking him to, and how he carried my luggage inside for me. Maybe deep down, he really is a little gooey.

"To *you*," Fredrik stipulates, and then chuckles. His wife rolls her eyes.

"He just needs the right woman to coax him out of himself," she says, looking at her eldest son with some sort of hope in her expression.

I bite my lip as I remember what Will said about him being into Emma, the librarian. I don't know if such a shy person could draw him out like Elsie says, but who knows? Maybe someone quiet and soft would give him the space to speak up.

"He needs to put himself out there," he argues, gazing at Lee, too.

I stifle a guffaw at how badly these two want grandbabies.

"Are you single, dear?" Elsie asks me suddenly. Her green eyes pin me with a penetrating look that lets me know I couldn't lie to her even if I wanted to.

"Yup."

"Elsie, don't you start," Fredrik scolds, but there's a sparkle in his eye.

"I'm starting nothing!"

Wait—starting something?

"Uh huh," he mutters sarcastically. Elsie slaps his arm with playful force.

"I'm not. It was just a question," she defends. "Cool your caboose."

I chuckle behind my mittened hand as the players assemble on the ice.

"Lee is perfectly capable of finding himself a nice girl. He doesn't need you setting him up with poor Lacey."

Wait, *Lee*? And *me*?

"Oh, no, no, I'm not interested in Lee," I cough out louder than necessary. I glance toward the Christiansen kids and Lars, but they didn't seem to hear me. Phew. "I mean he's fine, but not really my type," I add belatedly because these are his parents, and I don't want to insult them. I thought I got that point across when she suggested we go to the Holly Ball together, but maybe not.

Fredrik lets out a very Santa-like *huh ho huh ho ho* and slaps his knee. Elsie narrows her eyes at him, but that only seems to egg him on all the more.

"I know you're not," Elsie assures me. "I was just curious, that's all. You didn't mention anybody special at *fika* the other day."

"Right, yes. I've been too busy for a relationship," I explain, keen to keep the conversation moving.

Elsie eyes me for a moment, maybe expecting me to say more, and then she moves her focus to the ice where the game is taking place completely unnoticed by me. "You make time for the things you want," she says wisely as she watches the players shuffle around after the ball.

Her truth bomb sure hits its intended mark because my stomach drops. Now that I've had a moment to breathe here in Larkspur, I know that I only made time for work before Yvette gave me the axe. Here's my reminder again that the unhappiness and lack of fulfillment in my life is solely my own doing and solely in my hands for me to do something about.

"You're right," I murmur, almost to myself.

I wanted to be successful in my career, but during my short stay in Larkspur so far, I've already been happier than I've been in years. What Elsie and Fredrik are making me realize is that the thing I want most is the same thing they have.

My eyes drift over to where Will stands in his Larkspur Inn hoodie, smiling at something Svea is saying, and my heart does a little dance. Then, I think about what Lindsey said and wonder...could I ever really go for it? Sure, the circumstances aren't ideal, but couples have been through much worse, right? My future is completely up in the air right now, but he makes me feel warm and fuzzy and light in a way nobody else has.

"Will is single, too, you know," Fredrik pipes up, which causes his wife to bark out a loud *ha!* I startle at her lightning-fast reaction and then begin to blush when I process what he said.

"Well, if that isn't the pot calling the kettle black," she snickers. He smirks at her, and for just a second, I see an older version of Lee.

"Call it whatever you like, *Älskling.*"

I clamber for something to say, but everything I can think of would only make it sound like I'm trying to cover my butt. So, I just go with something casual, hoping that I'll come off as funny and nonchalant.

"Yeah, Will's alright if you're into the whole elf thing."

Thankfully, they both burst out laughing, so I do, too.

"Hey, keep it down over there!" Lars calls to us teasingly as our laughter dies off. I look over towards him and the Christiansen siblings, noticing that there are other tournament attendees who are eyeing me curiously.

"Respect your elders!" Fredrik shouts back through a grin.

My eyes meet Will's, and the tender smile on his face melts me like an ice cream cone in July. I don't think I could ever get tired of a man looking at me with so much affection and good humor. It feels like such a treat.

I'm thankful when my friends finally take the ice a half hour later because I have a legitimate spectator's sport right here in front of me, where I can watch Will's every move like a total lovesick creeper.

He's not as built as Lee or as agile as Lars, but Will is all I can focus on as they play against the other team of four. He moves gracefully for how awkward it probably is to shuffle around the ice on boots instead of skates, and after ten minutes of back and forth, he strips off his hoodie, and *holy bobbins* do my eyes feast on his strong torso and sculpted arms. Suddenly, this December day feels much more like a hot summer day at the beach, and I ain't complaining about it.

Will makes his way toward the goal where a defender or goalie or whoever is guarding it, and I surprise myself with how loud I shout when he winds up with his broom and sweeps the ball straight into the goal. Thankfully, his parents cheer just as loud.

But then, the opposing broomballer who was chasing Will careens into him, and both men come crashing down. Instantly, I'm on my feet and so are Elsie and Fredrik.

A resounding *ooooh* is heard from the other onlookers, but my heart is pounding too hard to notice. All I can think is *oh no oh no oh no* as I watch their teammates quickly check on the two broomballers splayed out on the hard, cold ice.

"Is he okay?" I blurt out to Elsie without moving my eyes away from the congregated people on the ice. I hear her reply but can't understand what she's saying, which causes me to swing my gaze to her worried face. She's muttering something into her mittened hands in a continuous stream as she keeps her eyes on where Will is lying on his back.

"*Älskling*, he'll be fine," Fredrik says to her, but he sounds just as scared.

"I should've made him touch the *tomte*," she blurts out in a breathy voice. Her husband puts his arm around her shoulders and brings her in tight to his side.

I want to say something to comfort her, but I've got nothing because I'm just as worried. I don't know what kind of injury he's suffered, but I automatically think the worst. Concussion, broken bones, paralysis. I start to panic, the blood pumping in my ears, realizing how much I care about this man. He's the last person to deserve something horrible like what I'm imagining. The mental barrier I've put up because of my temporary stay in Larkspur dissipates. It doesn't matter to me where I live right now. I just have to know that he's going to be okay. I'll *always* want to know if he's okay. If he's happy, content, living his best life. Distance won't change that for me.

Lars and Lee hook an arm under each of Will's arms and hoist him up, giving me the first view of his face. My stomach twists when I see the pained scrunch of his eyebrows and the way his mouth is stretched into a grimace. I watch with a racing heart as Lars and Lee help him off the ice, taking his weight so one of his legs braces on the ice and the other is kept raised.

"Oh, he must've hurt his knee," I say, but belatedly realize I'm speaking to no one because Elsie and Fredrik have abandoned their post and are rushing toward their injured son.

I hesitate to follow them for just a second because I'm not his family. I mean, I'm barely his friend, but ultimately, I make my way forward, too. I care about Will. I want to know for myself that he's okay. There's nothing wrong with that.

Weaving between other concerned people, I follow the Christiansen parents to where Lee and Lars have carefully lowered Will to the snowy ground. Everyone else stands around him in a tight circle of concern and love.

"I'm alright, I'm alright," he says to no one in particular. Despite his assurance, his normally warm voice is tense and strained.

"Is it broken?" Svea asks at my side.

"No, probably not," Lee answers in his usual surly way.

"Oh, *gudskelov!*" Elsie exclaims in relief and clutches her chest. Even in this serious moment in which I'm worried about Will, I can't help but think *gesundheit* in response.

"I'm fine. My kneecap just dislocated for a second. I'm good." Will even tries to get up, but Lee and Fredrik keep him down by the shoulders.

"Easy there, tiger," Lars says good-naturedly.

"Hey now, settle down," Fredrik chimes in.

Something about Will's stubborn tenacity has my heart ratcheting in my chest. I'm so glad he seems to be okay, but ugh, do I feel for him. I've never been one to sustain injuries given the fact that I avoid sports like the plague, but I can imagine that dislocating your kneecap is nothing to sneeze at when it comes to the pain department.

Wait—is it serious to dislocate your kneecap? Isn't that how the rest of your leg stays on? A little scrap of bone and some ligaments? My mind races, and the stupidest thing pops out of my mouth.

"So, they won't need to amputate?"

Six sets of eyes instantly land on me.

There's a beat of silence, and then Lars laughs from deep in his belly, followed by Svea and Fredrik. Elsie snickers as well, and Lee pins me with an *are you serious right now* look. It's Will's bright, though still slightly pained, smile that has me cracking up, too.

"No need to amputate, Lacey," he assures me appreciatively.

I nod, smiling too, and feel slightly embarrassed by my question but relieved to see him smiling. I've never really considered myself to be a ditz...but maybe I'm a ditz.

"So, what's going on?" a player from the other team calls from the ice. "Are you good to play, or do you forfeit?"

Sheesh. Have a heart, dude.

I wrinkle my nose at Mr. Tinman over there and then turn back to the group.

"You can't play the rest of the game," his mother decides, folding her arms. "Absolutely not."

Will tips his head back with a grieved sigh, exposing his neck to the winter sun shining down on us. I'm pretty sure I hear Lee curse under his breath so Elsie won't hear him, but I can't be totally sure.

Will dips his chin forward again. "Sorry, guys," he says to his team.

Svea loops her arm through mine. "I really wanted to beat the Wilsons, buttface, but we'll get 'em next year."

"Damn right we will," Lars agrees.

Lee says nothing for a moment, a sour look on his stony face. "I'll go tell them," he mutters, and stalks off toward the Wilsons.

"Let's get you to the hospital, Son." Fredrik offers a hand to help him up, but Will doesn't take it.

"I don't need the hospital. Just some ice and rest."

"Do as your father says," Elsie orders briskly, sending a chill up my spine. Oof, remind me to never get on her bad side. No wonder her kids speak so respectfully about her.

Will scowls almost as deep as I've seen Lee do and takes Fredrik's hand. Lars offers his hand as well, and the two of them get him up on his left foot. I'm about to ask if there's anything I can do to help at all when Will looks over at me.

"Here," he says, fishing his truck keys out of his pocket. "Drive the truck back to the inn for me. I shouldn't be gone more than an hour or so."

I step forward and take the keys. "Are you sure? I can drive you if you give me directions."

Will smiles sweetly at me, and my stomach flips. "Thanks, Lacey, but that's alright. I'm the one messing up your stay."

I frown at that. Messing up my stay? Is that all he's concerned about? Did he just...put me in the guest zone? Not even friend zone—*guest zone*?

Ouch. I thought we were at least friends, but...maybe not.

That stings more than it probably should, just because I only realized moments before how invested I am in him and his family. It isn't his fault if that feeling isn't mutual, but it still doesn't feel great. No one ever wants to feel like they aren't as important to someone who is important to you. It sucks that I've just figured out that I need to adjust my feelings so I won't get hurt.

"I'll make sure she's looked after Pappa," Svea says, her arm tightening slightly around mine. It's a friendly gesture that eases the sting of being put in the guest zone just a little.

"I don't need to be babysat," I tease, "but thanks."

Lee rejoins our little group, looking grumpier than ever with his eyebrows scrunched down like dark brown slashes. "Let's go," he commands.

Fredrik and Lee help walk Will to the parking lot with Elsie and Lars following them after they fold up the camping chairs. With a glance over my shoulder at the very happy Wilsons, minus the one cradling his elbow from the fall, I follow Svea to the parking lot as well.

"He'll be okay, right?" I blurt out against my will, but I can't help it.

Svea studies me curiously for a moment like I asked another ditzy question, but then she nods and gives me a comforting smile.

"Christiansens are tough, Lace, don't worry. As long as he didn't break something, I'm sure he'll be up and around in no time."

My stomach squirms a little despite what she said.

Svea offers to lead me over to the inn with her car, but I decline. I remember the way back, but I do feel strange climbing up into the driver's seat of Will's truck. I don't know much about men, but I do know that their trucks are important pieces of their identity. Will doesn't strike me as a guy who has a huge connection to his truck, but even so, I feel the touches of his personality sprinkled around the interior of the cab.

The air freshener clipped to the vent smells like vanilla cupcakes. There are a few random post-it notes and scraps of paper in the bottom of a cup holder, his slanted writing on them depicting lists of groceries and tasks. There's no trash or garbage anywhere I can see, and as I put the key in the ignition, I note the Larkspur Inn keychain on his key ring. The radio comes on playing O *Come All Ye Faithful*, and I take a moment to send him good vibes. Hopefully, Svea is right, and he'll be totally fine. Hopefully, I'll be able to keep my heart in check.

I strap in, put the truck into drive, and head back to Larkspur Inn without my favorite innkeeper. It doesn't feel right. Not even a little. Despite the radio, it seems quiet and empty, like a snow globe without any snow.

Is this how I'm going to feel when I leave? Will I be abandoning a big chunk of my heart here? I'm already attached to this town and these people, and I want a place in their lives whether I've earned it or not. Will may not think of me as much more than a guest in his inn, but he means more to me than that. His family means more to me than that.

I don't think I could replicate this little community and these people in Minneapolis even if I tried because whomever I meet won't be them. Wherever I end up won't be here.

What if I don't want to go back to Minneapolis, Debbie?

Chapter Fourteen

Will

Thankfully, nothing is broken. That's the good news. The bad news is I have to wear a clunky brace thing for a couple of days that's going to make doing anything a lot more difficult.

After an hour and a half at the ER, in which they took x-rays and checked me over, they gave me some crutches and sent me on my way. My parents have been adamant that I stay with them, but I argued that Lacey would be alone at the inn. I promised I would sleep on the couch and not try to crutch it up the stairs, and that was the only way they agreed to take me home.

My knee is throbbing and swollen, but the pain only reminds me of all the things I can't do that I told a lot of people I would. The Holly Ball is tomorrow night, and the most I'll be able to do to help set up for it tomorrow morning is hand people things. I'm not supposed to do any lifting or straining or even walk too much, so the limitations I'm suddenly finding myself under are really stressing me out.

I can't get groceries. I can't drive anywhere. I won't be able to do much at all around the inn because I'm supposed to rest and keep my knee elevated. Besides, even if I do get up, I'll really only have one hand to work with since the other one will be holding a crutch.

I've never felt so helpless in my whole life.

I'm used to being the guy who does it all, who never says no, who always helps. And now, I'm the one who needs help.

The worst part is that I was actually enjoying the Broomball game. Not because we were winning by a mile or anything but because I was playing in front of Lacey. A bigger part of me than I'm proud of was eating up her attention and her cheers. I wanted to win even more because she was watching. But instead, I was taken out and busted my knee, had to forfeit the game, and now I'm here, crutching up the walkway to the inn with my parents flanking me on both sides like I might go down like a sack of potatoes at any moment.

I love my parents. I love the way they raised us kids, and I genuinely like being around them. But I haven't experienced this type of helicopter parenting since I was probably in diapers.

"Let's go right in and get you comfy on the couch," Mamma says as we approach the porch steps. "We'll prop up that knee and get some ice on it."

I almost say a sarcastic "yes, ma'am," but I'm smart enough to keep my mouth shut. I should be grateful that they're so concerned about me, even though a bruised kneecap isn't that serious. Doctor Leffert said I should feel a lot better by next week, but that I should still take it easy for at least two weeks so I don't aggravate or reinjure it.

I take each porch step slowly with my crutches and left foot, slightly annoyed that Pa's hand is beneath my arm as a safeguard. When I reach the porch, the front door whips open, and Lacey stands on the threshold.

My heart stutters in my chest. She's a sight for sore eyes, poised there in black leggings and a lavender long-sleeved t-shirt. If my parents weren't right beside me, I know I'd have a lot of difficulty restraining myself from hugging her. I have a feeling she's a good hugger, and I could really use a good hug.

"How's the knee, chef?" she asks hopefully with a slightly hesitant smile. Out of the corner of my eye, I see Mamma cock her head slightly at her little nickname for me. It reminds me of the talks that Lacey and I have had about my future and where cooking comes into the plan and how I still haven't said a word about my passion to either of my folks. I'll get around to it eventually...maybe after Christmas.

"Nothing broken. I'll live."

Relief surges across her features as I limp forward, making me feel lighter inside.

"Av skadan blir man vis," Mamma says, which means, "injury makes you wise."

Lacey moves aside for the three of us as we come in and then closes the door behind us.

"Good thing there aren't more guests staying here right now," Pappa says as he shrugs out of his jacket. "We'd have all hands on deck here otherwise."

I bite my tongue at him admitting out loud that I do the job of multiple people all by myself. So, my parents are fully aware of how hard I work and don't think anything of it?

"We'll figure something out, Lacey; don't worry," Mamma adds in her most professional-sounding voice as she takes off her jacket as well. "We'll have Lee or Svea come by to take care of things."

A little bit of guilt sinks down my spine. How am I going to keep up with innkeeping duties? Hopefully, Lacey is good with slumming it a little. She seems pretty understanding.

"That's okay, honestly," she answers sweetly. "I know I'm a guest, but I don't need much. I'm a lot more concerned about making sure you're okay, Will," she says to me, her tone like honey.

My whole body goes still, and the pain in my knee leaves my awareness.

This woman is more concerned about me than she is herself. Even when it takes away from her comfort, she still wants to help. I matter more to her than what I can do for her.

That's the kind of woman you build a life with.

It's like a shot to the chest to realize it. Lacey is something special, and she's someone special to *me*.

More than anything, I wish my parents weren't standing here because I'm overwhelmed with emotions and things I can't do anything about.

If they weren't here, I'd let myself fall for her in a way I've never fallen for anyone. I'd fall for her and never want to leave her side again.

Lacey must see some of what I'm feeling in my expression because her cheeks flush all rosy.

"That's sweet of you, Lacey, but you're a paying customer, and this is a business," Mamma reminds her dismissively.

She makes a face at that, like she doesn't see things nearly as black and white as Mamma does. I realize I said nearly the same thing to her earlier when she offered to drive me to the hospital, and now I regret saying it. My family has never invited a guest into their home for *fika* or had a guest help a member of the family with something like Svea's boutique, and I certainly have never confided in a guest the way I have Lacey.

"Mamma, no offense, but Lacey isn't our typical guest. She's more like a family friend at this point," I tell her, my hands tightening on the handles of my crutches.

Pappa makes a thoughtful sound. "He's right, *Älskling*."

Mamma considers him for a moment, and then with one searching look at me, she nods. "But promise me that if you do need something, you'll let us know," she demands of Lacey.

"I promise," she says, and then smiles at me. My chest inflates with some nameless glow I've never felt before, and I smile back.

I want her to think of me as more than just the business owner of the place she's staying. I shouldn't, but I do. I shouldn't want to know where I rank, but I do. I'm in a dangerous place here, wanting something I can't have, but I really can't help wanting Lacey.

Mamma claps her hands then, startling me just slightly. "Alright, butt on the couch," she directs me, and I begrudgingly crutch forward into the living room.

My parents make a fuss over getting me settled. Boots off, jacket off, knee propped up with a couple of throw pillows. Lacey brings an ice pack from the freezer that she wrapped in a dish towel and hands it to me, seeming glad to contribute.

I give her a smile in thanks, wishing we were alone. But I know there's no use in telling my folks that they don't have to stay. In fact, once Mamma realizes there's nothing else she can do for me, I'm certain this afternoon will turn into *fika*. That or she'll try to find something to clean. I'm suddenly grateful that I caught up on chores yesterday.

"I'll make something for lunch," Mamma announces and marches into the kitchen while Pappa takes a seat on the opposite couch.

"Oh, I can help," Lacey says brightly, making that glow in my chest burn even brighter.

In a matter of minutes, Mamma and Lacey fall into easy conversation while they cook, their voices carrying across the dining room like a pleasant song. When Lacey's light laughter hits my ears, I almost sigh at the comforting sound of it.

"Not many women from the city would be so easy going about something like this," Pappa says quietly, catching my attention. He keeps his eyes trained across the house on his wife and Lacey as he continues speaking. "In my experience, people in general don't usually respond well when there's even a small issue with the place they're staying." A slightly confused smile tugs on the corners of his mouth as he looks over at me. "But she's been nothing but gracious and helpful to our family."

I nod, glad that I'm not the only one who's noticed how amazing Lacey is.

"It's a shame she's not staying," he adds, and looks back toward the girls.

My heart jumps up and lands in my stomach. He's the first person to say exactly how I feel about her, but that doesn't mean he's saying what I think he's saying.

"What do you mean?" I ask carefully.

"I mean..." Pa scratches his dirty blond hair. "She fits here, you know?"

"Yeah," I answer, and glance over the back of the couch to the kitchen. Lacey is listening to some story Mamma is telling with a beautiful smile on her face, like there's nowhere else on earth she'd rather be. "She does."

The gentle crackle of the wood stove pipes up between the echoey words Mamma speaks, and for the first time since the broomball game, I relax. But then, Pa says something else.

"Mamma keeps worrying about Lee never finding himself a wife, but I'm more worried about you, Son."

"What?" I blurt out in surprise. "Why?"

He gives me an almost sad smile. Leaning forward, he plants his elbows on his knees. "Ma and I have tried to instill a healthy work ethic into you kids, but sometimes, I worry that we did the job too well." He shakes his head but keeps his brown eyes on me. "You've said that you're too busy to date, but I'm telling you now, Will, that there are more important things in life than work." He nods toward the kitchen. "When you find the right one...well, she'll make everything...*better*. I don't want you to miss your chance just because you're too busy." Pa reaches over and pats my ankle with a wink. "Just something to think about."

Then, he gets up and joins the girls in the kitchen, leaving me to swim through the wave of thoughts he's left me with.

My parents stay for dinner. It's been a strange afternoon for me, in that I've been stuck on the couch while everything goes on around me. But hearing my parents regale Lacey with story after story of my youth has been enough to chip away what remains of the walls I had erected around my feelings for this woman. Every time she laughs or smiles, I feel those barriers crumble a little more.

And by the time my folks take off for the night, I'm more than smitten...more than sure of what I want. If I don't end up becoming a restaurant-owning chef, I'd be okay with that. But if I don't end up with Lacey, I know I won't get over her. It's a terrifying fence post to sit on. If I take the leap, it might be for nothing when she leaves. If I step back, my sky won't ever be as bright.

But what Pa said stays with me. I don't want to miss my chance either. I don't want to work myself to death. With Lacey by my side, I feel like I could do anything. With her, everything really is better.

How do I say this to her? Part of me wonders if I even *should*, but the bigger part that's crazy about Lacey feels the need to speak up. Speak my heart.

I take in a deep breath and let it out slowly, nerves encompassing my chest.

Just ask her out.

That's all. That'll let her know I'm interested. And if she says no, then I haven't totally embarrassed myself by pouring out these vulnerable feelings that I've never felt for anyone else.

I watch her stride into the living room with a bowl of popcorn. Evening has fallen, and the windows are dark. The white lights from the Christmas tree illuminate the room in a gentle sheen that makes me feel like we're in our own little world. What I wouldn't give to make that true...to suspend time and ask her to dream with me about what we could be.

She sits on the opposite couch and sets the bowl down on the coffee table. The cabinet next to the wood stove is open, where Netflix is pulled up on the TV and ready for us to pick a movie. It doesn't matter what movie she picks; I know I won't be able to focus.

"I'm kind of feeling like a Christmas movie," Lacey says cheerfully. I smile and hand her the remote.

"Pick whatever you like."

She grins, and I return it. I try not to stare at her while she browses, but all of her little expressions are so endearing. Each movie she considers has her face reacting. A thoughtful tilt of her head. A little scrunch of her nose. A cute squint that crinkles the corners of her eyes. And then, a gasp pops out of her as she finds the one she wants.

"Yes!" she exclaims, and I glance at the TV. "*Elf* is my favorite Christmas movie!"

I chuckle at that. "You're a big Will Ferrell fan, then?"

"No," she laughs. "I mean, he's great. I do like him. But that's not why I love this movie." She puts the remote down next to the popcorn bowl as the movie begins.

"Then why?"

Her brown eyes land on me, and I love how warm they make me feel.

"Because he's just so...jolly. It's infectious."

I laugh softly and reach for a handful of popcorn. "I thought you were going to say because his costume reminds you of me," I say through a mouthful of popcorn.

She giggles and covers her cheek with her hands. "Oh my gosh, you're right. You guys could be brothers."

I laugh louder this time.

"You're much cuter than Will Ferrell is though. By far my favorite elf." Her eyes go wide as pleasure fills me from head to toe. "There I go again. Sorry," she mutters in adorable embarrassment.

"Don't apologize, Lacey," I tell her with a smile. "I hope you don't mind me saying that you're not so bad yourself."

A flicker of surprise shows on her face before she blushes just slightly and smiles, despite how what I said doesn't describe how beautiful I think she is at all. Not even close.

Ask her. Now before you lose your nerve.

"Yeah? You think I'd make a cute elf?" she jokes.

"The cutest."

She giggles again, looking more pleased than ever, and wow. Just...wow. Outright flirting with her is like riding a loopy roller coaster. My insides don't feel right, and yet, I can't stop smiling from the thrill of it.

"I definitely can't sing as well as Zooey Deschanel though."

"I'll be the judge of that. Let's hear it."

That's it, man. Turn on the charm.

Lacey snorts. "You first," she challenges.

"What, you think I'm scared to sing in front of you?"

She shrugs and eyes me curiously. "You're not?"

I clear my throat and attempt to sit up a little more without moving my knee. I look her right in the eyes and bust out an intentionally off-key chorus of "Jingle Bells" that has her cracking up with laughter.

"Good, right?" I prompt when I've finished, and pat myself on the back.

"You have the voice of an angel," she agrees playfully. The brightness in her eyes has me thinking that she feels this, too. For the first time, I realize how badly I want her to. I want to believe that there's something real between us. Something mutual.

But the only way to know for sure how she feels is to ask her or to tell her how I feel first. My head knows how stupid this is. My head knows that getting involved with Lacey will likely end in heartbreak for one or both of us. But my heart is talking louder at the moment. For *once*, my heart is reminding me of how little I do for myself—how little I ask of anyone. How I always say yes to everyone else all the time and never focus too much on what I want.

Well, I want this woman. Despite all the complications...she's someone I can't talk myself out of pursuing. Her smile, her laugh, her encouragement to go after my dreams...it's everything to me.

I take a deep breath, preparing to lay it all out there for her, but then the phone rings. And all my hopes come crumbling down.

Chapter Fifteen

Lacey

Despite Will's injury, this is the perfect evening. The last person to watch a Christmas movie with me was my mom. I was a junior in high school, I think, and she and I cuddled under a blanket with hot cocoa.

It's been a long time since I've laughed with someone whom I jive with so well, especially since I haven't even known Will for a week. It seems kind of bonkers that I *haven't* known him longer.

I feel so at peace here on the couch, eating popcorn beneath the light of the Christmas tree and dimmed overhead lighting, daring to flirt with a guy that I can't keep myself from wishing was mine. How am I not supposed to like him when he sings badly just to make me laugh? How am I not supposed to fall for him when he smiles at me like I'm his favorite person? I know for sure that he's quickly becoming one of my favorite people, too.

In the middle of my unabashed laughter, my phone begins to ring in my pocket. Still chuckling at Will's version of "Jingle Bells," I take it out and see *Janssen Auto* on the screen.

"Oh, it's the auto shop," I say in surprise, and accept the call. "Hello?"

"Lacey, I have great news!" Lars blurts out. "I got a hold of my cousin, who lives in Watertown, and he has a radiator for your car. He's coming into town tomorrow morning for Christmas anyway, so he's bringing it with him. I'll have your car ready to go by the end of the day tomorrow."

My brain freezes instantly at the information Lars just excitedly told me.

"Looks like you'll be able to get to Sioux Falls for Christmas after all," he adds warmly, like he's just moved mountains for me. He kind of has, and there's a big part of me that's grateful, but...

I look over at Will, whose eyes are on me, too, and I can't feel anything but disappointment. I thought I had more time. I wasn't expecting to leave for days...and now?

"Lacey? You there?" Lars says in my ear.

"Uh, yeah—yeah, I'm here. That's great news, Lars. Thank you so much."

"Consider it an early Christmas present," he answers with a chuckle. "I'll see you at five o'clock tomorrow. Merry Christmas, Lacey."

"Merry Christmas," I reply quietly, and then hang up.

The living room doesn't feel so cheerful and perfect anymore. The warmth that had filled the room with our laughter has cooled, and I think my heart might be breaking a little.

"Your car is done," Will guesses roughly. I nod and try to give him the smile I should be sporting, but can barely manage it.

"He said it'll be ready at five tomorrow."

"Wow," Will says, his jaw tight. He clears his throat. "That's great."

I bite my lip and fidget with my phone.

Is it great?

It's supposed to be...but it feels much more like I've swallowed a skein of yarn whole.

Zooey Deschanel is singing "Baby, It's Cold Outside" on the TV, and it feels much colder inside of me right now.

How can I go? How can I leave and not be here while Will is injured? How can I miss the Holly Ball tomorrow night? How can I enjoy my Christmas if I'm not here with Will and his amazing family?

"I...I don't know," I murmur to my lap. "What about you? Your knee is—"

"Don't worry about me, Lacey," he interrupts softly as I look up at him. His green eyes have lost the glow that was there while we flirted and giggled.

I glance toward the TV as Buddy the Elf joins in singing, too, and ugh.

Don't cry, Lacey, for the love of all that is threaded and sewn.

"I guess, I just...I wasn't expecting to be able to leave so soon," I explain, despite him not asking for me to explain why I'm not jumping up and down right now.

Will is quiet for a long moment, perforated only by the movie playing in the background, and then he sits forward just slightly.

"Well, just because your car is fixed tomorrow doesn't mean you have to leave tomorrow." His sentence is measured and slow, like he isn't sure whether he should be suggesting the idea.

"Yeah," I agree weakly. "That's true." I let my eyes roam over his careful expression and realize what I don't see. I don't see happiness.

Is he sad that I could be leaving sooner than expected, too? Does he feel the same disappointment that I do?

I take a deep breath and feel a sheepish grin curl my lips up. "I'll stay for the Holly Ball if you wear your elf costume."

He blinks just once, processing what I said, and then his face splits into a beautiful smile. My heart beats hard in my chest as he laughs.

"That's a deal," he promises, his voice full of life again, "but only if you save a dance for this poor hop-a-long."

I grin and reach over with my pinky outstretched. "Absolutely."

He links his pinky finger with mine, and everything feels better.

"Lindsey, what do I do? I'm freaking out," I say in hushed tones into the phone as I pace back and forth in front of the bed.

Will and I finished the movie, and then I helped him close down the inn for the night. He said he could do it himself, but I insisted. It's not hard to turn off lights and lock doors. I made sure to put things on the coffee table for him in case he needed something in the middle of the night and then disappeared upstairs so he could go to sleep.

But there's no way I can sleep. Not when it's become so clear that I want to be here and not anywhere else in the world. Not just for Christmas, but possibly forever.

I told Linz about Will's injury and how he put me in the guest zone earlier, but then flirted with me to the max this evening. She suggested that he's conflicted, too—that he feels something for me but doesn't think he should do anything about it. Which is honestly, probably, a true insight. He's a business owner, after all, and what would the town think of him hitting on someone who's staying here? Or his family?

Would Mamma care? She seemed so concerned about him at the Broomball game in terms of his lack of dating.

But then....does it even matter what she thinks? Does it matter what *anyone* thinks? He and I could have something real and lasting...something I haven't found before with anyone else. That isn't something I feel like I should just walk away from because if I do, I have a feeling I would always regret it.

"Okay, deep breaths," Lindsey consoles me as I continue to pace.

"He's great, and I'm great, and we could be so—"

"Great?"

"Yes. But, ugh, Lindsey...I don't have the balls to just go right out and ask him what he thinks."

"Listen, alright? You're exactly right. This could be great. You said he seemed sad about Kia getting fixed sooner than expected. I think there's a super high chance that he's into you." I nod to myself, pacing faster. "So here's what I propose—"

"Oh no, no way am I proposing—"

"No, you dummy," she cackles. "I'm proposing that you come clean. Just say it. Say that there's hella potential between you two, but your life is kind of up in the air at the moment, so maybe you can stay in touch."

My nose scrunches up. *Stay in touch?* That seems lame, and...not enough. I mean, I guess I'll take what I can get in this weird situation, but...I want more than just a text here and there. If that isn't the truth kicking me in the shin, I don't know what is.

"And then once you kind of figure stuff out, you can decide whether to do the long-distance relationship thing or whatever."

A sigh rushes out of me and then I flop back on the bed. "I sort of hate the idea of long distance."

"Hooo boy, you really do like this guy. Remember the last dude you dated? You were basically long-distance dating him with how seldom you saw him."

"But I was cool with that. I didn't mind only seeing him sometimes. With Will, I...I would want to see him more than like once a month, or even twice a month." My cheeks flame after I blurt that out because it reveals to Lindsey, and also to myself, how deep my feelings go.

"Well, if that's the case, then something has to give, girl. One of you has to move to make it work. And I think it's kind of unfair to consider it at all without his input."

Damn her and her ability to say it like it is.

"Why are you always right?" I mutter to the ceiling.

She snorts. "Don't sound so excited."

I would be more excited if I had a plan. I would be excited if I knew where Will's head is at when it comes to me. I'm in this weird limbo where I have nothing left in Minneapolis for me but nothing anywhere else either. All I have are hopes and maybes and wishes... Is hope enough to start a new life? If I offer my little heart to him, will he receive it enthusiastically, or will he tell me to go back to the city?

After I hang up with Lindsey, I do my best to sleep. But when the sun peeks through the delicate lace curtains, I'm tired and unsettled. As I open my eyes, I'm hit with the reality of what today brings.

I could leave tonight. *Tonight.* I could leave after the Holly Ball.

It hurts my heart to think that I just spent my last night here. My nose tickles as I look over at my suitcase lying open on the floor. I don't want to pack up my things. I love Lindsey, and I do want to see her but...not yet. The fact that she understands that is what makes her my best friend.

My phone buzzes on the nightstand, and I grab it with a yawn. I'm deeply surprised to see that there's a text message from my dad.

Dad: *Forgot to tell you we're in Aruba for Christmas.*

I frown.

Well, that's one way to say he isn't expecting me for Christmas this year. Though, why would he at this point?

Lacey: *Copy that.*

Mom would be so sad that this is what our family is like without her. Last-minute texts to let each other know that we're good with not spending Christmas together. I still haven't told him I'm in Larkspur or that I was fired. The hard truth is that I lost both parents when she died. He was just never the same, even after Mariah came along. In some way, I feel like she's just a placeholder in his life. Maybe that's why she isn't a big fan of me—I'm a reminder of her husband's first wife. Can't say I blame her, really, because my mom and I are pretty awesome.

As I get up and brush my teeth in the bathroom, I can't shake the grief I feel for my nearly nonexistent relationship with my dad and how much I miss my mom. And when I go downstairs and see Will up on his feet and making coffee in the kitchen, I'm bowled over by another rush of emotions.

I'm going to miss him.

I'm going to miss his laugh, his green eyes, those little freckles across his nose, and the way the little bit of scruff coming in on his face is redder than his hair. I'm going to miss eating his food and hearing stories about his childhood and his family.

He swivels on his good leg and points a tired smile at me, but I can't get myself to return it. "Morning," he says, and that's all it takes for my eyes to start prickling. Just that deep sound, a little groggy around the edges, is enough to stir up a longing in my heart that I know isn't going to go away when I leave.

"Hey," I squeak out.

There's nothing left for me in Minneapolis.

No job. No friends. No family, not really.

I feel more attached to this small town than I do to anything else right now. I'm a little plant whose roots have no soil to hold onto. Could I settle here? Put roots down here?

"You alright?" Will asks from across the kitchen island.

And could *he* be part of my future? Could Will be what I need to live out my days happily here? Could I be happy here if he *doesn't* want to be with me and ends up with someone else instead?

"Lacey?"

I swallow hard, realizing that he's staring at me just standing like a statue as these thoughts roll through me. I clear my throat and try to ease my tense shoulders back a little.

"I'm fine. Sorry. Just...I got a text from my dad, and it's kind of messing with my head a little bit," I attempt to explain. "It's not a big deal. How are you doing? How's your knee this morning?"

Will's green eyes watch me carefully for a long moment, studying my face and my body language with so much focus that my knees go all wobbly. "My knee is much better than yesterday," he answers. "And if you're upset, then the text you got from your dad *is* a big deal."

Well, I never claimed to have a good poker face, did I?

I bite my lip, fighting back the sting of tears forming behind my eyes. "I just miss him," I murmur to the floor. "Not him *now*...but, I miss him from before. He was different before Mom died," I explain with a trembling, vulnerable voice. I sniff and look up to see that Will has limped around the island and is leaning on the edge of it closest to me. His focus on me keeps me talking. "He was fun, and...warm, and...*present*. Now, he's so distant that he didn't think to tell me he'd be gone for Christmas until now." I sniff and fidget with the hem of my flannel sleeve. "And I'm so distant that I haven't even told him I'm here." The tears brim and blur my vision. "Mom would be so sad by how broken we are now. If she was alive, I'd be ashamed to tell her."

A hot streak of wetness falls down my cheek, immediately followed by two strong arms pulling me in close to a big, warm, firm body that smells like the coffee he was just making. Without even a drop of shame, I take what he's offering me and hug him back tightly.

"Please don't cry," Will pleads into my hair. "I can't handle seeing you cry."

I choke out a baby sob because *could he say anything sweeter*?

"There's time, Lacey," he says softly. "There's still time to fix things with your dad."

I nod into his cotton shirt, unable to remember the last time I was hugged or comforted like this. Maybe Lindsey at my mom's funeral. It's been years since someone held me and made me feel safe and loved, and I haven't even known Will for long. How can this feel so perfect when there's so much more to know about him? How can I be so at peace with his arms around me when I only have a snapshot of who he is and not the full picture?

"I'm sure he doesn't like things the way they are either," he adds, smoothing one hand down my back. "I don't know anyone who wouldn't want more of you in their life."

My soul sighs like a lovesick teenager. I unashamedly snuggle into his warm chest a little more, eating up his comfort and compassion. I didn't quite realize how much I've craved his closeness. I was ogling him like crazy at the Broomball game, but this is different...this is pure. This is the feeling you want to feel as you're drifting off to sleep at night. His closeness is all I would ever need to feel at home.

I *do* feel at home. Right here. And there's no other place like it.

Chapter Sixteen

Will

I have no business holding her like this. I shouldn't be comforting her. But the second she started tearing up, it was a lost battle. Seeing her break down in front of me, so vulnerable and so innocent, completely unhinged the last bit of strength I had to stay away from her.

And now she's here...snuggled into me like she's meant to fit exactly inside my arms.

I should let go. I should step back and try to put a little space between us, but I can't. Or rather, I won't. This feels too right to stop. This is too perfect to pull away and try to pretend like it's nothing.

I stroke my hand down her spine again and then back up towards her shoulder blades, feeling the way her breathing is shallow and quick as she tries to stop her tears.

It's a horrible thing to witness her coming apart like this. She's only ever been chipper and perky, or full of conviction and encouragement. I've never seen her sad, truly sad, and it's like being whacked in the head with a hot, cast iron pan. There's nothing I wouldn't do for her to be happy, I realize.

"Thank you for saying that," she whispers into my shirt. "You know just what to say, don't you?" She gives just the tiniest little chuckle, but all I feel is dread because she's about to pull back.

"It's true," I say, doing everything I can to keep from burying my face in her sweet-smelling hair. "You're something special, Lacey. Even my dad said so."

She pulls back so quickly, I almost fall over, but manage to keep my balance on my good leg. Her astonishment is huge on her wet face as she looks at me.

"He did?"

I smile, daring to keep my hands where they are on her lower back only because hers are resting on my chest. "Just yesterday." The rest of Pa's words come to mind.

I'm telling you now, Will, that there are more important things in life than work.

When you find the right one...well, she'll make everything...better.

Lacey does make everything better. Even in this situation where my knee is injured, she's looked after me and made me feel valued and taken care of. She had a glimpse of my dreams and then showed me what they could really look like in reality. She's supported and believed the best in me from the very beginning.

How could I not want her? How can she not see how amazing she is? How can her idiot father not want to be more involved in her life?

"All of you Christiansens are so sweet," she murmurs, clearly pleased by Pappa's opinion of her as well as mine.

"He said that it's—" I shut my mouth because I don't want to talk about the fact that she's leaving—and leaving soon. Tomorrow, I assume, so she can be with her friend for Christmas. I reluctantly let my hands fall away from her and shake my head. "Never mind."

"No, tell me," she urges as I limp back a step so that her hands fall away from me. I already miss her being close to me, and it's a reminder of how much it will hurt when she's gone.

"He said it's a shame you aren't staying." I turn away to prevent her from seeing the pain on my face from speaking that sentence out loud and then limp carefully back to the coffeemaker. I pour two mugs of coffee with my back to her, but in the silence that stretches between us, I'm unsure whether she can tell how much I long for her. It's a longing that won't go away when she's gone. It's too strong.

When I turn back, holding a mug for each of us, I find her in the same place she was standing. She's staring at me, a question in her beautiful brown eyes. Without breaking our eye contact, I lean forward and place her coffee on the island.

Lacey swallows hard, seeming to steel herself. "Do...*you* think it's a shame?"

Her question is a loaded one, but there's only one answer.

"Yes."

Something akin to hope flickers through her expression that slices me clean through the chest.

"But it doesn't matter what I think, Lacey," I add quietly. "You're leaving. We both know that."

Her eyebrows scrunch together slightly, and she finally looks away from me, down towards the floor. She nods slowly. "Yeah," she agrees so quietly, I almost can't hear her.

I want to ask her to stay, but who the hell do I think I am to ask something like that? Even if maybe she feels this too, we barely know each other. I just happen to really, really like the things I do know about her...

When she doesn't say more and doesn't look back up at me, I gather all the strength I have to change the subject. There's no point in saying anything else about her leaving anyway. But it still hurts to end this conversation because at least while we're talking about it, I can fool myself into thinking there's a chance we could be something that would last a lifetime.

"I have to be at the community center to help set up," I grind out. "But I'll make breakfast quick."

Her head snaps up. "What? Will, no offense, but how are you going to help with that brace on your knee?"

I slug back a big mouthful of hot coffee. "I'll find something to do. I said I'd help, so I'm going."

Her eyes widen slightly as her mouth does a funny little wiggle. "What?"

"You sounded just like Lee. All gruff and serious." She stifles a giggle that makes my stomach flip. "Will, I'm sure most people in town know you had a bad fall yesterday. The Holly Ball people will understand if you skip out."

I shake my head. "I said I'd be there. If I end up just getting in the way, then I'll leave, but I gave my word, so I'm going to stick to it."

Lacey smiles softly at that, like she admires my honesty, but there's still a little glint in her eye that lets me know she's amused, too. "Well, I'll go too, then. I've never set up a ball, but I'm sure there's something I can do to help, right?"

I open my mouth to assure her that she doesn't need to, but then I close it. Her helpfulness is my undoing every time. Especially when I'm the one she's trying to help.

So, Lacey and I whip up scrambled eggs and toast while she asks me several questions about how I slept last night on the couch and how many times I had to get up for something, and on a scale from one to ten, how bad does my knee hurt today. I can't help but soak up her concern for me, even if I probably shouldn't.

Mamma calls as we're eating at the kitchen island and asks me all the same questions. Then Pappa gets on the phone next and tries to talk me out of going to help at the community center. It's a weird thing for him to tell me not to do something. Usually, it's the opposite. I guess it's nice of them to be concerned about me, but part of me wonders if they want me to take it easy just so I can heal quicker and get back to me being the yes-man I've always been.

My stomach sours as I hang up with my parents and attempt to finish my toast. There's a growing divide between me and my folks, I'm realizing. The more Lacey encourages me to dream and even plan, the further away I feel from the people who raised me. I don't think I can do both. I can't become the chef I want to be while doing everything for them and for everyone else. If I want to go after what makes me happy and fulfills me, then something has to give.

I don't want to have that conversation. I don't want to show them a vulnerable piece of myself and then have them guilt me into not pursuing it. I don't want them to attempt to change my mind because it wouldn't be good for the inn.

I want them to see that I have more potential than just an innkeeper or an errand-runner. I want them to believe I can do what I think I can. But it would hurt too much if they didn't. Despite Lacey's encouragement and enthusiasm about my cooking, my parents' disapproval would possibly do irreparable damage to our family relationship.

And when I think of it that way, my dream isn't worth the risk.

When Lacey and I show up at the community center, I'm surprised to find that my siblings are here. Lee walks past me carrying a box of Christmas lights and gives me a once over before nodding in a semi-pissed way that lets me know he still hasn't forgiven me for the snowball fight incident or my fall yesterday. I didn't expect him to, so it doesn't bother me in the slightest.

"Hey, buttface!" Svea shouts across the large gym. She's hanging paper snowflakes on the walls with Emma's sister, Caitlin, and one of the Llewellyn twins. Thankfully, they're her peers and not any of the women from the ladies' church group.

I wave as Lacey chuckles next to me.

People are bustling around the gym, setting up tables and moving chairs, stringing up Christmas lights, and working on the kids' corner where volunteers do crafts with them while their parents dance. There are tables being set up over to the left where the drinks and snacks will go, and I will my brain to not go down the rabbit hole of recipes I would fill it with. A little swell of pride fills me up to see everyone here, taking time out of their morning to make the Holly Ball the best it can be.

"This is so cool," Lacey says, looking around with a big smile. "You guys do this every year?"

"Yep. Everyone loves it. Quite a few couples have had their first dates at the Holly Ball," I tell her, then regret it because I immediately wish I could ask her to go with me.

"That's adorable," Lacey gushes and then claps her hands. "Okay, what should I do to help? Give me a task, chef."

I smile over at her, and she returns it, making me feel light. "Wish I could put your whisking capabilities to use here, big guns, but I don't think I can. Let's go see if Carly over there needs help setting up the kids' corner."

Lacey grins at me as I slowly make my way over, with her matching my pace as people weave around us. She eyes me as we go, and I can feel how uncertain she is about my assurances that I'm fine.

"You'll tell me if your knee feels worse, right?" she questions suspiciously.

"I'm fine, I promise."

Obviously, my knee isn't great, but compared to yesterday, it really does feel better. It's still a little swollen and definitely sore, but as long as I don't run a mile or tweak it further, I'll be good.

"You didn't answer my question, so I'm keeping my eye on you," she warns with a chuckle.

"Please do," I shoot back flirtatiously. Half of my heart breaks as I say it, but the other half lights up when she giggles. It makes me wish we were back at the inn—alone.

"Well, who's this?" comes a voice from my right. I pause at the sight of Clay Cox as he steps closer, his beady blue eyes trained on Lacey. "I saw you at the game yesterday," he says with a wide, friendly smile. He offers his hand. "I didn't get a chance to introduce myself after Will had to forfeit the game. I'm Clay."

Clay and I were classmates and even friends once. He's the kind of guy who comes off as a team player, but when it comes down to the buzzer, he'll always do whatever will make him look better. I can't say anything seriously bad about him, but there isn't much good to say about him either. From what I've heard and sometimes seen, he doesn't tend to have a girlfriend for very long. Svea called him a serial dater once, but as far as I know, he isn't a complete womanizer.

That being said, him talking to Lacey ignites a flame of jealousy that licks up my spine as she smiles politely and shakes Clay's hand. "Lacey," she says. "You probably didn't get a chance yesterday because I was too busy making sure Will was okay, and you were too busy wondering if his injury meant you won by default."

I nearly choke on my spit, and Clay's shoulders tighten in surprise at how she so quickly called him out on caring more about winning than anything else.

"Uh, yeah, I guess a lot was going on at once," he replies in a fumbled way, like he isn't sure he can salvage his image.

Lacey smiles again and nods like she understands, but I see the little bit of snark in her expression. It floods me with happiness and fondness for her.

Clay clears his throat as he glances at me and then decides to press on with whatever reason he came over here for. "So, Lacey, you got a date for the Holly Ball tonight? I'm available if you'd—"

"That's sweet of you to ask," she interrupts, astonishing Clay. "But I'm already going with Will here."

I keep my face as unchanged as possible, not just to go along with what Lacey said so Clay takes a hike, but also because on the inside, my heart is doing back flips.

He looks over at me in displeasure, but then he smirks. "You're going with Will? He can't even dance with his knee all messed up." He steps closer to Lacey. "Why don't you go with me, honey? I'll show you a way better time."

I can't help making a face. *Honey.* Adrenaline begins to pump throughout my body, dulling the pain in my knee, but before I can say or do a single thing, Lacey answers him.

"I hate to break this to you, Clay, but I'm interested in a lot more than how well Will can dance. I actually really enjoy his company, and I can't say the same about you."

Clay's eyebrows rise halfway up his forehead as the tension in my muscles eases away. He frowns at me in defeat and sends an irritated look Lacey's way. She just smiles at him pleasantly, and I fall for her a little more.

"Let me know if you change your mind," he mutters, and then ambles off toward where Svea and the others, who are hanging decorations.

"I'm not changing my mind," Lacey says, and as I swing my gaze to her, I catch her rolling her eyes.

"You're feisty sometimes," I point out, impressed.

She laughs and squeezes my forearm. "Sometimes. I hope you don't mind me using you as a scapegoat."

"Not one bit."

Lacey beams up at me, and I smile back because even though she's leaving tomorrow and that fact hangs over my head like a storm cloud, there's no one else I'd rather go to the Holly Ball with. And I sure as hell don't want to see her dancing with anyone else.

She stays by me the entire time we're at the community center. Part of me thinks it's because she really is keeping an eye on me, but she did say that she enjoys my company. Putting Clay in his place and defending me came so naturally to her, and as we help Carly Gustafson with the kids' corner and then help plug strings of Christmas lights together, I'm drawn to her even more.

Serving my community with her by my side just feels...easy. I have a strong suspicion that I could do anything with her, and it would feel like this. It's like my dad said—Lacey makes everything *better*.

And apparently, I'm her date tonight, bum knee and all. The bit of panic I've been feeling since I hurt myself yesterday dissipates as she and I laugh and talk while we work. It reminds me of the way cooking relaxes me and takes my mind off of everything else. It's the first time I've ever had that feeling outside of cooking, and that, if anything, is what makes me realize that I'm in for nothing but heartbreak when it comes to Lacey Murdock.

Chapter Seventeen

Lacey

T he gym is looking festive. It's very Winter Wonderland, with white lights strung all over and snowflake decorations. I can't wait to see it with the overhead lights dimmed. I think it'll be romantic and ethereal tonight when the music starts and people dance.

I've never been to a dance like this, though I guess prom sort of counts. I went with my friends, for the record, not a date, and I wouldn't change that for anything. But tonight, well, I get to go with Will after all, and I'm not even a little disappointed. Why would I be? He's amazing.

And he thinks it's a shame that I'm leaving.

He probably has no idea how close I was to climbing over the kitchen island and kissing him smack on the mouth when he said yes, it's a shame. It was just one tiny hint that he wants me to stay. Another tiny hint was him being more than willing to go with me tonight. Clay, AKA Mr. Tinman, could've dropped some lines of Shakespeare or Rumi and it wouldn't have persuaded me to go with him. Will is the only guy I'm interested in dancing with tonight, even if it's in a limited sort of way because of his knee.

Without realizing it, I start humming Whitney Houston's "I Wanna Dance With Somebody" as Will and I spread a light blue paper tablecloth over the refreshment table. He was adorable singing so unbelievably off-key last night. I can't remember the last time I laughed that hard, and he wasn't bothered in the slightest. In fact, he seemed pleased.

I'm going to miss him so much.

I never thought I wouldn't be happy to get Kia back, but all morning, I've had this overwhelming sense of pleading in my heart for time to slow down. Even if I stayed for Christmas, I still need to go back to Minneapolis after that. I still need to go and figure out what I'm going to do with my apartment and how to go about starting my own business instead of trying to get hired somewhere else. I'm definitely not looking forward to any of that.

I just want to forget about all the unknowns waiting for me in Minneapolis and be present *here*, where things feel like they make more sense than not. I want to go to this ball tonight and have the most amazing time and not think about how it's my last night in Larkspur. I don't want to think about when the morning comes and I have to pack up and be on my not-so-merry way.

"Gotta go to work. Keep an eye on him," comes Lee's gruff voice from my right as he walks by, heading for the exit.

I smile at the back of his dark head because he hasn't said one word to Will since we got here, but it's clear that Lee cares about his brother. He's got a little gooey spot beneath that rough and tough personality.

"So, how do we get Lee and Emma together?" I ask Will as I round the table toward him.

Will cocks an eyebrow at me in surprise, but then he chuckles. "Beats me. I jokingly said I was going to ask her to the Holly Ball, and he nearly decked me."

I snort, but there's a teeny tiny little bit of jealousy that flicks me in the stomach. Just for a second, because then I remember that I'm the one going with Will. Even if it's just as friends.

"Is she coming tonight?"

"She usually does," he replies as he looks around the gym to see what else needs to be done.

"Good, I want to meet her."

Will laughs softly and looks back at me with warm eyes that melt me inside. "You're more than merrier to try and get her to talk to Lee outside of the library, but I'm not holding my breath on that one."

I rub my hands together. "You underestimate me, William."

"Did you just call me *William*?"

"That's what Will is short for, right?" I place my hands on my hips and meet his gaze with a jaunty lift of my chin.

He studies me for a second with laughter in his eyes, making my heart beat a little harder. "Mamma is the only one who calls me William, and that's only when I'm in serious trouble."

"Your full first name and middle name?"

He shrugs. "Maybe."

"William David?"

Will shakes his head, smiling.

I step closer to him as I guess again. "William...Andrew?"

"Nope."

"William Frankenstein?"

"What?" He laughs from his belly. "Not even close."

I laugh too and push his arm playfully. "Come on, tell me. I give up."

His smile softens as his laughter dies down. He reaches forward and touches a few strands of my hair. I feel every bit of me inside and out standing at attention as he looks into my eyes. "It's William John."

I don't know why knowing his full name seems so intimate. It's just a name, but it feels like he's giving it to me in a way. Trusting me with it. It's a name I know I'll always hold dear.

He gently moves my hair back behind my ear, which sends a shiver down my spine in the best way and then quickly drops his hand. That tender expression has vanished, and in its place is something heavier and shuttered.

"Now I know what to call you when you get in trouble with me," I say, trying to lighten the mood back to what it was.

"I don't plan on getting into any trouble with you."

I smile. "You're related to Svea. I'm sure some of her troublemaker blood runs in your veins, too." I look across the gym to where Svea is chasing a kid around, playing tag instead of doing anything productive. "Hey, that reminds me!" I turn my focus back to Will. "We still haven't gotten her back for salting your coffee."

He chuckles and shifts his weight slightly. I glance down at his braced knee and realize he's probably been on his feet too long. "Let's go home and make a plan," I suggest, and feel only a small swoop in my stomach when I notice that I called the inn *home*. I put that thought down for now so I can pick it up later to think about more. "You should get off your feet for a while anyway."

Will sighs, shifting on his feet again, and glances around the gym. The only ones really doing anything are a few guys in the far corner who are setting up sound equipment. Just about everything else is taken care of. He seems to begrudgingly agree because he nods with a tight smile.

"Let's go, chef."

He falls into step beside me, nodding or waving at this person or that as we head towards the doors we came in through. I peek back over my shoulder at Svea, wondering what kind of prank we could pull on her when I see that Clay has joined in on the game of tag. Hmm. So, maybe he does have a heart. Could've fooled me, honestly. I almost threw up in my mouth a little when he called me *honey*. Gross. I mean, he isn't bad looking. Clay has a nice straight nose and sort of sandy blond hair that looks like he spends a lot of time styling it. He's not horrible to look at, but the whole not caring about Will's injury and then basically putting him down for it so that I would go to the Holly Ball with him instead? Eh, that's pretty horrible in my book. I'd much rather play a prank on Clay than Svea, I realize.

Will and I grab our coats from where we put them down out of the way, and then he holds the door open for me, even though he's the one limping. I smile at him and make sure to go slow across the parking lot to where his truck is. The sun is high above in the sky, shining down on the little patches of snow here and there on the pavement, making them sparkle.

He hands me the keys, we get in, and then we're on our way back to the inn with him trying to discreetly rub his knee in the passenger seat.

"You alright?" I ask. "That was a lot of standing and walking around."

"I'm fine," he replies, as I knew he would. "Tylenol wore off, is all."

"I was going to bring some, but I forgot. I'm sorry."

"No worries, Lacey," he assures me as I turn onto Main Street. "And thanks for coming along this morning. You were a big help."

I beam over at him as we pass Svea's Boutique. "It was fun, actually."

"And you like my company, so that helps."

I fight the urge to flirtatiously smack his arm. "Hey, you're getting a little cocky there, William John. Don't let it go to your head."

Will chuckles at that. "So, what's your plan for revenge on Svea?"

I slow to stop at the four-way and thoughtfully tap my fingers on the steering wheel. "We could get her a gag gift for Christmas. Something she would be embarrassed to open in front of your parents," I suggest with a mischievous grin. "Like a bikini or a thong or something."

"You're just as evil as she is."

I laugh as I press down on the accelerator. We trundle through Main Street, passing the Karlson's Butcher Shop and Alma's Diner. I suddenly wish I had thought to check out all the local businesses. Besides Svea's Boutique, I notice a few other shops that sell tchotchkes, gift cards, and local goods like honey and jams.

"Ooh, we could put hot sauce in her Christmas dinner."

Will laughs again, but I catch him looking over at me like I'm onto something. "In her hot cocoa. That would be only fair."

"It really would," I agree. A familiar electronic jingle sounds from my coat pocket. Keeping my eyes on the road, I take it out so I can glance at the screen.

Janssen Auto.

"Oh, I think it's Lars," I say in surprise, and hold it out toward Will. "Do you mind?"

He takes it, all levity gone from his expression. "Of course." He swipes to accept the call and then taps speakerphone.

"Hello?" I answer. Will moves the phone between us.

"Hey, Lacey. It's Lars," he greets jovially. "I hope you're ready for an early Christmas present because your car is done!"

My stomach instantly twists and I barely remember to turn left where I need to. "Oh, wow—I thought it wouldn't be done until tonight.

Isn't that what you said?" Not that it really matters, I guess, but I can barely formulate a coherent thought at the moment.

"Yeah, that's what I said, but I got here bright and early and worked my butt off to get it ready for you," he explains, like he's literally giving me the best Christmas present I could've asked for when in reality, it's kind of the opposite.

Larkspur Inn comes into view, and my heart sinks down to my toes. "You didn't have to do that, Lars."

"Ah, you're basically a friend of the Christiansens now, just like I am," he insists. "Just promise me you'll get where you're going in one piece this time." He chuckles to himself. "At least there isn't a big chance of you hitting any more albino deer on your way."

I wouldn't be surprised at this point. "You never know," is all I can manage to respond with.

"Listen, I'll come by in a bit to pick you up, how's that? You're at the inn, right? I'll give you a ride to the shop, then you can get your car and make it to Sioux Falls before dark."

Lars, ugh.

He's totally killing me here.

I glance over at Will, but his face is pointed out the window. I pull into the driveway and put the truck into park.

"Oh—uh, that's really nice of you, but I was planning on going to the Holly Ball tonight." I switch off the truck and offer the keys to Will, who gives me my phone. Keys in hand, he swings the passenger door open without a word or even a look my way and gets out. The door slams hard, making my heart jump.

"Is that right? I guess I figured you wanted to get out of dodge as soon as possible," Lars almost confusedly says in my ear.

"Not that I don't appreciate you working so hard—I just—I'm going with Will, and I don't want to stand him up," I explain quickly, guilt eating me up because Lars really went above and beyond for me when he absolutely didn't have to. I don't want him to think I'm not grateful.

"You're going with Will? That's awesome," he says, his tone instantly lightening. "He works too hard, you know? You guys will have a great time."

My eyes follow Will as he hobbles up to the side door of the inn. "Yeah, it"ll be great," I agree numbly.

"Well, let's still get you squared away with your car today, okay? Then, you can go first thing in the morning or whenever you want to."

"That sounds good, Lars. Thank you."

"I'll swing by in about a half hour. See you then."

"Alright. Bye."

"Bye."

I hang up and lean my head back against the seat.

My car is done early. Extra early. But that changes nothing. The plan is still to stay the night. I'm going to attend the Holly Ball with Will. And then, in the morning, I'll...?

I heave out a distressed sigh.

In the morning, I'll pack and...

Tears begin to well in my eyes.

In the morning, I'll pack my things and...and then I'll go. I'll go spend Christmas with Lindsey, where she'll help me navigate what I should do next.

I sniff, trying to keep my emotions from becoming too much, and then I get out of Will's truck and go inside.

The side door opens into a small mudroom. I hang up my coat and take off my boots, noticing the two doors ahead that stand ajar. One is a half bath, and the other is a laundry room with a desk tucked into the corner. The hall turns to the right and into the kitchen, where I find Will rummaging through the refrigerator.

"You should get off your feet," I say, the words coming out weaker than I intend. "I'll cook something for lunch."

He continues to rummage, but he speaks over his shoulder to me. "I want to cook. You need to pack anyway." His voice is cold and so unlike him that for a moment, I don't know how to respond.

"Will, I'm not—"

"It's fine, Lacey," he growls, and finally seems to find what he was looking for. Will tosses a few items on the counter next to the fridge and then closes the door, all with his back to me. "It's not like the Holly Ball was going to be an amazing time with my knee the way it is. And now you can see your friend for Christmas."

Wait—is he upset? Is he mad because he thinks I'm backing out on going with him? I step closer, my brain whirling as I try to put the pieces together.

"Lars will be here soon, so just go." He clears his throat. "I'll make up something for you to eat on the road." This time, he uses his professional voice, the one that's all polite and not at all like we know each other. It hurts more than I want to admit.

"Will, I'm not leaving tonight."

My words have him freezing in place, lunch preparations forgotten. I move a little closer, still speaking to his back.

"But if you don't want to go to the dance with me, that's okay."

His shoulders tense, and he carefully turns around. His face is tight, eyes shrouded like he's pulled back from me. "Maybe it's better if we don't go together," he says quietly.

It's not what I expected him to say, and it hurts like a thousand needles stuck into my skin. I expected him to tell me that *of course*, he wants to go with me and that he's glad I'm not leaving tonight. But in the silence that fills up the kitchen between us, I realize he isn't going to take it back.

"Why?" I press with a pounding heart.

Will swallows, leaning back against the counter to take the weight off his knee. "It would probably be inappropriate, being that you're a guest here."

There it is again. Back in the guest zone. I clench my jaw to keep the hurt from showing on my face.

"Right," I mutter bitterly. "It would be so inappropriate if someone thought we were friends."

He doesn't disagree with my statement, which just feels like another blow. Why is he being like this? Who is this man?

"You should just leave today, Lacey."

My chest aches like he has my rib cage in the palm of his hand, squeezing the breath out of me. My throat burns as I try to keep a sob from escaping. Because he wants me to leave. He not only wants to go to the Holly Ball alone, but he also wants me to pack my things and just go.

But I don't want to.

At least I didn't before I walked in here. Now I'm wondering if I should put my foot down and make him eat his words. Now I'm wondering if I should go tonight and dance with Clay, just to make him see what he's missing out on. That would be cruel, but this moment is pretty cruel, too.

"You really want me to leave?"

His lips press together tightly for a moment before he answers me. "I don't *want* you to, but I also don't want you to feel like you have to stay. You should be with whomever you want to be with for Christmas."

The breath rushes back into my lungs. His words, however politely spoken, give me hope. I step closer. "And if I want to be here?"

He blinks. "Do you?"

I close the distance between us and nod. He looks down at me, those green eyes still a little guarded.

"Are you sure?"

"This is where I want to be, Will. If I go to Sioux Falls today, I'll regret it, I just know it." My hands tingle to reach out and touch him, but I restrain myself. "I'd be kind of a third wheel with Lindsey and her fiancé anyway," I admit, even though that isn't remotely true. They've never made me feel like a third wheel. "I'm not saying that I have any right to be with your family for Christmas, but I do want to be *here*."

Will rolls his teeth over his bottom lip. "I was planning on inviting you if your car wasn't done in time," he says softly. "I didn't want you to spend Christmas alone, and I still don't."

Warmth floods me, and I give him a wobbly smile. "Then I guess I need to do some Christmas shopping."

"No one is expecting you to give them presents, including me."

"Too bad, chef. It's happening."

Chapter Eighteen

Will

After Lars shows up and Lacey goes with him to get her car, I let out a huge, heaving, stressed-out sigh.

I don't like how I just acted. I can't believe I told her to leave. I can't believe I actually said those words. The hurt on her face was...nearly unbearable. I've never thought of myself as a jerk, but in that moment, I absolutely was. What kind of idiot pushes away a woman like Lacey? Especially when apparently, she wants to be here for Christmas?

I limp over to the couch and lay down, hating myself.

The issue isn't that I want her to leave, it's that I want her to *stay*. For good. And that's just not something I can bank on happening. I'd be a fool to think that if I stuck my neck out and told her how she fits here in Larkspur that she would just up and move here. It's one thing to dream about being a chef and having a restaurant, but it's another thing to dream about Lacey being a permanent fixture in my life. I need to adjust my expectations so that she won't leave with my heart in her hands.

My phone buzzes in my pocket, and I take it out to see a text from Lee.

"Hmm," I say out loud, because he almost never texts me.

Lee: *She's nice.*

Oh, boy. Here we go.

Will: *Yeah, Emma's great.*

I know that reply will rile him up, and even though I'm in a miserable state of mind, I can't help messing with my big brother.

Lee: *No, Lacey, you idiot. Glad you finally asked her to go to the Holly Ball.*

Will: *Well, that's not exactly how it happened, but yeah. It's not a big deal.*

But it kind of is. I'm not about to assume it's a date because I need to keep myself in check, but still. I haven't gone to the Holly Ball with anyone in years.

Will: *Wait, how did you know that?*

Lee: *You know who my best friend is.*

Damn it. Lars and his big mouth. I swear, he's just as bad as Grandma Janssen in the loose lips department.

Lee: *Just be careful.*

Lee's warning is vague, and I hate that he's that way sometimes. He could be warning me to be careful because of my knee or to be careful with Lacey. I don't really want to find out which one he means, but then again...he's my brother. If I can't talk to him about things, then what good is he? At least I know he won't blab my business all over town like Lars would.

Will: *Yeah...I like her.*

Admitting it feels like a heart attack.

Will: *I know I'm an idiot.*

Lee: *Everyone knows you're an idiot.*

I scoff at that, but then another text comes through.

Lee: *You're only an idiot if you let her become the one who got away.*

Lee: *Gotta get back to work. Later.*

I sigh and toss my phone on the couch next to my bad knee. He's one to talk. He's in love with Emma but won't do anything about it. And what's his excuse? She's shy and might turn him down? He doesn't think she feels the same way? Well, I might be biased, but it's far worse to be pretty sure it's mutual and for her to be an out-of-towner that you'll likely never see again.

I'm not the kind of guy to start something I can't finish. And I know that with Lacey, I want to finish it. I want the whole thing, not just a small bite. She's beautiful, funny, selfless...everything I could ever want.

How will I ever find someone better than her? How will I go for my dreams and not think of her constantly because she was the one who encouraged me to do it?

She's made such an impact on my life in such a short amount of time. That kind of thing shouldn't be ignored. And according to my slightly hypocritical brother, it would be a mistake to let her go. I definitely do agree with him, but it doesn't change anything. She's here for Christmas, and then that's it. I would feel like such a loser if I asked her to stay and she didn't...if I told her how I felt and what I think we could be, only for her to leave anyway.

What am I going to do?

I don't want to put myself out there and get shot down. But I can't have her if I don't ask...right?

All I know is when she does leave and my life goes back to normal, it won't feel right anymore. If I have to go back to running this inn day in and day out, running this errand and doing that thing for my parents, and if I don't speak up about going after my dream or going after Lacey...it will hurt like hot grease on a sunburn. But if I go for it all, for my dream and for Lacey, I might still end up with what I had before she showed up on my doorstep.

I stare up at the ceiling, finding a small comfort in focusing on the wooden beams because it reminds me of working alongside Pa. Maybe that's where it all went sideways with them. I went from working *with* my parents to working alone and basically against my will. I wasn't lying when I told Lacey that they never asked me if I would take over Larkspur Inn. It was just assumed, and I never said no. Now, it just feels too late.

But, what if I left to pursue my dream? What if I didn't give *them* a choice in the matter? Maybe I could find a replacement to run the inn, and then I could...I could go to Minneapolis and work in a real kitchen. I could save up for my own restaurant and see Lacey whenever I wanted to. Could I really do that? Abandon my hometown? Leave my family here? It's not like I'd never come back, but...would things ever really be the same between my parents if I decided to leave?

I love my family. As much as they stress me out and ask for too much sometimes, I love them. I would miss the hell out of them if I didn't see them all the time. And the idea of leaving this town...this town where I grew up and where I always envisioned myself living, well, it makes me nauseous. Larkspur is a tight-knit community. I doubt that I could find something similar in Minneapolis, even if moving there meant Lacey and I could be together.

I smack myself on the forehead. No, I want to be in Larkspur. I want my restaurant to be here. I want to serve my community, and I know that they would give me their support. I just need to get my folks on board.

And I need to figure out what this is between me and Lacey. I don't want to look back in ten years and wish I had just said something. I need to find a way to convince her not to disappear from my life. I'm afraid that if she did, I might never find the courage to finally say no to my parents.

It's nearly time to leave for the Holly Ball, and I'm so relieved that Lacey told me I didn't have to wear my elf costume. Lee would never let me hear the end of it if I showed up in that thing. I took one step at a time up the staircase so I could shower and get ready in my room, and now all that's left to do is put on my suit jacket and shoes.

I'm nervous. Really, really nervous. Lacey has been getting ready for twice as long as me, and I know when I see her all dressed up that I'm going to fall even harder for her.

She was gone more than an hour after she left with Lars, and when she came back, her arms were filled with gift bags and things she had picked up in town. Before I could insist she didn't need to get me and my family Christmas presents, she asked for tape, scissors, and wrapping paper, and then disappeared upstairs.

I want to apologize to her for the way I acted earlier, but I don't know exactly what to say. Maybe I can make it up to her tonight.

I take one last glance in the bathroom mirror and then limp my way out to the hallway. Lacey still hasn't made an appearance, so I pause at her door. I can faintly hear music playing from inside as I lift my hand and knock.

"One second!" she calls out, and then the music stops. A moment later, the door opens, and I realize how unprepared I was to see her like this.

She's curled her brown hair and left it down, laying nicely over her almost bare shoulders. Her eyelashes look longer and darker than normal, so that they frame her coffee-colored eyes and make them pop. And her dress...her dress has me gulping and forgetting how to breathe. It's a shimmery sort of fabric, dark green in color, and it accentuates her curves without looking too tight on her.

Vacker, I think, which means "beautiful."

I clear my throat, realizing I'm just standing there staring open-mouthed, and focus back on her eyes. "You look—" But I can't finish my sentence because I finally see the way she's looking at me.

"Wow," she says. "You clean up nice, chef."

Butterflies instantly zigzag in my stomach.

She likes what she sees; how about that?

"So do you, big guns."

She grins then, breaking the spell that we were both under.

"You ready to go?"

"Yeah, let's go." She closes the door behind her and unnecessarily matches my pace going down the stairs.

I made sure to take Tylenol so that my knee doesn't totally ruin the night. At the bottom, we put on our shoes and coats, and then we're on our way out the door.

"Let's take my car," she offers, and I follow her down the front walk to where her car is parked on the street.

The night is dark and cold, the street illuminated by the streetlights and the glow of the inn's Christmas lights. I don't notice a damn bit of it because I can't take my eyes off of Lacey. She's beautiful even without all the extra effort she put in, so seeing her like this feels like I've won the lottery as far as dates go—platonic or otherwise.

She drives through town to the community center, whose parking lot is already nearly full.

"Shoot," she says as she looks for an open space. "I was hoping we could find a spot closer to the door so you don't have to walk so far."

"It's alright," I assure her. "You'll catch me if I fall, right?"

"Absolutely, I will," she replies with a chuckle.

Lacey finds a space along the back row and parks. My nerves come back to the forefront of my mind as I get out of the car. But her beautiful smile pointed at me helps me relax just a little.

"Shall we?"

Together, we weave through the rows of vehicles to get to the front doors. The music invites us in, and I have the delight of watching Lacey take in the transformed gym. She gasps as she looks around, seeming enchanted by the space now that the overhead lights are off. The Christmas lights are strung along the walls and over the designated dance area, forming a lighted canopy. The room is buzzing with laughter and conversation just over the volume of the music, and an odd sense of contentment fills me up to see that people are already dancing. Even in the low lighting, I recognize my parents cutting a rug. I smile at that and point them out to Lacey, who laughs.

"Look at them go!" she exclaims as they waltz in a circle, and then she grabs my hand and urges me forward to get a better look. I see the Gustafsons are already here and so are the Janssen's. Lars's older brother, Anders, is dancing with Grandma Janssen and looking a little put out about it.

Groups of people are gathered all over the gym, some eating cookies and punch, some just talking. The kids' corner is full of kids and a few parents who are helping with the coloring contest and cookie decorating station. I spy Svea next to the refreshment table talking to

Emma's older sister, Caitlin, but I haven't pinpointed where Lee is yet. Maybe he's working a little late since he was here this morning to help set up.

"Everything looks so amazing," Lacey says to me, standing close so I can hear her. I catch a scent of her shampoo or whatever she has in her hair and have to actively restrain myself from moving in closer.

"*You* look amazing," I blurt out, and feel my cheeks heat up.

Great. Real smooth.

She giggles and reaches out to adjust my tie. "I know I said you didn't have to wear the elf costume, but now I'm kind of regretting that."

I snort. "Of course, you are. You have a thing for elves."

She yanks on my tie, pulling me toward her slightly. "Excuse me, I do not."

The flirting is back, and I'm all for it. I'd much rather lose myself in this than in the reality of her leaving, especially after my behavior this afternoon. "You're the one obsessed with me wearing that costume."

"Okay, now we're exaggerating. I'm not *obsessed*. I just think you're cute—" She clamps her mouth shut as I snicker.

"Oh, believe me, I've noticed."

She narrows her eyes at me and shakes her head slowly, but she's fighting a smile, and it makes me feel lightheaded. I reach for the zipper pull at the top of her coat and tug it down an inch.

"Take this off, or you'll get warm. You can put it over there." I point to a sectioned-off area where people have piled their coats on a couple of tables.

"Sounds good. No dancing without me," she instructs, pointing a finger at me.

"Wouldn't dream of it." I watch her move around a couple of small circles of people, removing her coat as she goes.

"Lookin' sharp, bro," Svea says from behind me. I turn and smile at my sister, who's wearing a gold, knee-length dress and a braid down her back.

"Hey, Svee."

"Our parents are the life of the party yet again," she says, nodding toward where Pappa is twirling Mamma around. We watch them for a moment, both admiring the relationship they have. Not many people are that in love after being married nearly four decades. As far back as I can remember, they've been inseparable.

When I look back to Svea, her eyes have strayed to the side of the gym. She smirks, smacks me on the arm, and points to where our brother is standing. He's on the other side of the gym from us, and not surprisingly, he's gazing at Emma, who looks beautiful in a black dress that cinches around her waist.

"What are the odds this is the year he asks her to dance?" she muses as we look at poor, lovesick Lee.

"Oh my gosh, are we talking about Lee and Emma?" comes Lacey's excited voice as she joins us. I chuckle as she clutches my sister's arm and scouts out where Lee and Emma are.

"Maybe if you dance with Lee, it'll make her jealous," Svea suggests, but she cackles in response.

"Like he would say yes if I asked him to dance."

I smile to myself because he wouldn't. And that's good because I want to be the only one who dances with Lacey tonight.

"Ah, I have to go heckle him. I'll see you guys later," Svea says, and then she's off to mess with Lee.

Lacey laughs as my sister pulls him by the arm onto the dance floor. The look of pure annoyance on his face might as well be my Christmas present from him.

"What do you say, Will? Are you ready to put that knee to the test?" she says, turning toward me.

"I'm ready."

She takes my hand, and I don't let it go until we're under the canopy of lights. With a timid smile, she reaches up and places her hands on my shoulders. I smile and put mine on her waist. We sway a little back and forth to "It's Beginning To Look A Lot Like Christmas," and I can feel my heart beat in every limb. She looks so beautiful under the soft glow of the Christmas lights. I wish my knee didn't hurt and I could twirl her around and dip her, but I can't. I hope so badly that one day I'll get another chance to do that.

"Not bad," she says with a smile, easing my fears a bit that she's bummed by my injury.

"Could be worse, I guess."

"Much worse," she agrees. Something catches her eye to the left, and then she busts out laughing. I look over my shoulder to where Svea and Lee are dancing and see that she's stuck a sticky note on his back that says "kick me."

"Oh, she's gonna get it," I say as I laugh, too. "Lee hates getting pranked, especially in public."

"She's fearless, isn't she?"

"I'm surprised she's made it this far in life, actually."

Lacey laughs as my parents waltz by behind her. I'm suddenly flooded with relief that she's going to stay for Christmas. The thought of her being at the table for Christmas Eve dinner tomorrow night makes me warm inside. Christmas Eve and Christmas Day are reserved for family time, and we usually spend both days cooking, watching Christmas movies, playing board games, and spiking the eggnog when Mamma isn't looking. I can see Lacey fitting right in with everything, and in this moment, I decide that I'm going to do my best to put aside all my fears about what comes after. I'm going to choose to enjoy Lacey's presence in my life for as long as I get to have her, whether that's for the next 48 hours or the next 48 years.

Chapter Nineteen

Lacey

"I'm gonna ask him," Svea says to me as we grab cookies and punch from the refreshment table. Her parents are still going strong on the dance floor, and every time I see them cutting a rug, I find myself wishing yet again that I had what they have.

"Ask who what?" I glance over my shoulder to where Will is chatting with Lee and Lars. I can't help myself. The man looks fine in a suit. Well, he looks fine in an elf costume or a pair of jeans and an old sweatshirt. But the suit is just...handsome. He's a knockout.

"Lars. I'm gonna ask him to dance."

My head whirls back to my friend. "What? Really?"

She nods seriously, nerves written all over her face. "It's just a dance, right? It's not like Lee would get upset over just dancing."

"You're absolutely right. Yes. Ask him to dance," I encourage her excitedly. It's a great idea—what better way to get Lars to notice her than by asking him to dance while she's looking so gorgeous? I don't think he's seen her yet because he just got here a few minutes ago, and I can't wait to see his tongue roll out of his mouth and his eyes turn into hearts. It'll be my favorite moment second only to the way Will reacted when he saw me all dressed up.

It still makes me all giddy when I think about it. The way his eyes widened when I opened the door and how he slowly took me in like he had never seen anything so amazing before. It's one of those things I'll never forget. And then to feel his hands on me as we danced...sigh. I'm so smitten. I'm so in trouble.

"Okay. I'm doing this," Svea says to herself, taking a few deep breaths like she's pumping herself up.

"You got this." I rub her shoulders like she's about to enter a boxing ring, and to the tune of "Walking In A Winter Wonderland," she makes her way toward the guys.

I watch with bated breath and there—Lars sees her! He visibly gasps, his jaw drops, and wow. *Wow*, they belong together. There's no way he isn't into her. I grin like a maniac as Svea moves forward, the skirt of her shimmery gold dress swishing as she walks. She's halfway to him, and then to my complete shock and horror, a young woman saunters to Lars's side and laces her fingers through his.

Everything stops around me as I gape at what the hell is happening. Svea stops too, just a second or two, and then joins Lee, Will, Lars, and apparently, his date. My heart breaks for Svea as she makes small talk with them all for a minute, and then she excuses herself. I watch her book it toward the bathrooms and without a thought, I follow.

No, *no, no...that's not how it was supposed to go for her.*

He was supposed to dance with her and realize how perfect they are together and then maybe ask for Lee's blessing or something. Instead, my friend is heartbroken and probably humiliated. I wind my way through the random attendees, and thankfully, when I open the door to the bathroom, there's only one stall occupied.

"Svea?" I ask gently.

I hear a sniffle in reply and clutch my heart. I walk over and stand on the other side of the stall door.

"Svea, I'm so sorry."

"She introduced herself. 'I'm Amber, Lars's girlfriend,'" she chokes out. "Like I don't know who she is. Ugh, I've always thought Amber was mean like that." She sniffs again, and then I hear the high-pitched squeak of the toilet paper holder moving.

His girlfriend? Not just his date? That's so much worse.

"I'm such an idiot, Lace." She blows her nose loudly. "All I wanted was one dance, you know? But the only thing I could do was pretend like everything is fine when it just isn't..."

I pull on the handle of the stall door but it doesn't budge. "Let me in, Svea. You need a hug."

The lock turns a moment later, and when I open the door, she's sitting on the floor against the wall, curled up with her knees to her chest, a puddle of gold tulle and sadness. Her makeup is smeared under her eyes, and she looks truly crushed. I step in, trying not to cry as well, and squish in next to her. She instantly leans her head on my shoulder and cries.

"One day, he'll figure it out," I whisper, clutching her hand.

"No," she whispers. "I just need to get over him and move on."

I close my eyes and lean my head against the wall. I want to tell her not to give up. I want to tell her that the way he looked at her tonight wasn't her imagination, but maybe she's right. Maybe it would be better if she dated someone else. Maybe then he'll start to realize what he's missing out on.

"You're so amazing, Svea. You're beautiful, and funny, and smart, and you have a business about to launch. You're a catch, girl. Don't let Lars get you down, okay?"

She nods against my shoulder but says nothing for a couple of minutes as she sorts herself out. Eventually, she takes in a deep breath and then slowly lets it out. "Okay. Help me fix my makeup, and let's get back out there."

"You sure?"

"Yeah, I'm sure."

I get to my feet and then reach down to help her up as the bathroom door opens, letting in a few measures of Christmas music before it swings shut and blocks it out again. A woman I recognize from setting up this morning pauses when she sees us at the bathroom mirror.

"Oh, Svea what's wrong?" she questions instantly.

Svea gives her a grim smile in the mirror. "I'm alright, Caitlin. Just a dumb crush that I need to get over." She waves her hand like it isn't that big of a deal. "You'd think I'm a teenager, crying in the bathroom like this."

Caitlin comes closer and slings an arm around Svea's shoulders. "Boys. Can't live with them, can't live without them."

"Lacey, this is Caitlin. Remember Emma from the library? This is her older sister," she introduces as she wipes a paper towel under her eyes.

"Oh, it's nice to meet you," I say with a genuine smile. I didn't get that good of a look at Emma at story time the other day, but I would not have guessed this was her sister. Whereas Emma has black hair, fair skin, and glasses, Caitlin is taller, with eyes that look almost too blue, long blonde hair, and tanned skin that seems even tanner against the white sequin halter dress she's wearing. "Emma's here tonight, right?"

"Somewhere," Caitlin replies and removes her arm from Svea. She heads into a stall and closes the door but keeps talking anyway. "She's such a wallflower. I don't even know why she comes; she never dances."

Maybe because she's waiting to see if Lee will ask her to dance?

Or she wants to see him in a suit. The Christiansen men know how to wear a suit, that's for sure.

"It's still fun to go even if you don't dance," I suggest. Svea blows her nose and then looks herself over in the mirror one more time. Besides her cheeks being a little splotchy, she seems to have pulled herself together, even if her eyes are still sad.

Caitlin snorts as she exits the stall. "That's exactly what she says."

Hmm, someone doesn't seem to see eye to eye with their sister. Although, maybe that's normal. I wouldn't know I guess, being an only child.

"I haven't officially met Emma. Can you introduce me?" I ask as Caitlin washes her hands.

"Yeah?" she volleys back, surprised. "Are you a bookworm, too?"

I shrug because I've been known to read a book or two in my spare time. Not that I've had much spare time except for very recently.

She shakes her head like she can't fathom being a book lover, her blonde hair moving in waves, as the three of us leave the bathroom together. "She's over here I think," Caitlin says over the music, and we follow her lead to the other side of the gym where a slightly uncomfortable-looking Emma stands near the wall. Her black dress seems a size too big for her, like maybe it was borrowed or she doesn't like to show off her body too much. Her dark brown eyes are darting around the dance floor behind her glasses, taking everybody in. As we get closer, I can see the canopy lights reflecting in the lenses.

"Hey, this is Laney," Caitlin incorrectly introduces.

I smile at Emma, who gives me a shy smile in return. "It's Lacey, actually. Nice to officially meet you. I was at story time on Tuesday," I tell her warmly. "The library looked amazing."

I notice that Svea seems to very purposely keep her back to where Lars and his girlfriend are still talking with Lee and Will.

"Oh, thank you," Emma replies, so quietly I almost can't hear her over the music and talking. "Your family always makes Christmas story time so special," she squeaks out to Svea.

"I'm going to find Gavin," Caitlin says, sounding bored by our conversation, and then she's off.

"She's still with Gavin, huh?" Svea asks, and from the surprise in her tone, I take it there's a story to be told about them.

Emma nods and smiles tightly. She awkwardly moves her hands behind her back, like she doesn't know what to do with them.

"What about you, Emma? Do you have a lucky guy?" It's sort of an obvious question that I already know the answer to, but I'm going to ask it anyway because I need an opening to suggest that she ask Lee to dance. Am I going to hell for meddling? Maybe.

"Me? Uh, no. No, I'm single." She blushes beet red and tucks her straight black hair behind her ear.

"Me too," I say, hoping to ease her a little. I look over my shoulder toward the Christiansen brothers, and as I do, my focus snags on Svea's knowing gaze. "Not to be weird, Svea, but your brothers look handsome tonight."

She fake gags, and I'm pleased to see that she isn't completely bogged down by what happened with Lars, at least not at this moment. I laugh at her and then look back at Emma.

"Lee looks bored over there. You should go dance with him."

If Emma was blushing before, that was nothing compared to now. I'm pretty sure the poor thing breaks out into a literal sweat at my suggestion.

"What? Dance with—with Lee? That's, uh, that's alright. I don't think he knows I exist. It would be weird," she blurts out nervously.

I smile at her genuinely. "Are you kidding me? You look dynamite tonight, and I've caught him looking at you several times. Right, Svea?" I really have caught him staring at her, so it's about time these two introverts get together.

Svea grins at me. "Yeah, I thought about offering him some eye drops at one point."

That makes me snort, but Emma's terrified expression doesn't change one bit. I glance over my shoulder and see that Lars and his date have gone to dance, so I try another tactic.

"Well, I should get back to my date over there." I shoot Svea a look that I hope she interprets as instructions to follow my lead.

"Do you think Lee found the 'kick me' sign yet?" she asks instead, her expression full of anticipation.

"I don't know." I look back to Emma. "Why don't you come join us, Emma? It would be rude to leave you over here alone."

"Yeah," Svea chimes in before Emma can reply. "Let's go."

"Uh...okay. Sure," she says, her small voice full of uncertainty, but she follows us over to the guys, and I shoot Svea another glance to see if she's caught on to what I'm up to. I take her smile to mean that she does.

As we approach, I see Lee visibly stiffen when he notices that Emma is with us. I can practically feel Emma's entire body blushing next to me as we stand opposite Will and Lee.

"Hey guys," I say, and Lee tears his gaze away from Emma long enough to narrow his eyes at me suspiciously.

"Hey," Will says, smiling at me so sweetly that I temporarily forget my plan regarding Lee and Emma. "How's the food?"

I grin up at him because of course, he would want to know if the snacks are any good. "Not bad, but I know someone who could've whipped up something better." I wink at him, feeling flirtatious.

"Do you cook much, Emma?" Svea asks, which switches my attention back to the task at hand.

"Well, just for myself, yeah." She avoids making eye contact with Lee, and it makes me want to squeal like a little girl. She likes him so much. And he likes her, too. If Lars and Svea aren't going to happen tonight, then at least there's still hope for Lee and Emma.

"Like what?" Will asks, interested.

"Just...food. Nothing that exciting," Emma replies awkwardly, her fingers gripping the skirt of her black dress.

"You look nice," Lee pipes up unexpectedly, looking straight at Emma. *Yes! Touchdown!*

I mean, "nice" isn't that great of an adjective, but he complimented her of his own free will. This is a big deal.

Emma's eyebrows rise above the rim of her glasses in surprise, and she blushes a deep crimson as she fidgets with her dress even more. "Oh...uh, thanks. It has pockets." She stammers out, and her hands disappear into said pockets. Oh my gosh, she's so cute.

"Seriously, pockets are a girl's best friend. Who needs diamonds? I just want pockets," I throw out with a chuckle.

"Oh, by far, I'd rather have pockets than diamonds," Svea jumps in seriously. "Yes, diamonds are pretty, but come on. Pockets are a daily need. Especially in women's clothing." My affection for her grows a bit because of our enthusiasm about pockets.

I catch Will giving his brother laser beam eyes and surreptitiously nodding his head in Emma's direction, but Lee doesn't take the hint. Maybe if I dance with Will again, Lee will ask Emma. Here goes nothing.

"How's your knee doing, Will? Got another dance left in you?"

"I sure do."

"Awesome." Will and I leave our little group but stay close enough to see if Lee gets up the courage.

"I'm impressed," Will says as we start to sway a little.

"I have no idea what you're talking about," I claim innocently, and he laughs softly.

We watch Svea keep the conversation going, with Emma seeming to agree with whatever she's saying. Lee looks unbelievably disinterested. He keeps looking around the gym, and I want to choke him.

"Come on, come on, just *ask* her!" I mutter to myself.

"Easy, big guns. Give them a minute."

Someone approaches the three people we're spying on, and my eyebrows scrunch together when I realize it's Mr. Tinman. He says something to each of them, and then Svea takes his hand, and they join the dance floor.

"Interesting," Will comments.

"Yeah..." I watch Svea and Clay dance for a moment in total confusion because she seems to be enjoying herself. She's laughing and smiling to the max when I know for a fact that Clay isn't that charming. But then, I see Lars and his girlfriend dancing nearby, and I can't keep the grin off my face.

Yeah, girl. Make him jealous.

And he does look jealous. Every time Svea laughs, Lars looks over at her. He may have a girlfriend, but it's pretty clear there are some feelings happening there. Maybe he's dating this other girl because he can't act on his feelings for Svea. You know, cause Lee would kill him.

Oh, bobbins, Lee—

I snap my head back to where Lee and Emma are, but to my dismay, I see them still standing there very much not dancing together. But then, I see Lee's mouth move. I gasp.

"He's talking to her," I squeal, clutching Will's shoulders tighter. We're both so focused on trying to read lips that we're barely dancing.

"She said something, too," Will says, just as excited as I am.

"Oh my gosh, it's happening. They're falling in love."

He laughs at me but doesn't disagree.

Like creepers, we do our best to eavesdrop on their conversation. Emma's expression is still shy and guarded, but her eyes are lit up like they're talking about something she loves. The only way to tell that

Lee is stoked about it is the tiny upward tilt to his mouth and that he's angled his body towards her a little more. Oh, this is going so well. Yes!

"I've only ever seen them speak to each other at the library. This is amazing," Will tells me, pleased but also astonished.

"It's true love," I gush. "I knew it."

Will chuckles, and my breath catches in my throat when I feel his thumbs just gently stroke back and forth over my sides. I look up at him to see a soft expression on his face. "You're always encouraging people to go for it, aren't you?"

I try to calm my pulse when I realize how close we've gotten to each other while we were distracted by Lee and Emma. I smile because, yeah, I guess I am always telling people to go big or go home.

"I'm just a natural cheerleader, apparently."

His smile cracks wider and then softens again. My interest in his siblings fades to the background because neither of us makes an attempt to put any distance between us. We've danced a few times tonight already, but this is by far the most intimate one.

"*God Jul*, you two!" Elsie sings out as she and Fredrik dance a lap around the outer edge of the dance floor. I don't think I've seen them stop dancing for longer than a few minutes all night.

I chuckle at them. "I love your family, Will."

"I know it's hard to tell with Lee, but you've won over each of them. When I called Mamma to let her know you'll be with us for Christmas, she was really excited."

"She was?"

He nods, still smiling softly at me beneath the lights overhead.

Aww. Well, that feels nice. Two years ago when I was last with my dad and Mariah for Christmas, I never really got the impression that either one of them was terribly excited to see me. Mariah certainly made it seem more like an inconvenience for me to be staying with them, even though I did my best to keep out of the way.

"Well, now I'm extra glad that I got everyone a Christmas present."

"That just means I have to get you something."

I shake my head. "You've given me so much this week, Will. You don't owe me anything."

And then it happens. His gaze drops to my lips. Just for a second, but I saw it. Just one glance is all it was, but it was enough to let me know that he's interested. Just the thought of kissing him sends a thrill of electricity throughout my body.

Maybe I'll have to take my own advice tonight. Maybe tonight is the night that I go for it.

Chapter Twenty

Will

The Holly Ball is in full swing. Everyone is having fun and letting loose on the dance floor. Christmas music pervades the gym, but so does the feeling of community and camaraderie. Even with my knee, which is getting sorer and sorer, I'm enjoying myself.

But in this moment, I wish Lacey and I weren't here.

I wish we were alone, and I could try to explain the complex feelings I have for her.

I wish it was just us so that I could dare to hope that I might be enough of a reason for her to stay in Larkspur.

In this moment, I'm over what I should and shouldn't do because she loves my family. Because she recognizes every good intention I've had towards her.

You've given me so much this week, Will. You don't owe me anything.

I don't know if it's possible to love someone so quickly, but the words she just said make me think that I could. I'm not used to anyone showing me this depth of genuine gratitude, and I've done far less for her than I have for my family and community. If anything, she's done more for me. I feel like I've gained a right-hand woman while she's been at the inn. Everything I've done, she's been a part of in some way, always wanting to help and never wanting to be an inconvenience. She was helping Svea and jumping in with me to make dinner even before I injured my knee.

She's never asked anything of me, and I'm realizing that there's nothing she could ask for that I wouldn't want to give her. Not because

I'm a yes-man who always has to help, but because I'm falling for her hard, and I want her to be happy. My heart clenches in my chest.

I want her to be happy.

That's a terrifying thought because her happiness doesn't necessarily include me. And yet, if she's happier in Minneapolis where there would be a bigger market for her plans and her dreams, then I want her to do that. It would be selfish of me to ask her to do anything that doesn't align with what she wants.

My hands bring her in just slightly closer as we dance. I don't want to let her go, but...the fact that I'm willing to put aside my own happiness for the sake of hers means that this could absolutely be the kind of love I hoped I would find one day. It's a cruel trick of luck that I found the woman I could love for the rest of my life, and I might have to let her go.

"What are you thinking about? Your face is all thoughtful," she says with a sweetly curious smile. I look back into her beautiful brown eyes with an aching heart.

I want to explain but not here. Not with a hundred people around us and music dulling the words I would say...the words I'm not even sure I *should* say.

"I just want you to be happy," is what comes out of my mouth.

Lacey rears back just slightly in surprise and a little confusion. "I am happy."

I swallow hard as we gaze at each other. Mamma and Pappa waltz by again, and the song changes to another Christmas tune that couldn't matter less to me right now.

"Here?" My voice comes out low and vulnerable. Her answer has the potential to break my heart. I hold my breath as she briefly considers my question, and then she smiles a smile so warm and soft that my insides get all gooey.

"Yes. I'm happy here."

I press my lips together to keep myself from asking a question I definitely shouldn't ask.

With me?

"Are *you* happy here?" she asks me, and despite her gentle tone, the question catches me off guard. Even more than that, I realize my answer throws me for an absolute loop.

I'm happy wherever you are.

I clear my throat and force a smile. "Yeah, I'm happy here. This is where my family is."

Lacey's hands squeeze my shoulders just once. "Just not at the inn," she clarifies.

"Right."

"Have you talked to your parents about it? I didn't want to bring it up yesterday when they were over just in case, but I really wanted to when your mom and I were making lunch."

I let out a tense little sigh. "No, I haven't. I think after the holidays, I will."

She nods in agreement, and we both fall silent as we sway through the rest of the song.

"Not bad, Mr. Hop-a-long," she teases as I release her.

I chuckle and steer her back over to where we left Lee and Emma, but my brother is now standing there alone. "Where did Emma go?"

Lacey stops abruptly, seeing the same thing I do. Lee doesn't look disappointed, just neutral as usual, like he didn't just talk to the girl of his dreams.

"What happened? Do you think she said no?"

"I'm betting that he didn't ask her to dance, and she got pulled away."

She sighs in exasperation. "Bobbins! What is his problem?"

I let my eyes fall over her slowly, memorizing the way she looks in that dress, and feel my stomach turn over. "If he takes that step, there's too big of a chance she could reject him. I think he's more comfortable being in limbo where nothing wagered is nothing lost."

"That's not the saying!" she fires back, full of feistiness again. "It's 'nothing ventured, nothing gained.' And Lee is gaining nothing because he's venturing nothing."

And so am I.

"Lacey," I say gently, and take her hand so she looks away from Lee and back at me. "He'll figure it out. Maybe he's just not ready."

Her face softens, but there's still some fire in her eyes about the situation. "You should go talk to him," she suggests more calmly.

I chuckle. "You're nosy."

She narrows her eyes at me flirtatiously. "Hey, either you go talk to him or I do. And we both know that he'll get an earful from me."

I squeeze her hand. "Alright, alright. Go see if you can steal Pappa away for a dance."

She nods seriously and heads off into the crowded dance floor. I limp my way over to Lee, who avoids eye contact with me even when I make it to his side. My knee feels swollen and achy, and I hope Lacey will be ready to leave soon.

"Don't say a damn word," Lee growls in my direction, though he's still not looking at me.

"About what?"

Lee side-eyes me because he and I both know my innocence is feigned.

"I was just curious what you talked about," I throw out as nonchalantly as I can. A smile crosses my face when I see Pappa teaching Lacey how to waltz off to the side while Mamma gets a drink from the refreshment table. Clay and Svea are still dancing, and I don't quite know how I feel about it. Like I said, he isn't a terrible guy, but I know he isn't good enough for my sister.

"Books," he answers irritably, like it's costing him years of his life.

"Nice." I bob my head, again going for nonchalance, and look around for where Emma disappeared to. "Did you ask her to dance?"

He shifts on his feet next to me and pushes his hands into the pockets of his dress pants. "No."

When he makes no attempt to explain, I glance over at him. "Because..."

Lee shoots me a glare and then looks away again. "I didn't want to come on too strong."

I snort loud enough to be clearly heard over "Jingle Bells", and he shoves my shoulder. I wobble on my good leg. "Hey—easy!"

"You deserved it."

"Lee, come on. Sure, she's shy, but it's just a dance. It's not like you're telling her you're in love with her."

He shakes his head with his jaw clenched, like I'm being the ridiculous one in this situation. "You know just as well as I do that getting involved with someone who may not want you isn't a good idea." He eyes me like he knows all my secrets, and even though I want to deny what he's saying, I can't.

The teasing expression I had on my face slides off.

"She's nice, Will, but don't be an idiot."

I frown at him. The music and chatter around us quiets in my ears. "Isn't that a little hypocritical? If I'm an idiot for falling for Lacey, then you're an idiot for not going after Emma."

Lee's shoulders stiffen at the point I just made, but then he unexpectedly huffs out a quiet laugh. "So we're both idiots. Great."

His sarcasm eases me enough to laugh, too. "Yeah. Great."

Lacey and I make our way up the porch steps of the inn about forty minutes later. The Christmas lights strung on the eave illuminate a few stray snowflakes that fall as the breeze shakes them off the trees. The icy glitter and the soft lighting just make Lacey look even more breathtakingly beautiful.

She steps ahead of me to the door while my steps falter. Even in her black puffy coat, I'm in awe of her.

"Will?" she asks, noticing that I've stopped. Her voice is sweet and caring, as warm as a hug.

And for some reason, right there standing on the porch looking at the woman I may or may not be falling in love with, I think of my older brother. I think of how much he holds back from taking a chance on the one thing I know he wants. I see him on the edge of the dance floor, talking to his dream girl about her favorite thing, but not taking the risk to ask her to dance.

I could do the same thing. I could stand on this porch in two days and wish Lacey safe travels as she packs up her car and pulls away. I could let her go without putting my heart on the line.

Or, I could step out from behind my fear of rejection and inner turmoil about what I should or shouldn't do, and man up enough to be vulnerable and open with her. And then just maybe, *maybe*, she'll reciprocate. Maybe then she'll start to seriously think about where I could fit into her plans.

"I think you're incredible," I begin, my heart pounding. "I think you're beautiful. You're funny, and selfless, and sweeter than honey."

I hear her sharp intake of breath but decide to press on with my heart in my throat.

"I'd have to be a blind fool not to notice how special you are, Lacey."

The porch decking creaks as she takes a step closer to me. In the soft rays of the Christmas lights, she looks otherworldly and angelic.

"And, more than anything, I...I wish things were different." My breathing begins to quicken as she moves closer again, only a few feet between us. "If things were different, I'd—I'd..."

I'd kiss you. I'd beg you to stay. I'd promise you a lifetime of love and happiness.

One more step brings her in so close to me that her head tilts back so she can look me in the eyes.

"I think you're amazing," she murmurs, holding every scrap of my attention on this chilly porch. "I think you're dedicated, and talented, and honest." Her brown eyes shine with tears, but she grins. "And I think you're hands down the cutest elf I've ever seen."

I snicker and fight the urge to lean my forehead down against hers.

"If I forget for just a second how up in the air my life is right now, I feel completely..." She sniffs even as she smiles up at me. "I feel so completely good when I'm with you."

It's a soothing balm to my soul to hear her say these things.

She feels this, too.

"I do, too," I whisper back. I can't stop myself from reaching up and tangling my fingers through her curled hair. She leans into me, cuddling in close to my chest with her hands resting on the front of my suit jacket. I trail my fingers from her hair to her cheek and let my free arm move around her back.

"How do you wish things were different?" she asks gently, vulnerability transforming her already beautiful features into something hopeful and genuine.

I glide my thumb over her cheek with a pounding heart. "I wish you weren't leaving." It's painful to say it out loud, but I mean it.

She leans into my hand and closes her eyes. I take in every bit of her face. Her smooth complexion, the flare of her eyelashes as they rest on her rosy cheeks, the slight furrow of her eyebrows as she takes in what I said.

"I wish that, too," she whispers, and then opens her eyes again. "I love it here, Will. Larkspur is amazing and so is your family and so are you, but...I left my life in Minneapolis in complete shambles. I have to go back and figure things out."

"I know." The winter breeze picks up around us, but it isn't as cold as the words she just said. "Like I said earlier, I want you to be happy."

Lacey searches my face for a moment, hesitating like there are words just on the tip of her tongue. When she finally speaks, her voice is so soft that I almost can't hear her.

"*You* make me happy, Will."

My heart jackhammers throughout my body. I clutch her tighter to me as I let that sink in. I've been hoping so much that I could be the one to make her happy, and here she is now, telling me exactly that. The sun could freeze over right now, and I would still feel warm.

Her hands grip the lapels of my suit jacket as something apologetic crosses her face. "I want you to be happy, too. I want you to do all the things you've been dreaming about. And if I get to be there one day when you achieve them, I would feel pretty damn honored."

If?

It's that one word that knocks my whole world off kilter. She's speaking hypothetically now. She isn't promising me anything either way. Maybe it's unfair of me to be disappointed that I didn't get the straight answer I want to hear, but I can't help it. I clear my throat, mentally scrambling to get away from this vulnerable conversation.

I remove my hand from her face and loosen my hold around her back with my other arm. "And one day when you're off living your dream, I hope you sometimes remember that one time you hit an albino deer and got stranded in a little snowy town for Christmas." I try to say it with levity, but I know it falls flat.

She's leaving. She's leaving without any assurances that she'll ever come back. A dull ache hits me square in the chest, and I step away, finding it impossible to hide how crestfallen I am.

"Will..." she says gently, but I limp past her to the front door.

I want her to be happy, I remind myself as I unlock it. If leaving makes her happy, then I guess I just have to deal with it.

"Come on," I say over my shoulder. "Let's go in. I'm tired, and my knee hurts."

Playing the injury card seems to do the trick because she follows me inside without another word. But as soon as the door closes, she grabs my wrist.

"Will, please..."

Please, what? Please don't be upset that you're leaving with my heart in your pocket?

"It's okay, big guns," I tell her, but it's not. It's just not. I turn away from her toward the stairs, and her hands slip from my wrist. "It's been a long day. I'm going to bed." I'll be damned if I'm not sleeping in my own bed tonight, even if my knee is throbbing right now. "Feel free to stay up if you want, just turn out the lights when you're done." My tone has reverted to the professional one I used when I first welcomed her into this house. I hate myself for doing that, but my heart is breaking as I slowly ascend the steps one at a time.

"William John, do *not* put me in the guest zone." Her stern voice cuts through the air like a knife, and I turn in surprise halfway up the staircase. She's standing at the bottom with her hands on her hips, her furious eyes narrowed at me.

"The guest zone?"

"You and I both know that I'm a hell of a lot more to you than just a guest here at the inn. So don't treat me like one," she demands in that feisty tone I like so much. "You said so yourself, remember? I'm more like a family friend. Is that true, or were you just trying to be nice?"

If only she knew how much more she is to me.

"You're right. I'm sorry," I murmur. I can't explain that I'm just trying to protect myself. I can't tell her that I'm about to break down from the thought of being someone she leaves behind.

Lacey nods at my apology and then reaches over and turns the deadbolt on the front door. "I'm not staying down here alone like a loser," she announces, and despite how torn up I am right now, I can't help but smirk at her.

She climbs the stairs, and I resume my ascent as well. She reaches the top right at my side, and I shift slightly in her direction to say goodnight, but I'm instantly overcome by the sweet scent of Lacey just before a very soft pair of lips land on mine.

I forget everything.

My knee doesn't hurt. My heart isn't broken. My to-do list no longer exists.

All there is to think about now is how warm her mouth feels kissing mine, how heavenly she tastes as I kiss her back. I lose myself in her. I disappear into the euphoric feeling of her fingers on my face and in my hair. And when she pulls back just a little, all I can hear is the pounding of my heart in my ears. I'm breathless, arms wrapped around her like they're meant to be as I look her in the eyes. She's blushing and trying to catch her breath, too. There's a spark of light in her expression that I wish would jump off her face and onto my own.

But it doesn't because reality seeps back into my brain as I look down at her.

I can't go all in with her, not like this. I can't give my heart to someone who isn't going to stay.

Feeling unsteady on my feet, I let my arms fall from around her and step away. Confusion crosses her brow as I shake my head.

"We can't do this," I mutter, mostly to myself.

"Because I'm a *guest*?" she asks, fire returning to her eyes.

"Because you're not staying." Her shoulders sink slightly, and my stomach sinks too when she doesn't correct me. "We shouldn't have done that," I say, knowing every single word is a lie because I can still feel the warmth of her on my lips, and it just makes me want to kiss her again.

"Will—"

"Let's call it a night before we make any more mistakes." As soon as the words leave my mouth, her jaw drops. There's a deep hurt on her face that I purposely put there, and I know I'll have to live with that for the rest of my life. "Goodnight, Lacey."

I limp down the hall to my room and close the door, and only then do I hear Lacey's door close as well. Little do I know, it's the last time I'll hear her footsteps in this house.

Chapter Twenty-One
Lacey

I close the door and then lean my back against it. My heart is beating so hard that I can feel it in my stomach. I glance around unseeingly as I try to process what I just did.

I kissed him. I shouldn't have thrown myself at him like that, but I couldn't stand him putting me in the guest zone one more time, so yeah, I kissed him. Mouth on mouth, big ol' smooch, fully committed to getting him to admit that I'm something important to him.

Did it work? Absolutely not. Instead of getting him to see what we could be, he called it a *mistake*. I've never been hit in the face, but I felt like he delivered a knockout punch when he said it. My head instantly started pounding, and everything started spinning as my hopes came crashing down.

I'm such an idiot. I pulled a Lindsey and banked on it working—expecting that kissing Will would change everything. Well, it changed everything alright, just not in the way I wanted it to. I wanted a happily ever after with him, but he pushed me away, even though he said he wished I wasn't leaving. He was the one who touched my hair and my face on the porch and looked at me with such sorrow at the thought of me leaving that I almost kissed him right then and there.

But I guess when it came right down to it, Will couldn't see past the fact that I can't promise to be a permanent fixture in his life, even though I want to be.

My eyes land on the little yellow gnome on the dresser, and I slide down to the floor. How am I supposed to look him in the eye tomorrow morning? What am I supposed to do—just pretend it didn't happen? That's impossible. *Impossible.* It was the best kiss I've ever had. I couldn't act like it was nothing to save my life. How am I supposed to spend Christmas with his family now?

The answer is clear. I can't.

I can't be around him and act like I'm not hurt and humiliated and still half in love with him. It would be easier to just go now so I can lick my wounds on the way to Sioux Falls. Lindsey will help me pick up the pieces of my heart when I get there, and then I can go back to Minneapolis and figure out my life.

Don't cry, don't cry, don't cry...

I guess I was wrong about things happening for a reason. Maybe my accidental pit stop in this town was just meant to redirect me toward my passion of creating and had nothing to do with Will and his amazing family. I was foolish to think otherwise, I know that now.

All that's left to do is leave.

My stomach rolls and clenches as I get on my hands and knees and crawl over to my suitcase. I stare down into it, seeing only a few worn garments and a pair of socks. Everything else is strewn around the room and bathroom, and with each thing I collect and deposit into my suitcase, the more nauseous and grief-stricken I feel.

This isn't home, Lacey, I remind myself.

This is just some weird fever dream that I'll wake up from as soon as I click my heels together three times. There's nothing here that is meant for me, including Will. I need to stop holding onto some farfetched idea of what we could be. He very clearly isn't willing to chase that dream with me.

I'm about to zip up my suitcase when I look down at the dress I'm wearing, and then my heart breaks a little more.

I should text Svea to say goodbye. I should, but...I can't. She won't understand why I'm leaving so suddenly unless I explain everything.

I change out of my dress and dig out something to wear for the ride. I'm just asking for it driving at night again, but I can't stand to be here in this house. The rejection is palpable, and everything I see just makes me think of him or his family.

I touch the lace curtains one more time, then the yellow gnome, and with tears in my eyes, I quietly slip out of the room and take one step down the stairs at a time. Each one creaks, but not as loudly when I go slowly.

At the bottom, hot tears drip down my cheeks as I look around one more time. The Christmas tree lights are on, but everything else is dark as I spot the Christmas gifts I wrapped and put under the tree. Hopefully, each one will be received happily and not sadly because I won't be there when they open them. With that, I turn the locks and leave the house.

I sob all the way to where Kia is parked and throw my suitcase in the back seat before getting in. I turn the ignition and reach for the shifter, but that's when I stop. The feeling in my gut is saying that this isn't right, that I shouldn't go like this. I should wait until the morning and say proper goodbyes to him and his family.

But the humiliation I feel trumps everything else right now. Will rejected me, plain and simple, and I'm under no obligation to stay when I don't want to.

So, I shift into drive and pull away from the Larkspur Inn.

I thought the drive would help me make more sense of things, but all it did was exhaust me. I rolled into Sioux Falls around midnight, thankfully without any accidents. I texted Lindsey when I stopped for gas an hour outside of Larkspur and promised I would explain my late arrival in the morning. When I pulled into her driveway, she came right out and hugged me tight because she knows me well enough to see the pain written all over my face, even under the cover of night. She got me settled in her guest room, and I quickly got ready for bed and was asleep before my head hit the pillow.

But now it's morning, Christmas Eve morning, and all I can think about as I shower is that Will woke up to an empty house.

Is he sad? Upset? Annoyed that I left without saying goodbye or even leaving a note? Did he knock on my door hoping to talk or smooth things over but opened the door to an empty room?

I guess it doesn't matter because I won't be seeing him again.

The spray of the shower head disguises my tears until I get out and dry off. Then, my face doesn't dry no matter how many times I wipe it.

I've been through a few breakups in my life, but I have never felt as legitimately heartbroken as I do today. Honestly, I don't know what I expected to happen. He told me himself that he's too busy to date. It's not like kissing him would change that. It's my own fault that I gave him the opportunity to turn me down. I should've just taken the hit to my pride and let him treat me like a guest instead of anything else. Then, I wouldn't be coming apart at the seams and trailing thread across a state line.

I get dressed and make the bed, hating that this room, though beautifully decorated with picture frames and soft linens, doesn't feel as homey as the one I had at Larkspur Inn. I miss his mother's handmade quilt and his grandma's handmade lace curtains. I miss that little yellow gnome on the dresser and the history of the original tile in the bathroom. Lindsey's house is well taken care of and well updated, but I miss Will's kitchen island and the wood stove in the living room. I miss the Christmas tree and all the family ornaments on it. I miss the way I felt in that house, even though I had no right to feel so at home there.

I had no right to kiss Will and expect that our different, separate lives would somehow magically make sense together.

The knock on the door startles me, but I call out, "Come in."

The door opens, and my best friend stands there holding two mugs of coffee. Her straight, dark caramel-colored hair is pulled into a lopsided ponytail on the top of her head. She's wearing a red and white reindeer flannel nightshirt and reindeer slippers. She gives me a sympathetic smile. "Morning, Puff Daddy."

I shake my head at her reference to my puffy eyes, and she comes in, offering me one of the mugs.

"You look like you could use a shot of Bailey's in there," she says as I take a sip. I really could. "You ready to tell me what happened, or should we pretend a bit longer that you don't want to talk about it?"

My lower lip quivers. "I kissed him," I whisper, already about to start boo-hooing.

Lindsey's blue eyes narrow slightly. "You kissed Nowheresville dude?"

I nod, tears flooding my eyelashes.

"Judging from the tears, he was either a horrible kisser, or he didn't kiss you back."

I shake my head and get down on the floor, going slowly so I don't spill my coffee. Lindsey gets on the floor, too, as I set my mug carefully on the rug. I lay down on my back, and my best friend does the same. It's what we always do when something is wrong. We lay on the floor and talk it out until things seem better.

So, that's what I do. I tell her everything. I tell her about the Holly Ball and how he was gobsmacked by how I looked. How we danced and talked about wanting each other to be happy. How I kissed him, and he called it a mistake.

"And you just...left? Without even a note? That's harsh, girl."

"What was I supposed to do, Linz? Go knock on his door and tell him to his face?"

Out of my periphery, I see her shrug. "Fair enough. I don't know why I feel bad for him. He's the one who messed everything up."

"Uh, have you been listening? I'm the one who messed everything up. If I had just kept my lips to myself, none of this would've happened."

"Ah, what fun is keeping your lips to yourself? If I hadn't kissed Jack, he would've never made the first move."

I still don't know how he can keep up with her. Jack is one of those level-headed, easy-going guys who don't get too upset about anything.

He's steady, reliable, and, frankly, a little boring. I'm sure Lindsey's antics keep him on his toes.

"Yeah, well, Will isn't Jack apparently," I mutter to the ceiling. My back hurts, but I'm not getting up yet. Not until Lindsey and I are laughing about something stupid, and I feel like I can face the world again.

"I'm sorry you kissed an idiot, Lace. Maybe it's for the best since you said you didn't want to do the long-distance thing," she suggests.

My chest aches. "Yeah."

Lindsey lets out a long sigh, the kind that shows how much she's hurting for me. "You know what I would do if I were you?"

I turn my head to look at her. "What?"

She rolls onto her side to face me. "I'd go back and tell him what's what."

I snort. "I know you would."

"He just sounds like a guy who has to get his head on straight and needs help to do it."

I give her a suspicious smile. "And what exactly would you say to get his head on straight?"

She cackles and rolls onto her stomach. Supporting her upper body with her elbows, she gets right into it. "I'd say, 'Hey, Buddy, don't be dumb. I'm a catch, and you're an idiot if you release me back into the wild. There's plenty of fish in the sea, but I'm a *shark*, baby'"

I clutch my stomach as a grateful laugh erupts out of me. "A—a shark?" I gasp out.

"Damn right, you're a shark," she insists seriously even as I laugh more. "Don't sell yourself short, Lacey—you're at the top of the ocean food chain. You're a shark who could have any fish she wants. Don't let the idiot you're hung up on make you think you're a minnow."

I shake my head as I catch my breath. "Whatever you say, Linz."

"Trust me. If you gave him the fish spiel, he would easily see that losing you would be the biggest mistake of his life."

I reach over and pat her shoulder. "Sure he would."

"Is that what you want?" she asks more seriously. "Do you want him to change his mind about you?"

I sigh, looking up at the ceiling again. "I want him to change his mind, but it shouldn't take me harassing him to do it."

"Personally, I think he deserves a little harassment, but I get what you're saying. He should be able to make his own choices."

I'm afraid he already has made his choice, and that choice isn't me.

"Hey," Lindsey says gently, nudging my arm. "What are you gonna do, Lace?"

I close my eyes and take a few deep breaths in and out, trying to find a place of calm as I settle on the answer to her question. "I'm going to go back to Minneapolis, get out of my apartment, and find a cheaper one so that I can start my own business." Saying those words out loud feels equally painful and healing. "I'll start an Etsy shop and sell clothes and accessories online until I have enough money to open a brick-and-mortar store."

Lindsey plops down on her back again and laces her fingers through mine. "You're a badass, Lacey. Nothing is impossible for you, you know that right?"

I squeeze her hand. "Tell me that again when I actually have to do all of it." And do all of it without the people I left behind in Larkspur, people I won't stop thinking about for the rest of my life. It's a hard thing to realize, especially because Will doesn't call or text, not even to make sure I got to Sioux Falls safely.

None of the Christiansen family members make an effort to reach out. Svea doesn't call to tell me how crappy it was that I left without saying goodbye. There are no Merry Christmas or *God Jul* texts. So, I spend the holiday with Lindsey and Jack, feeling like my time in Larkspur really was a fever dream, and my feelings about Will are pointless for me to dwell on.

I guess what happens in Larkspur stays in Larkspur.

Chapter Twenty-Two

Will

"I just don't get it," Svea exclaims as she paces in front of me. "Why would she leave so suddenly? Without saying goodbye?"

I can't bear to look at my sister. She's upset because Lacey is gone, and I am too, but Svea has no idea what happened last night. She was still dancing with Clay when we left, and I hate that Svea didn't get to say goodbye then either.

If I hated myself before for telling Lacey that our kiss was a mistake, that's nothing compared to how much I hate myself now.

"I'm gonna call her," she decides, reaching for where she set her phone down on the coffee table.

"Just give her some space, Svee," I tell her with a sigh.

She frowns at me, looking like she might cry, and then goes back to pacing. "I thought we were friends," Svea continues, this time sounding less confused and more hurt.

I can feel Lee looking at me from across my parents' living room. He's standing next to the Christmas tree with his arms folded, trying not to seem worried but failing. Mamma and Pappa are in the kitchen working on food preparations for Christmas Eve dinner. I would normally be in there, finding joy and comfort in cooking, but I can't. I skipped helping tear down the Holly Ball stuff and the set up for the Christmas Day Dinner at the community center this morning, too. That's how I know I'm really messed up. That's how horrible I feel.

After I closed the door to my room last night, I almost went back out to her. I almost apologized for what I said because it wasn't true.

Kissing her was far from a mistake. I sabotaged the best thing that's ever happened to me, and I don't deserve a second chance to get her back. I deserve the consequences of my actions, which is her absence from this town and my life.

"Are you sure nothing happened?" Svea asks, pausing her pacing to face me where I sit on the couch.

"I'm sure she had a reason for leaving the way she did," I mutter. "Maybe she thought it would be easier. Some people hate goodbyes." It's a horrible and untrue explanation, and the words taste sour on my tongue.

"But she said she was staying for Christmas," Lee's gruff voice pipes up.

"Pappa made her a *Dala* horse," Svea adds sadly, almost to herself.

"Doesn't seem like Lacey to go back on her word," he adds. I can feel the question in his tone. His policeman brain is trying to work out this situation like it's a case he's been assigned to at work.

I swallow hard, briefly contemplating telling my siblings what happened. Being dishonest doesn't come naturally to me. My conscience is squirming with the secret I'm keeping.

When I showed up late this morning without Lacey, Mamma was so disappointed. She's taken a liking to Lacey, just like everyone else has, and I know she was looking forward to opening her home and our Christmas traditions to her. But my stupid mouth ruined all of that, and now my family is paying the price just as much as I am.

We miss her, plain and simple.

Svea plops down on the couch next to me with a sad sigh. "It totally sucks realizing you didn't mean as much to someone as you thought."

My eyes close in shame. I did this to my sister. I ran Lacey off, and now Svea is suffering because of it.

"She got everyone Christmas presents," I murmur to the floor. It hurt like hell to pack them up this morning so I could bring them over. "She wouldn't have done that if she didn't care about us."

"She did?" Without another word, Svea darts off the couch and slides onto her knees in front of the Christmas tree. She starts rifling through the wrapped presents, looking for the ones from Lacey.

"Svea," Lee warns, always about authority and following the rules.

"Aha!" She holds up a brown bundle and chucks another one at Lee, who catches it despite his disapproval. "I wanna know what she got us." She pushes a small rectangular box in my direction and then tears into her present. The brown paper falls away, and in her hands is a glass picture frame with dried yellow rose petals between the glass panes. Where the picture should be is a note that Svea reads aloud. "'Svea, here's a picture frame for whenever we get around to having a picture taken together. Thank you for pointing me back toward my love of sewing and creating. I don't know where I would be without you, and I hope you know how much you're loved by me and all the people around you. Love, Lacey.'" She sighs. "It's so pretty. I wonder where she got it?" She holds the frame to her chest and murmurs, "How did she know yellow roses are my favorite flower?"

"Lucky guess, probably," Lee answers with a huff.

"Go on, open yours," Svea urges him from where she's still kneeling on the floor.

He rolls his eyes like he isn't at all curious about what Lacey got him, but he unwraps the small bundle anyway. His eyebrows furrow together as he brings out some kind of metal badge with a post-it note stuck on it.

"What is it?"

"It's an antique Sheriff's badge," he answers Svea curiously.

"Come on, tell us what the note says!"

He brings the note closer to read. "'Mr. Christiansen, thank you for coming to my rescue that first night. I'm sorry if I annoy you, but I think of you like the brother I never had. You already have a police badge, but this one made me think of you. I hope it gives you the courage to go after what you want in life. Love, Lacey.'"

My head squeezes like a lemon in a citrus juicer as Svea gets up to take a closer look at the badge.

"Wow," she whispers. "How did she find this? At the thrift store, you think?"

Lee shrugs thoughtfully. "Wasn't expecting her to get me something so personal."

But that's how Lacey is. She's just special that way, and in so many other ways that I will never get to experience again.

"Well, now I can't wait to see what she got you." Svea whirls around and claps her hands at me to get to it.

With a sigh, I reluctantly pull the box toward me and open it.

I move the tissue paper aside and find a whisk inside. The handle is made of wood and the wires are gold. Beneath it is a note that I'd much rather not read out loud, but I know Svea won't let me get away with that.

"'Will, without you, this week wouldn't have been half as amazing as it was. Thank you for teaching me some of your family recipes and sharing your dreams with me. I wanted to get you an apron with 'The Swedish Chef' embroidered on it, but there wasn't time. So here's a whisk, and when you use it, I hope you think of me. Love, Big Guns.'"

My eyes linger over her swooping handwriting as my stomach churns painfully, like it's filling up with battery acid. She couldn't have written anything better to me, but it hurts much more because of what I said to her that made her leave.

Svea and Lee both stare at me for a long, silent moment as I drop into an even deeper pit of self-loathing because there are so many things in Lacey's note that they don't know about. I watch it dawn on my siblings that maybe I have the closest relationship with her, and I never said anything.

"Care to explain, bro?" Svea asks, squinting at me suspiciously.

"Not really." I fold the note and stuff it in my pocket.

"Big guns?" Lee questions curiously.

I clear my throat and close the lid of the box. "Just a nickname," I mutter in reply.

"What dreams did you talk to her about?" Svea demands, stepping closer.

"What's The Swedish Chef?"

The questions irritate me. Each one hurts like a knife in my chest. Not just because I have personal things I've not spoken to them about, but also because I told every one of my desires to Lacey. I opened my heart to her and shared vulnerable things I've never said to anyone else. And she wrote down my ideas and helped me dream to my heart's content because she believed I could accomplish anything.

Åh nej, what have I done?

"Children, come eat!" Mamma calls from the kitchen.

None of us move.

"We're talking about this later," Lee says in a low voice, and then nods me and Svea toward the dining room.

We leave our gifts in the living room and follow the delicious scents coming from the other room. On the dining room table, our folks have laid the table with Swedish Christmas foods. They've made a ham and Swedish potatoes—basically mashed potatoes baked in a pan with breadcrumb topping—but everything else is the traditional *julbord*, which is a Christmas-style *smorgasbord*. There's pickled herring, beet-root salad, bread, meatballs, and sausage. It all looks delicious, but I feel a healthy amount of guilt that I didn't help prepare any of it. Maybe there's still time to help Mamma make *risgryngrot*, or rice pudding, which we usually have for breakfast on Christmas morning.

"*God Julafton!*" Mamma exclaims, which means, "Merry Christmas Eve."

We file into the dining room and take our seats, me moving slowly because of my knee. Despite all the good food, I don't feel even a little hungry. But I pile things on my plate and try to make it look like I'm enjoying myself as everyone else digs in, too. All I can think about is Lacey and how she was supposed to be at this table. How we were going to put hot sauce in Svea's cocoa. I keep my head down and stay out of the conversation until Mamma brings over the *pepparkakor* cookies. They're a kind of gingerbread cookie, Svea's favorite.

One by one, we follow the tradition that Mamma taught us. Pappa goes first. He holds up his cookie in one hand, makes a wish, and then taps the cookie with a finger from his other hand until it breaks.

"Ah, damn," he says when it breaks clean in two.

Mamma is next, and after making a wish and tapping her cookie, it breaks into three pieces. "Wow, yes!" she exclaims, because if the cookie breaks into three pieces then your wish comes true.

I take a healthy swig of *glögg* as Lee takes his turn, and Svea does, too. Lee's breaks into four pieces, and Svea's breaks in two.

"Go, Will!" Svea says excitedly, and I hold up my cookie.

I wish Lacey would come back.

I tap with my finger, and the cookie breaks into three pieces.

"Yeah, buttface!" my sister shouts and pats my shoulder.

I force a smile because I don't believe my wish will really come true. I don't deserve for it to come true.

Mamma claps her hands and stands from the table. "So, who will be *Jultomte* this year?"

I fight back a groan. *Jultomte* is the Christmas gnome. One of us dresses up like a gnome and gets to hand out the presents. There is truly nothing I want to do less right now. I'd like to drown myself in my cup of *glögg*.

"Aha, Will," Mamma decides happily, and pushes in her chair.

I don't know exactly what happens to me then. Something snaps. I can't do it. I can't dress up like an idiot one more time for the sake of my family. I never say no when they need me to do something, and today, I'm too depressed and angry at myself to go along with it. I just don't have it in me.

"No." The word feels weird in my mouth, like it doesn't fit right.

She stops mid-stride across the dining room and so does Pappa, who was hot on her heels.

"What?" Svea pipes up, like I just blurted out a swear word in front of our parents. "Will, come on, you have to."

Anger pulses through my body. "No, I don't. Someone else can do it." My teeth are clenched, and I'm sure my face is turning red. I can't look my mother in the eyes because if I do, I know I'll just feel like a little boy who is misbehaving. But I'm not a little boy, and I should get to say no sometimes.

Lee kicks me under the table with a death glare, but I don't budge.

"William John, what is going on with you?" Mamma asks, totally aghast that I actually said no to her.

I shake my head and sigh. "I'm just tired, Mamma. I do everything for everyone, and I can't do it anymore." I look up at her slowly, hoping she hears the exhaustion in my voice instead of just the fact that I'm disobeying her. She's in total shock at my behavior and my words.

"Son," Pa says sympathetically.

"Please, Pappa. I'm done doing everything. It's too much. I need a break."

Svea's jaw drops, and Lee loses the death glare. They realize it isn't about not wanting to dress up like *Jultomte*.

Everyone is looking at me in silence, hardly believing that I'm speaking up for myself like this. I guess I might as well just get it all out there because what good would it do me to save the rest of how I feel for another time?

I clear my throat. "You never asked me if I wanted to run the inn."

Mamma frowns in confusion.

"You didn't give me a choice. You just assumed that I would take over for you guys, and I was happy to do that because I love you two more than anything. But it isn't what I want to do for the rest of my life." My heart pounds hard against my rib cage as the silence weighs down on my shoulders. "If you had asked me, I would've said yes. But not forever. I would've said I'd take over until you found someone else because I have my own dreams that none of you know about." I glance at my siblings, too. "No one has ever thought about me enough to ask what I want."

The stillness of my family members makes it feel like the whole room is frozen in time, and it helps me keep talking.

"I want to cook, alright? I want to open my own restaurant. *That's* my dream. *That's* my passion. Not making beds and dusting and catering to yuppie tourists." Getting the words out gives me strength, and I think of the notebook Lacey and I wrote my ideas down in. "I want to cook the food of our ancestors. Swedish cuisine. I want to share our family heritage through food."

Mamma's hand slowly moves from her side to cover her heart. She's getting emotional, and I can't stand to see her cry, so I hurry on to the next bit before I chicken out.

"But I can't do that if I'm busy running the inn full time and doing everything else you need me to do for you and for the community in addition to that." I take in a deep breath, willing the tension clutching my body to subside. "I want to step back from the inn. I'll work until you find a replacement, but that's all. My goal in life is not to be an innkeeper, Mamma. I'm sorry, but it's just not."

She sniffs, her face crumpling slightly as Pappa wraps an arm around her.

"Sheesh, buttface. Way to ruin Christmas," Svea mutters with a chuckle. "Ow!" Lee gives me a nod, apparently having kicked her in the shin under the table on my behalf.

"And...there's something else, too." I hesitate to bring up Lacey, but they should know why she isn't here. "I kissed Lacey last night."

Svea gasps and is instantly on her feet. "Oh my gosh! You *kissed* her!?" she screeches in excitement. Lee cringes at the high-pitch and volume, and pulls her back into her chair by her arm.

"Will, what were you thinking?" Mamma questions in astonishment.

"I'm thinking that I'm in love with her."

This time, every family member gasps in unison as I blush in front of them.

"You've barely known her a week," Lee unnecessarily reminds me with his eyes wide.

"I know."

"Wait, wait, wait," Svea chimes back in, waving her hands like windshield wipers. "If you kissed her, and you're in love with her, why did she leave? Did she not feel the same?"

I scratch the back of my neck. "Uh, no, it's not that. I might have said some things I didn't mean because I knew she wasn't going to stay here permanently..."

Lee stares at me for a moment, and then he barks out a single *ha* that has me narrowing my eyes at him. "So, you kissed her and then messed it all up."

"Correct," I mutter. "I don't know how to get her back."

I look at each one of my favorite people, silence falling again until Mamma straightens up with a determined expression on her face. "Freddie, put on some coffee. We're going to sort this out."

"What?"

"You heard me, Will. We're going to get this figured out. Lee, clear a space. Svea, grab some paper and a pen. We have a plan to make."

"Yes!" Svea shouts and hops up immediately. Lee does as Mamma says, and I sit there completely dumbfounded.

They're going to help me? On Christmas Eve? Before we've even opened presents?

My throat gets a little dry as they come together for my sake. I...I really love my family.

"Mamma, we don't have to do this now," I tell her as she helps Lee move plates and dishes out of the way.

"Of course we do," she insists firmly. "And when we go to the Christmas Vigil later tonight, we'll all be praying for you and—and this new life that you want to live." She swipes at her eyes and then gives me an apologetic look from across the table. "I never meant to make you feel so burdened, Will. I'm so sorry."

I reach over and take her hand. "I know, Mamma."

"We'll make this right."

Svea comes back with paper and a pen, her eyes all lit up like this is the best day of her life. "Alright, buttface. Let's get her back."

Chapter
Twenty-Three

Lacey

Spending Christmas with Lindsey was a welcome distraction. I went along to her parents' house on Christmas morning, and it was so great to see them. They've always treated me like a daughter, which was exactly what I needed after my tiny text conversation with my dad. After brunch, Lindsey, Jack, and I went back to their house, and the rest of the day was filled with hot cocoa, holiday movies, popcorn, Christmas cookies, and Christmas music. My bruised heart soaked up every second of it, and I tried not to think about Will.

But now, it's eleven at night, and my friends have gone to bed. I can't tell if it's the sugar keeping me awake or just the misery I've been trying to avoid all day. Either way, my brain is wide awake and so is my heart. And my heart misses the Christiansens. My heart misses the way I felt at home in Larkspur. My heart misses my dad.

This morning at brunch, I watched the way that Lindsey's dad just adored her. He laughed at every silly thing she said and listened to her so intently. My dad used to do that, too, back before Mom died. He used to light up when I walked in the room, like I was his favorite thing. Well, second favorite thing, because I know my mom was his first favorite.

I could tell my parents anything. They were always there for me when I needed someone to listen. But now I only have one of them left, and only barely. The truth is though, it isn't all his fault. I haven't made much of an effort to reach out. Sure, I could blame that on Mariah, but ultimately, I'm just as complicit in the distant relationship I have with him.

He's all I have left of the life we had with Mom, and tonight, he's the closest thing I can get to talking to her. And I really, really wish I could talk to her.

I'm dialing Dad's number before I can talk myself out of it, not knowing if he'll even pick up. Sometimes, Mariah answers his phone. Also, there's probably a couple of hours time difference down there in Aruba, but oh well. The dial tone is ringing, and I'm not hanging up.

Just when I think it's about to go to voicemail, my dad picks up. "Hello?" He sounds tired and groggy, like I woke him out of a dead sleep.

"Hi, Daddy," I say softly. "Sorry it's so late, I just...miss you."

There's a beat of silence in which I'm not sure if he's still trying to wake himself up, or if he's surprised, or if he just plain doesn't know what to say. In the background, I hear Mariah pipe up irritably, "Who the hell is calling at this hour?" Probably for the first time ever, he ignores her and speaks to me.

"I miss you, too, Lacey. Is everything okay?"

Tears well up in my eyes. "No. I mean, yes, I'm fine. I'm with Lindsey for Christmas, but..." I swallow hard as my chest inflates with all the things I haven't told him about this week. And then, I open my mouth and just say it all. "Yvette fired me last week. It's not even fair that she fired me, but she did, so I packed a bag, and I started driving to spend Christmas with Lindsey, but then I hit Albie, and my car was messed up, so I had to stay in this cute, little town until it could be fixed. Lars said it was going to be done after Christmas, which was a bummer at first, but then I became friends with the innkeeper, Will, and his amazing family. And then, he hurt his knee, and my car got done early, and we went to the Holly Ball together, and then I kissed him." I stop to take a deep breath and then keep going. "He said it was a mistake, which hurt my feelings, so I left and drove the rest of the way to Lindsey's, and I've been here two days and I—" I pause for a moment to just cry like a lost little girl. "I don't know what to do, Dad. Everything is so out of sorts, and I wish Mom was here to talk to, but she's not. And you guys are in Aruba for Christmas, which is totally fine, but I—I miss you. I miss what we were like before she died, and I want it back, Daddy."

I sniffle and wipe my eyes as I catch my breath from all that word vomit. Dad says nothing for a long moment, probably trying to process everything I just blurted out. I'm sure none of it makes sense to him, but it still feels good to say it all. He can't be a part of my life if he knows nothing about it, so this is my way of opening that door a little wider.

"Honey, you've just been through it, haven't you?" he says finally, and the endearment relieves me so much. I can't remember the last time he called me that. "Back up, start from the beginning. Let's talk this through." He sniffs on the other end of the line. "We can pretend she's on the phone with us, too, okay?"

That has me blubbering all over again because it's the sweetest gesture.

So, I go back through my little speech and fill in the details. He asks me questions and helps me make sense of things. It heals me in a way I only hoped it would. Despite being thousands of miles apart, I can feel his attention and his concern for me. Apparently, my word vomit broke the log jam between us because this is the most we've said to each other in years.

"Sounds like Will is conflicted," he suggests thoughtfully. "He kissed you but then backed off because you were leaving, right?"

I go back in my mind one more time to replay that horrible exchange as I pace around the darkened guest room with my phone pressed to my ear.

"We can't do this."

"Because I'm a guest?"

"Because you're not staying."

"Yes," I reply to my dad. The tears are gone now, and it's all business as we hash this out.

There's a pause and then, "Hmm."

"Hmm, what?"

"Well, it seems like he pushed you away to keep himself from getting hurt."

My heart pounds. "Do you think so?"

"That's what it sounds like to me."

I keep pacing, my tired head whirling. It's fair to want to protect yourself. I can certainly understand that. But...Will said some awful things in order to protect himself. Does the reason justify the hurt he's caused me?

"What are you thinking?" he prompts patiently. Ugh, I've missed this man. It's like going back in time talking to him like this. It's like gaining back an old friend you didn't think you'd ever see again.

"I...I'm thinking that protecting himself doesn't excuse the things he said." That sounds harsh even to my own ears, but it is what it is.

"You're right, Lace. He hurt you, and there's no excuse for that. But it's pretty clear that you still have strong feelings for him."

I throw myself backward on the bed with a big sigh. "I know."

"I think it would be worth talking it through with him. I'm not saying the way he acted was right because nobody hurts my daughter, but I think that if you can be happy with him like I was happy with your mom, then it's worth finding out for sure where he stands."

I sniff at the mention of his and Mom's marriage. "I miss her."

"I miss her, too," he whispers back roughly. "Every day." He clears his throat. "A love like that doesn't come along very often. So, if you think you could have that with Will, then you owe it to yourself to figure it out."

"You're right, Daddy."

I don't want to let go of Will. The idea of never seeing him again or talking to him again makes my stomach feel like I've swallowed a handful of sewing needles. If my Dad, being far removed from the situation, thinks it would be worth trying to work things out with Will, then I probably should. I really do think it could be a love like my parents had, the kind that lasts a lifetime and lives on after death.

If I can reassure Will of how I feel and what I want, maybe he'll give us a chance.

I guess I have a pit stop to make on the way back to Minneapolis.

My nerves are running haywire when I hit the road the next day.

This is it. I'm gonna tell the dude how it is.

I rehearse what I'm going to say the whole way there.

Will, I think we could have something great. You're awesome, I'm awesome, and we would be awesome together. I know my life is in Minneapolis, but I'm not tied down there anymore. I want to move here, to Larkspur, and have a brand new start. I'll get a job doing whatever, and we can see where this goes. I don't want to look back on my life and regret not taking a chance on you.

Ooh, that's good. If that doesn't speak to him, I don't know what will.

That doesn't mean I'm not feeling like I'm about to puke when I approach the city limits though.

"Deep breaths, Lacey," I mutter to myself as the Larkspur welcome sign comes into view, the one I blew past on my way out of town two days ago.

Will isn't the only one on my mind. I need to see Svea, too, and apologize for leaving without saying goodbye. I need to make sure that I haven't burned any bridges, the most important bridges I've ever built. I need to hug her and maybe hug Lee, too, if he'll let me, and I need to go see Mamma and Pappa. I need to make everything right, whether Will wants to take a chance with me or not.

I pass the Larkspur welcome sign, and that's when I hear the sirens. I look in the rearview mirror to see a police car behind me, sirens blaring and lights glaring.

What? Was I speeding? Maybe I was weaving. I'm certainly distracted enough.

I pull over to the side of the street and put Kia in park, nervous for an entirely new reason. I've never gotten a ticket. If I ruin my good driving record I'm going to be so disappointed.

The squad car pulls over behind me, and in the rearview mirror, I see a policeman get out. A very familiar-looking policeman.

My heart leaps. It's Lee!

I roll my window down as he walks over. I don't know why I'm surprised, but he doesn't greet me with a smile or even an ounce of surprise or recognition. He's doing his job here, so I'm not expecting him to be chipper. I also skipped town without warning, so there's a big chance he's mad at me.

"What seems to be the problem, Officer?" I say to him, and I can't stop my grin because it's good to see his moody face. He glares in at me, and that has me wondering even more why he pulled me over.

"Get out of the car."

My grin vanishes. I blink in total confusion. "What?"

His serious face tightens as he stares at me. "Get out of the car. Now."

The blood drains from my face as he steps away and opens my door.

Oh, bobbins. I must've done something seriously bad. He gestures for me to come out with an impatient wave of his hand, and I unbuckle my seatbelt with dread. I climb out on wobbly knees, and then he slams my door closed. I shiver from more than just the chilly December air.

"Lee, what did I—"

"You're coming with me." It isn't a question. It's a matter of fact.

My entire body straightens. "I'm—*what*?"

"Now," he growls out, surly as ever, and all I can think is that I've really pissed him off. He's definitely more sensitive under the surface than I thought if my leaving has him twice as grouchy as usual...assuming that's even what has him so ticked off. With a hand on my bicep, he ushers me towards his police car.

"Wait, Lee, I'm sorry for leaving so suddenly," I blurt out as he half frog marches me along the shoulder of the road. "I should've said goodbye, but—"

"Save it," he mutters, and opens the back door.

"But, Lee—aren't you supposed to read me my Miranda Rights or whatever?" He urges me forward, and I slide into the back seat. "Don't I get to speak to a lawyer or something? What are you even arresting me for?"

The door shutting is the only answer I get before he gets into the driver's seat. Without saying another word, he pulls out and then takes the next right into town.

What the bobbins is going on? Is he really arresting me?

My heart pounds in the back of the police car, the same one he gave me a ride in the night my Kia slid into his life.

"Is it because of Albie? Am I being charged?" I exclaim through the grate.

Lee says nothing, and I start to panic.

"Please, Lee. I won't last a day in prison. I'm a gentle soul. I'd never make it."

His stony silence continues, ramping up my panic even more. But instead of heading to the police station, which I'm pretty sure is off Main Street somewhere, Lee turns down a familiar road and stops the car outside of Larkspur Inn. My heart sighs to see it. It's only been a couple of days, but I feel like it's been a year since I pulled up to this house in the back of Lee's police car that first night.

But...if he brought me here then that means he's *not* arresting me. Phew. No prison time for this girl. Thank goodness.

"Lee...what's going on?"

He eyes me in the rearview mirror and then gets out of the car. When he opens my door, there's a teeny tiny little smirk on his face, like he enjoyed the hell out of making me squirm.

"Are you kidding? I thought you were arresting me!"

"Never said I was arresting you."

I dart out of the car and fist my hands on my hips. "Seriously?"

He shrugs. "Consider it payback for faking an injury at the Snowball Fight."

My mouth pops open, but then I throw my head back and laugh. "I shouldn't be surprised that you like to get even."

"Hope you've learned your lesson." He cocks one dark eyebrow at me, but I can see the twinkle in his eyes, a twinkle that reminds me of his sister.

Behind us, the front door opens and closes. Lee nods toward the sound, and when I look over the roof of the squad car, I see Will standing on the porch. My pulse picks up, but I still narrow my eyes back at Lee.

"You could've just told me you were bringing me here."

He closes the car door. "No fun in that."

I shake my head at him, fighting a smile, and then attack him with a tight hug around the middle.

"Oof," he huffs out as I squeeze him. He pats me on the back twice and then peels me off of him. Lee steps away and points me around the hood of his cruiser, side-eyeing me in that uncertain way I've missed.

The cheerfulness of Lee's ruse ebbs away as I move around the hood to the sidewalk leading up to the porch of the inn. There on the top step is Will. His hands are in his pockets, weight still leaning a little to his uninjured leg, wearing a slightly nervous frown.

The last time I saw him, he was pushing me away, saying that we can't pursue something together because I was leaving. Well, now is the time to set him straight. That's what I came here to do, right?

I take a deep breath in and then blow it out nervously.

Okay. Remember what you wanted to say.

I throw my shoulders back and start forward. The closer I get to the porch, the more my knees tingle and weaken.

Will, I think we could have something great. You're awesome, I'm awesome, and we would be awesome together.

I breathe in and out deeply as I close the distance between us, which shrinks even more when he carefully steps down to the sidewalk, too, and keeps coming toward me.

I know my life is in Minneapolis, but—but?

Shoot. I don't remember the rest.

I stop when we're a few feet from each other, but he doesn't. Pretty green eyes intent on mine, he reaches for me and takes my face in his warm hands.

Bobbins, and needles, and thread, oh my...

"Lacey," he murmurs, his brows furrowing with emotion, "I'm so, so sorry."

I gulp that apology down like water. I drink in his contrite expression, and just like that, want to I forgive him. How can I not when he realizes he made a mistake?

"I was an idiot." He searches my face like he hasn't seen it in years. I take him in, too, every last bit of his lightly freckled complexion and reddish stubble. "We're not a mistake. We're..." He swallows hard and smoothes his thumb across my cheek. "We're perfect together. I'm falling for you, Lacey. All that matters to me is that you're happy, even if it isn't here with me. Please forgive me for being a coward and saying things I didn't really mean."

I blink back a few tears, and he leans forward, kissing me on the forehead like I'm the most precious thing to him. My heart melts and squeezes. And here I thought I was the one who would be giving a speech.

"I forgive you," I whisper, and he instantly pulls back to look at me.

"You do?" His expression is beyond surprised.

"Uh...yes? Is that okay?" I tease, chuckling.

"Of course...I just thought it would be a little harder than that. I...I have more to say."

I smile. "Alright. Go on, then."

His familiar face is close to mine, and he speaks quietly and slowly. "If going back to Minneapolis is what you need to do to be happy, then I won't stop you. I want you to follow your dreams like you've encouraged me to follow mine. So..." He moves his hands from my face, across my shoulders, and down my arms. Taking my hands in his, he pierces me with a longing look and says, "Dream with me. Dream with me about what we could be."

I beam up at him through watery eyes. The snowy pine trees and snow-covered inn behind him have me feeling like we're in our own little world. That is, until a car comes hurtling down the street and screeches to a halt next to Lee's police car. He throws his hands up as Svea hustles out of the driver's side.

"I could arrest you for reckless driving," he threatens, but his sister ignores him and heads straight toward me and Will.

"Did I miss it? Am I too late?" She rushes up the sidewalk, her dirty blonde hair flying behind her.

"No, Svee, I was just getting to that part," Will assures her with a sigh.

"What part?" I ask, turning towards Svea as she joins us. Lee stays by the hood of his cruiser with his arms crossed over his chest, trying to seem like he isn't interested.

"The part where he begs you to stay because we have a plan," she answers with a huge grin.

I swing my gaze to Will. "A plan?"

He smiles sweetly. "Yeah, I have a plan. And it involves my sister here."

I look back at Svea, who's still grinning like the devil himself.

"Wait, did you say the 'dream with me' part? 'Cause you said that was important."

I bite back a laugh, but I can't fight the absolute joy that comes over me. They talked about this. Will talked to his siblings about how to make everything right with me. I can't believe it.

"Thank you, Svee. I got this, okay?" he says to her, making his eyes go a little wide to get his point across.

"Oh, right. Right. I'll be over here when you're ready for my bit." She goes and stands next to Lee, who I can tell is still contemplating arresting her for reckless driving.

"What in the world is going on?" I ask Will, who shakes his head slightly as smiles. He squeezes my hands and grows serious again.

"I talked to my parents," he says quietly. "I told them I don't want to run the inn anymore, and that I want to open a restaurant."

I gasp. "How did they take it?"

"They're okay with it." His green eyes are bright and hopeful, and *ugh*, I'm at least forty-six percent in love with this man. "We talked it out and...yeah. We're good."

"Will, I am so, so happy to hear that."

"Come on, hurry up!" Svea shouts excitedly from behind us. I glance over my shoulder to laugh at her and see Lee giving her a rough nudge.

Will tugs on my hands to turn me back to him. "I know we haven't known each other very long, Lacey, but there's something here."

My heart warms in my chest despite the December chill. It's the warmth of hope.

"When you know, you know," comes Lee's deep voice, but he says it without the usual edge. I smile at him over my shoulder because I think it's sort of his way of giving his blessing. But I also see something else in his expression, something softer. Something that looks an awful lot like understanding and self-reflection.

"He's right," Will agrees, and I turn back to him. "I want to explore it with you. I want to go after my dream with you by my side, and I want to be by your side as you go after yours."

I smile up at him because that sounds so amazing. There could be nothing better than that.

"So, dream with me about what your life could look like here in Larkspur." A hopeful expression comes over his handsome face that bumps me up to fifty-nine percent in love with him. "I see you helping me with starting this restaurant. I see you working with Svea and—"

"That's my cue!" Svea bounds forward, making me laugh. "I totally want you to be my business partner, Lace," she butts in with bright eyes. Excitement dances on her face as she continues. "You know all the ins and outs of the fashion world, right? But you also are super skilled at creating stuff, so it's perfect! *And* I happen to have a second bedroom in my little apartment above the boutique that needs a tenant." She shakes me by the shoulders. "It could literally not be any more perfect!"

Wow. It really does sound perfect. I'd be part of a business where I can do the thing I should've been doing all along, but I can also help with marketing and the business aspects as well.

"Are you serious? You're offering me a job and a place to live?"

"Yeah!"

I look back at Will. "And you want to be with me?"

"Very, very much."

There's nothing wrong with any of this. Not a single thing, but it's easy to forget that we can't snap our fingers to get to that point. Going back to pick up my life and move it here will take time.

"I still have to go back and find a sub-leaser for my apartment and everything," I remind him tentatively.

"I don't care if you have to go back as long as this is where you end up." He swallows hard, but his eyes go tender. "With me."

"Are you sure?"

He touches my jaw with gentle fingers. "I'm sure."

Before I can give my resounding acceptance speech, the sound of another car pulling up distracts me. I look over my shoulder as Will groans. "What now?" he mutters.

The car parks, and Elsie gets out, holding something in both of her hands. "Wait!" she shouts and rushes toward us. "You need to touch the tomte!"

"Mamma, really?" Will complains, but I can't help snickering.

"Both of you," she instructs when she reaches us. Svea backs up with a smirk, and Elsie thrusts the little gnome statue at our still connected hands.

He sighs and does as Mamma says, and so do I. She glows with pride and hope then, and I'm so relieved that there aren't any hard feelings about me ducking out of their Christmas. She steps back with her hands clasped beneath her chin and a smiling Fredrik joins her. Lee still keeps his distance over there, but he hasn't left, so apparently, he's interested in what I'm going to do.

"Well?" Svea urges excitedly.

I beam back up at Will. "This is where I want to be, Will. Here with you and your family."

He smiles wide and tugs on the tomte in our hands so that I come closer. "You sure, big guns?"

"Positive, chef."

And then, with the *tomte* and the future at our fingertips, he kisses me. In front of every member of his family, he kisses me, and this time when we pull away, he doesn't say it's a mistake. This time, there's only joy when he looks back at me.

Pappa, Mamma, and Svea cheer and hoot for us, but it's the slamming of a car door that catches everyone's attention. Lee starts up the engine and pulls his police car onto the street, apparently satisfied with how our story is about to begin.

Epilogue

Will

I 'm a nervous wreck as I pace back and forth through the renovated kitchen. My mind is frantically going through the list of things we had left to do this morning before the grand opening. I barely slept last night from nerves and excitement. But everything seems under control. The kitchen is prepped, and the line cooks know the menu backward and forward. The wait staff has the dining area under control and had plenty of test runs with the P.O.S. system. Everything is clean and where it should be.

The original plan was to renovate the inn and have an in-house restaurant, but the more I thought about it, the more I realized it wouldn't be enough space to do the menu I wanted to do. So, I looked into other places in town and was lucky enough to use Mamma's connections at church to land this spot. When the church expanded a few years ago and got its own building, they kept this space as an extra meeting place but haven't used it much. So now, I pay my rent to the church, which I think is amazing, and they were more than willing to let me make the changes I needed to as long as I footed the bill. Thankfully, a lot of community members and businesses donated almost everything I needed to get this place up and running.

I check the time and see there are just minutes to go, so I think through my mental list one more time. In the middle of it, I realize that six months ago, I was doing the same thing. Except back then, my list included things like laundry, dusting, and errands. I take a deep breath, feeling grateful that the inn is no longer my responsibility. It hasn't been since my parents found someone to take it over five months ago. Without the inn, I've been able to throw myself into preparations for this restaurant. It's been a crazy amount of work, but I haven't done it alone.

Pa helped me hook up the appliances in the kitchen and clean out the ones we kept. Mamma helped me pick out paint colors for the dining space and decided where the pictures of our Swedish family should go on the walls. There are a handful of gnomes scattered throughout the dining room and a couple of *Dala* horses as well. Lee helped me sand down the tables and restain the hardwood floors. Svea helped paint the walls the colors Mamma chose, a rich navy blue as accent walls and a warm cream on the rest.

A little of my nerves settle as I step out of the kitchen and see all the people gathered outside the front doors and down the sidewalk of Main Street. My parents are first in line, with Svea clutching Mamma's arm excitedly. Lee stands just behind them, his arms folded as he looks around at the crowd. No doubt he's keeping an eye on them, making sure no one is getting too rowdy. I see the Gustafsons and Grandma Janssen and all our neighbors and friends, every one of them here to support my dream. Beneath my nerves, I'm happy. This is really happening.

"Where is he?" I hear from behind the kitchen door. I turn around as it opens, and there stands the love of my life.

She's been by my side every step of the way as I've put my dreams into motion. She was there when I met with the church board and toured this space for the first time. She picked up every time I called her in the middle of the night so I could run an idea by her. She taste-tested every single menu item and helped me write the descriptions for each dish. She's been here every evening this week as it all came together. And she's here now, looking as nervous as me.

Despite how much is on my mind and the fact that I'm minutes away from opening those doors, all I can do is stare at Lacey. Without her, none of this would be happening. If she hadn't skidded into my life that one December night, I would still be unhappily running the inn and letting my boundaries be trampled on by my family. She's changed everything, and the last five and a half months with her living here in Larkspur have been the best of my entire life.

I was scared that she would move here, and then she would change her mind about living in a small town, but she's thrived here—both professionally and personally. My family has basically adopted her at this point, and she's a staple for every fika. On top of that, she hasn't shied away from becoming a part of the community. She rallied several community businesses and the Chamber of Commerce to go in on an electronic billboard that scrolls through all the local business adver- tisements 24/7. It's right on the highway, and as the spring months thawed the permafrost, Larkspur has seen an increase in tourism. Mamma told me that Patty, the woman who took over the inn, is booked solid this summer and into the fall as well. And with Lacey's help, Svea's Boutique has taken off, too. Lacey has worked some marketing magic so that they're bringing in sales online as well as in the store. She spends most of her time working at the boutique and creating garments. Every time she finishes a piece she's been working on, I get to see the pride on her face, and it fulfills me as much as it fulfills her.

She makes everything better. With her by my side, there's nothing I can't do.

After we settle into a routine here at the restaurant, I plan on asking if she wants to move in together. Right now, I'm living with Lee, and even though it isn't bad, I'm ready for the next step with Lacey. I love her so much, and there isn't a day that goes by that I take her presence in my life for granted.

"Hey—there you are. Come with me really quick," she demands in a rush as she grabs my hand and pulls me back through the kitchen door to the office. Her urgency and seriousness has me worrying that something is wrong, but the minute she closes the door behind us, she breaks into a beautiful smile that has my heartbeat rising.

"What's going on?"

"I have something for you, chef." She goes to my desk and opens the bottom drawer, pulling out a folded piece of white cloth. "Here," she says, putting it in my hands with an even bigger smile.

I unfold it, not sure what to expect. I hold it up and quickly realize that it's a chef's jacket. Over the left breast, I see my name embroidered in black thread. Above that is the logo for the restaurant, The Swedish Chef.

Lacey squeals as I stare at it. Pride rolls me through me because she made this for me. She believes I can do this. She believes that I really am a chef, and this is what I'm supposed to be doing with my life.

"Put it on!" she urges, and holds it open so I can slip my arms into it. "There," she says confidently when she's done up all the buttons for me. "Now, you're ready."

I look down at myself and then back up to Lacey, whose eyes are brimming with happy tears. "I couldn't have done any of this without you."

She shakes her head, smiling softly up at me. "You could have, Will, but I'm so glad I'm here by your side to watch you achieve your dream."

"My dream would be nothing without you, Lacey." I stroke her cheek. "I love you so much."

Her coffee-colored eyes turn misty. "I love you, too."

The nerves and pressure dissipate completely when I lean down and kiss her. The feelings I had for her that first week have only deepened with time. She's my best friend, and I intend on marrying her when the time is right. I want to have a home with her and build a life together. We've talked about it already, and once our careers are established, we're going to take those steps together. Until then, I'm happy to spend our evenings talking and laughing on the couch at Lee's house or Svea's apartment.

Lacey pulls away and swipes at her eyes. "Okay, let's get you out there."

I take a deep breath in and slowly blow it out. "Yeah. It's time."

Lacey intertwines her fingers with mine as we go back through the kitchen to the dining room. She squeezes my hand tightly and then lets go so I can throw the doors open and officially start off this crazy dream of mine.

With my family grinning through the glass in front of me and my forever girl behind me, I unlock the doors to an excited crowd. Gathering my nerves and stuffing them down, I embrace the joy and call out, "Welcome, everybody, to The Swedish Chef!"

Acknowledgments

I'm going to start this off by saying thank you to my editor, Tiffany. Despite studying English in my college years, I apparently still have no idea where to use a comma or not use a comma. Thank you for your enthusiasm and for being so gracious about answering my many insecure questions.

Thank you to my beta readers for taking the time to read this as I wrote it. This manuscript wasn't selected by Hallmark for publication, but you all were totally on board with me publishing it myself. Your feedback makes every book better.

Shout out to Dawson, MN for being the inspiration for the town of Larkspur. Gnometown, USA is such a quirky little place to live, and I couldn't keep my brain from creating back stories.

Of course, thank you to my favorite husband, Jon. Your support is never taken for granted. Thanks for going on this journey with me. I love you.

About The Author

Katie Stearns is a contemporary romance author and stay at home mom from southwestern Minnesota. She and her husband and two young daughters live on six acres in a 122 year old farmhouse with their German Shorthair Pointer, Porkchop.

She writes stories that pack an emotional punch, with an emphasis on positive portrayals of mental health.

In her free time, she enjoys reading, baking, and photography. You can often find her behind the wheel of the family mini-van, schlepping her kiddos back and forth to school and ABA therapy. She's always daydreaming about the next story.

Also By Katie Stearns

On The Dotted Line

Water Under The Bridge
Burning Bridges